BRUNO'S CHALLENGE

BRUNO'S CHALLENGE

AND OTHER STORIES OF
THE FRENCH COUNTRYSIDE

MARTIN WALKER

THORNDIKE PRESS
A part of Gale, a Cengage Company

A Cengage Company

The following stories first published as Vintage e-Short Originals by Vintage Books, a division of Penguin Random House LLC, New York: "A Market Tale" (2014), "The Chocolate War" (2018), "A Birthday Lunch" (2019), and "Oystercatcher" (2020).
Thorndike Press, a part of Gale, a Cengage Company.

Thorndike Press® Large Print Mystery.
The text of this Large Print edition is unabridged.
Other aspects of the book may vary from the original edition.
Set in 16 pt. Plantin.

LIBRARY OF CONGRESS CIP DATA ON FILE.
CATALOGUING IN PUBLICATION FOR THIS BOOK
IS AVAILABLE FROM THE LIBRARY OF CONGRESS.

ISBN-13: 979-8-8857-8173-2 (hardcover alk. paper)

Published in 2022 by arrangement with Alfred A. Knopf, an imprint of The Knopf Doubleday Publishing Group, a division of Penguin Random House LLC.

Printed in Mexico
Print Number : 1   Print Year : 2022

To Julien Montfort
and Caline Sokolow,
whose wine store and friendship
have been a constant source of
my well-being

CONTENTS

CONTENTS

BRUNO'S CHALLENGE

It was market day in St. Denis, and Bruno Courrèges, the town policeman, was strolling between the stalls along the rue de Paris on his morning patrol with his basset hound, Balzac, at his heels. He was shaking hands with the men along the street and exchanging the *bise* with the women from twelve to ninety when he saw his friend Ivan at Maurice's vegetable stall, clutching his stomach.

"Putain de merde," Ivan gasped when Bruno asked what was wrong. "I've got the most terrible pain in my gut. I had a few twinges last night, but this is — aargh." He fell to his knees, his shopping bag spilling strawberries and heads of lettuce.

Bruno was about to call the *pompiers,* the local fire brigade that also provided the emergency medical and ambulance service, but realized there was no way they could get through the crush of stalls and shoppers that filled the rue de Paris. He put an arm around Ivan and half carried him down the narrow alleyway that led to the rue Gambetta, where he commandeered Maurice's handcart, loaded Ivan aboard and began pulling him back to the main square in front of the *mairie*. He called Fauquet, owner of the local café, to help. With Balzac trotting ahead to clear their path over the pedestrian walkway beside the bridge, they hauled a groaning Ivan over the river, through the parking lot in front of the bank and into the medical center.

"Bruno, you may have to do the cooking tonight." Ivan gasped as they set him down and the receptionist went in search of a doctor.

"Don't worry about anything, Ivan," Bruno said automatically. "Let's just see what's going on with you."

The doctor on duty was Fabiola. She ignored Bruno and bent over Ivan to ask what the problem was, and he pointed down to just above the groin. She opened his shirt and put a stethoscope to his belly while her other hand took his pulse.

"Ambulance, urgent, for Périgueux hospital, possible burst appendix," she called out to the receptionist.

"It's the golden wedding anniversary of

Patrice and Monique," Ivan said through gritted teeth, his face creased with pain. "I can't let them down. I've already bought the chicken, cheese and wine. Thirty guests, some canapés with the *apéro,* soup, chicken tarragon with puréed potatoes, salad and cheese, yogurt mousse with strawberry . . ."

Ivan broke off to groan, and Bruno said, "Ivan, I only cook for small tables of friends. There's no way I could manage thirty. Let me see if I can get someone else to help out."

"You cook for thirty at the tennis club all the time," said Fabiola, before telling Fauquet to ask Dr. Gelletreau for a pack of sterilized instruments.

"I can put together one simple course with lots of help," Bruno said. "But this is a special occasion. Patrice was on the council when they hired me, and Monique taught me half of what I know about cooking. We've got to do well by them."

"Sounds like you owe them your best efforts," said Fabiola as the ambulance arrived with a brief burst of its siren. She grabbed her medical bag as the *pompiers* came in with a stretcher. Dr. Gelletreau handed her a sealed pack of instruments, which Ivan eyed with alarm. She had to go with Ivan in case his appendix burst on the way.

"Don't be silly, Bruno," she said. "You can pull it off. You have friends. Sort it out."

Ivan pressed a key into Bruno's hand, winced and then said, between gasps, "I was going to make that tomato soup of Pamela's and something with strawberries for dessert. The wine's in the pantry, and Stéphane will drop off the cheese." He closed his eyes and squeezed Bruno's hand. "Thanks, I knew I could count on you."

Ivan was laid out in the back of the ambulance, Fabiola joined him, and they were off.

Fauquet turned to Bruno and said, "Fabiola's right, you know. You can handle the dinner. Still, it's a pity this happened after the Japanese girl left."

Bruno shook his head sadly. Ivan had, over the years, introduced the palates of St. Denis to the wonders of global cuisine, thanks to his love life. He had gone on vacation to Spain and returned with a Belgian girl who added to his restaurant's menu many different ways with mussels, from *normande* and *à la crème* to Rockefeller. She made a broth called *waterzooi* that was very warming and tasty on a wintry night. Then he had gone to some Italian beach and returned with an

12

Austrian girl, or perhaps she was German, and suddenly St. Denis understood what a glorious dish a well-flattened Wiener schnitzel could be in the right hands, washed down with a glass of Grüner Veltliner. Then in Turkey he had fallen for a Spanish girl, and Bruno still yearned for her *gambas al ajillo* and her dulce de leche.

When Ivan had announced that his next destination would be Thailand, the gastronomic fantasies in the town ran wild, only to be dashed when he returned with a young Australian woman he'd met on the island of Ko Samui. But hope soared again once the locals tasted what Mandy could do with her fusion cuisine that blended Malay, Vietnamese and Thai dishes. St. Denis went into mourning when Mandy left to begin a wine course in Bordeaux, but then came a wonderful surprise. Miko, a Japanese teacher of French, enjoying an Eiffel scholarship to study French culture, ate at Ivan's restaurant, stayed for the summer and enchanted the customers with yakitori chicken and shrimp tempura.

So now, with Miko gone, much as the locals admired Ivan's way with the familiar dishes of the Périgord, the gastronomic pride of France, they could hardly wait for his next vacation. Indeed, there were lively discussions as to whether he should be sent to India, Tuscany or Hong Kong. There was even talk of crowdfunding to help finance his trip. But Miko's departure had sent the usually cheerful Ivan into a mood that St. Denis decided to call introspection, for fear that it might turn out to be a real depression, and then where would they be? And this spring Ivan had taken no vacation at all, consoling himself by offering his customers the occasional *moules à la crème, paella à la mode de Consuela* or, on one treasured occasion, *pad krapow moo saap,* a Thai gem of fried basil and pork.

Bruno stopped at the Hôtel de Ville to tell the mayor, his employer, that he would be otherwise engaged that day. The mayor simply nodded; Fauquet had already called him.

"Since I'm one of the guests tonight, I'm very happy you're stepping in," the mayor said. "Let me know if you need a hand peeling potatoes, setting tables or any other unskilled work."

Bruno thanked him, left his uniform jacket and cap in his office and went back to the market to recover Ivan's shopping bag. He let himself into the restaurant and went straight to the pantry to see what other supplies he would need. On the counter beside the stove, he found a copy of the menu, written in Ivan's italic hand.

Kir royal de Ch Lestevenie et canapés de pâté de chevreuil

La soupe froide de tomates à la mousse aux herbes

Poulet à l'estragon avec sa purée de pommes de terre et ses haricots verts

Salade verte et ses fromages du coin

Mousse au yaourt et coulis de fraises

Café

Vins

Brut, Ch de Lestevenie

Bergerac Sec de Ch des Eyssards, 2020

Ch la Vieille Bergerie, cuvée Quercus, blanc, 2018

Ch Bélingard, réserve rouge, 2016

Ch de Monbazillac, 2015

Marie Duffau, hors d'âge, Bas-Armagnac

Bruno thought he'd better get some copies made, when his phone vibrated in the pouch on his belt. It was Pamela, the woman from Scotland whom the town had first nicknamed the Mad Englishwoman from her habit of coming to Fauquet's for her morning croissant on horseback, and then doing the London *Times* crossword, while Fauquet tried to stop the horse from eating his roses. She was now the joint owner of the local riding school and a respected member of the *chambre de commerce,* which had done more to integrate her into St. Denis than the gentle and reasonably discreet love affair Bruno had enjoyed with her. It was she who had given the recipe for the tomato soup to Ivan.

"Bruno, I've heard the news," she began. "Fabiola called me from the ambulance. I can make my soup and take some of the strain off you. I'm going to buy the tomatoes now. Are you in the restaurant?"

He said he was and would wait for her arrival. Then he opened the huge fridge. There were thirty chicken breasts, eight one-liter pots of Greek yogurt, four of crème fraîche and four labeled chicken stock, four kilos of unsalted butter, two of *demi-sel* and two dozen eggs, which Bruno had delivered to Ivan from his own chickens the previous day.

In the pantry, he found what looked to be ten kilos of old potatoes and the same amount of new ones, another five kilos of

16

green beans, a couple kilos of shallots, five kilos of yellow onions and two of red and a long tress of a dozen heads of garlic hung from a beam. There was a bottle of Armagnac, six of the brut and six of the Eyssards white, another six of the Quercus and twelve of the red. At a quick estimate, Bruno reckoned that Ivan had already spent some three hundred euros on drink.

Balzac, sniffing around the restaurant, had paused by the door that led out to the yard and gave a tiny yelp. Bruno went to open it, and Balzac scampered out to relieve himself on a patch of grass beyond the paved section. Ivan had not yet opened this area for summer lunches and dining, but there was more room here than in the small restaurant. Bruno paced the area and thought that if he placed the tables along three sides of a square, serving would be easy, and everyone could see everyone else, particularly the golden-wedding-anniversary couple at the center.

He found a broom and swept the terrace clean. There was a climbing vine along one wall, a wisteria had been trailed across another, and there were roses on the old stone wall that divided Ivan's yard from the house to the rear. There was plenty of basil, parsley, chives and tarragon in the herb

17

garden. Bruno plucked off a leaf of tarragon, sniffed and enjoyed the slightly numbing, aniseed taste when he chewed it. Good, it was the real French version, the sativa.

There were three iron bars running the length of the garden, well above head height, on which Ivan would sometimes hang lanterns, Bruno recalled. He'd try to find those, but before he could look, he heard the door to the street open and Pamela's voice calling his name.

"In the garden," he called in reply. She arrived with Gilles, Fabiola's partner, and put down what looked like five kilos of tomatoes before embracing him.

"Fabiola called from the ambulance to say you might need a hand," Gilles said.

"Looks like you're planning to feed them outside," Pamela said. "Good idea, always better at this time of year. The weather forecast is excellent, and it means the smokers won't have to make constant trips outside. Now, what's on the menu and what do we need to buy from the market?

"I'll do the soup, prepare the strawberries and make the Monbazillac sabayon and leave the main course to you," she said, after studying the menu Ivan had left. She went into the pantry and looked at the supplies.

"I don't see any venison pâté," she said.

"I think he was planning to use mine," said Bruno. "I'll bring a few jars from home."

"Good," said Pamela, halfway out the door. "I'll get the menu photocopied while you two move the tables and chairs outside."

"Funny how Pamela always likes to take charge," said Gilles, once the door had closed behind her. "It must come from running the riding school. But then Fabiola is the same. Do you think they were born that way?"

"No," said Bruno. "I think it probably comes from their experience with men like us. Let's get these tables moved."

Pamela reappeared just after the furniture was in place in the yard and wanted to know where Ivan kept his tablecloths. Bruno replied that he'd never seen him use them.

"You can't have a golden-wedding-anniversary dinner without tablecloths," Pamela said. She would go home and return with some of her own. Gilles was told to polish the wineglasses and ensure the cutlery was clean while Bruno prepared the *haricots verts.*

"Do them in butter, *façon conserve,*" she said as she left. "They're so much better that way."

First, Bruno began to drain some of the yogurt in a colander lined with paper towels. Then he cut the ends off three kilos of the *haricots* and turned to the bags of tomatoes. He put the four biggest red and the four yellow tomatoes to one side and turned on the oven to two hundred degrees Centigrade. He knew Pamela's recipe well, so he sliced the rest of the tomatoes in half crosswise, deseeded them before laying them sliced side up in two roasting pans, drizzled olive oil over them and slid them into the oven, setting the timer for forty minutes.

Despite Pamela's instructions, he thought he could leave the *haricots* until the evening, so he went looking for Ivan's lanterns. At the top of a storage cupboard full of crockery, he found three long electric wires with lightbulbs and several Chinese lanterns of different-colored paper, all neatly flattened and packed. He opened them up, found a stepladder and went into the garden with Gilles to fix the bulbs and lanterns to the bars. They were still at it when Pamela returned with the tablecloths.

Under her direction, they spread them over the tables and let her lay out the first set of cutlery with the soup spoons on the outside, before telling Gilles to do exactly the same layout with the other twenty-nine. She went to the kitchen to prepare the strawberries, and when the timer buzzed, Bruno took the roasted tomatoes from the oven and left them out to cool. Then he blanched and peeled the four big yellow and the four even-bigger red ones and seeded them, diced the flesh and put that in the fridge.

"What time does the dinner begin?" she asked. "I have to exercise the horses."

"Seven," Bruno replied, "with drinks and bits of toast with venison pâté, then we'll sit everyone down for the soup at seven-thirty. I think I can manage alone except for the serving. I'll come back about five to peel the potatoes, start on the chicken and make the salads."

"I'll be here by seven to finish the soup and make the yogurt-and-herb mousse," she said. "I can make the strawberry coulis while everyone is eating the main course. What are we going to do about servers? For thirty people you'll need at least three, preferably four. You and me make two, and Gilles, can you help?"

"Of course," he replied. "I'll be here at six. I may not be much of a cook, but I can peel potatoes, wash the lettuce and open wine."

21

"The mayor, the baron and I are all invited tonight, so we can help serve, and with you and Gilles assisting, we can easily handle it," Bruno said to Pamela. "In fact, the mayor already volunteered. Everybody will have heard about Ivan's illness, so they'll be happy to pitch in and help. Thank you for what you've both done so far. See you later."

Once they had gone, Bruno locked up and then called Patrice at home to say Ivan had been taken ill, but the dinner would still go ahead. Then with Balzac close behind, he set off on another patrol of the market that was now winding down, with the townsfolk and stallholders all asking after Ivan. He told them there was no news yet from the hospital, but he'd put something on the town noticeboard as soon as he heard. As he headed back toward the *mairie,* he was waved over by Stéphane at the cheese stall.

"I heard you're cooking instead of Ivan," Stéphane said. "I have a whole Tomme d'Audrix and thirty *crottins* of goat's cheese. When do you want me to drop them off?"

"Call me when you're ready to leave," Bruno replied. "And it's not just me; Gilles and Pamela have also stepped in, and the mayor and the baron will be helping."

"Really?" came a familiar voice from

behind Bruno. "So the whole town is rallying to make sure the golden-wedding-anniversary feast goes ahead. That's great, a nice heartwarming and feel-good story on a slow news day," said Philippe Delaron, the local reporter for *Sud Ouest,* camera at the ready and notebook in his hand.

"I hear you were with Ivan when he collapsed and carried him over the bridge to the medical center," Philippe continued.

"No, Fauquet and I wheeled him there in Maurice's handcart," said Bruno, impatiently. "I have to go."

"I'll see you later at the dinner. Patrice and Monique have asked me to drop by and take some pictures for the family album. What's on the menu?"

"Just what Ivan planned," said Bruno, before heading into the *mairie* to tackle the morning's paperwork. It seemed to grow by the week. He sighed, sat down and thought about opening that morning's mail while scanning his emails. But instead, he pulled out a notepad and wrote down the timings of the various components he'd have to cook. Twenty minutes for the potatoes, then two minutes more to mash them with milk and butter, thirty or thirty-five minutes for the chicken plus another five or ten minutes for the sauce and fifteen minutes for the beans.

Drinks and canapés at seven, the soup at seven-forty, so the main course should be served at eight-fifteen and the salad and cheese at nine, the dessert at nine-thirty, then coffee and Armagnac at ten. But there would be speeches, certainly from the mayor and the eldest son, probably from one of the grandchildren, and no doubt cards from distant friends and relatives to be opened and read aloud. So he would assume it would go on until closer to eleven, but the only hot dish was the chicken, and if he planned that for eight-fifteen, the various other tasks and timings would fall into place. The job suddenly seemed less daunting.

Balzac was just taking his usual place under the desk for one of his many naps when the phone rang, and Stéphane said he was ready to drop off the cheese. Bruno grabbed his hat and went out into the hallway, where Claire, the mayor's secretary, turned up the radio. "Listen, it's about you," she said.

It was indeed a feel-good piece that Philippe was doing live for the listeners of France Bleu, Périgord's lunchtime magazine show, about a small town rallying to save a golden-wedding-anniversary dinner, when the restaurateur had been taken ill. The town policeman would be cooking, and the mayor and the local landowner, the baron, would be serving. Philippe then read out the mouthwatering menu, and the piece ended with a statement from the mayor about the splendid public spirit of St. Denis.

"And Ivan, if you're able to hear this, the whole town wants you to get well soon," he added, with a final flourish.

A very slow news day, thought Bruno, as he returned to the restaurant to receive the cheese from Stéphane. He put the sparkling wine and the white wines in the fridge, and then his phone vibrated in the pouch at his waist. It was Fabiola to say that she'd heard from the hospital and that Ivan's appendix had been removed in time, and he was expected to make a swift and successful recovery. Bruno drafted a short bulletin, returned to the *mairie* so Claire could type it up and then went downstairs again to pin it on the noticeboard. He also put his head around the door of the café to tell Fauquet the good news, which was probably a more efficient way to spread the word.

Shortly before five, he left for home to shower and change and feed his chickens before heading back to Ivan's with four big jars of his homemade venison pâté. He stopped to get six fresh baguettes, still warm, from the *boulangerie* on the way. Juliette, the manageress, handed him a large cake box, wrapped with red ribbon, that she wanted to offer to the feast. She had heard Philippe Delaron's description of the menu.

"It's a chocolate cake that should go perfectly with the strawberry dessert I heard you're making," she said.

Once in Ivan's kitchen, Bruno washed his hands and started to cook. He began by cutting each of the chicken breasts into four pieces and then put two hundred grams of butter and two wineglasses of olive oil into a pan and onto the stove to melt. He placed two dry roasting pans over the flames to heat up, and poured the melted oil over the heaps of chicken breasts, rotating them to ensure they were all coated.

Once they had browned in the hot pan, he put them aside, tucking sprigs of tarragon around them, until it was time to make the sauce. Once that was done, he'd need thirty minutes to bake them. So he started on the *haricots* as Gilles came in and asked how many potatoes he should peel. Five kilos plus a big one for luck, Bruno said, knowing the people of St. Denis had good appetites. Then he began peeling and chopping a dozen shallots and then a head of garlic, chatting with Gilles about this and that, determined to damp down the sense of nervousness about this daunting transition from cooking a meal for six or eight friends to catering for thirty paying customers.

Pamela arrived at six-fifty, went to the garden for chives and basil and then began whipping egg whites into the yogurt to make the herb mousse for her chilled soup. Bruno began slicing the baguettes and smearing on chunks of the venison, and Gilles then laid them on various serving plates. Patrice and Monique arrived at seven sharp, and Bruno led them out to the terrace, where the sparkling wine was waiting in ice buckets. He began opening bottles and making kirs as the rest of the guests trooped in. Gilles emerged with the canapés, and soon the scene was buzzing with activity as the couple's two great-grandchildren darted around and the teenage granddaughter began playing audiocassettes of 1960s and 1970s music on a boom box. Bruno hadn't seen such cassettes for years.

He helped Pamela, carrying out the trays of soup bowls, while she put a bowl at each place setting. Then he went inside to start on his sauce, setting the oven to one hundred eighty degrees Centigrade. He put two Le Creuset casserole dishes onto the heat with butter and olive oil along with the two handfuls of shallots. He had a liter of chicken stock heating in a saucepan, and when the shallots were ready, he added five tablespoons of Dijon mustard, six tablespoons of sherry vinegar, a generous wineglass of cognac, then added salt and pepper, a whole bunch of tarragon and a liter of crème fraîche. Finally, he added the browned chicken and put the big roasting casseroles into the oven, covered with their lids, and set the timer for thirty minutes.

He had two kettles of boiling water ready for the potatoes, which he chopped so they would cook faster. The rest of the boiling water he salted and used to boil the *haricots* for four minutes and then drained them, saving about half a liter of the liquid. Into yet another roasting pan, he melted a stick of butter and tossed in the minced shallots and garlic, salt and pepper. Once they had softened, he added the beans, stirring them in thoroughly, and then the chicken stock, turning the gas up high to reduce the liquid to a syrup.

"They all seem very happy, lots of reminiscences and toasts," said Pamela, coming back into the kitchen and reporting that Gilles was attending to the wine. Without being asked, she checked that the potatoes were cooked and began to mash them, adding milk and butter. Bruno looked at his watch; it was eight-ten. The *haricots* had developed that lovely mellow, nutty flavor that he liked, so he turned off the heat to let them rest just as the timer pinged and he pulled the big casseroles of chicken from the oven, stirring in the last of the tarragon leaves.

Pamela had the plates lined up in rows on the counter, and as Bruno served out the chicken and beans, she added the mashed potatoes and took out the first two plates to the guests of honor. She came back with Gilles and the big tray, loaded four more plates onto the tray for him to carry out and for her to serve. Bruno continued filling the plates and, within moments, Gilles and Pamela were back for four more, followed by the baron and the mayor who each took two plates. Within just over five minutes, thirty people had been served, or rather twenty-nine, since Bruno was slicing the cheese for the salad course.

"Stop it," said Pamela. "I'll do that. Go out and join them. They invited you and they want you there, eating with them."

Bruno nodded and went out to take his seat at the end of one of the tables and was startled when the rest of the gathering rose to their feet and started applauding. He called Pamela and Gilles to join him. Pamela immediately put down her knife, took off her apron and made a little curtsy as the diners gave her a huge cheer.

"Well done, Bruno, Pamela and Gilles," cried Patrice. Monique came around from her seat to kiss Gilles and Pamela on both cheeks, murmuring her thanks. Then she kissed Bruno firmly on the lips as the other guests whistled and cheered.

"Bruno saves the day," cried the mayor.

"Ah, mais non," said Monique, turning with a pout of her lips and a flash of her eyes that made Bruno suddenly think how she would have looked fifty years ago. "Bruno saves the night!"

It was a success. Even the great-grandchildren said so, before they curled up with Balzac on an eiderdown that Pamela had brought down from Ivan's living quarters upstairs. The grown-ups finally staggered out close to midnight, having stuffed themselves on Pamela's strawberry gratin and the chocolate cake, topped off with glasses of Armagnac.

I'm exhausted, Bruno thought as he

loaded Ivan's enormous dishwasher, which had room for only half the dirty dishes. I'm very glad I don't do this for a living. Rather than drive home he went upstairs to Ivan's bed, cuddled up to Balzac and tried to sleep. But there was something sticking into his ear from beneath the pillow. He pulled it out and saw that it was a typed manuscript. It fell into sections, one entitled "Miko" and another "Gudrun." The pages were filled with lists of ingredients. It looked like a cookbook, filled with recipes.

Bruno glanced at the title page: *The St. Denis Cookbook.* He turned the page and saw a list of chapter headings, each one named after a woman — Birgit, Consuela, Gudrun, Mandy, Miko and Mum. Then came the dedication: "For my mother, Natalya, who loved Tolstoy, Tchaikovsky, Chekhov, Lenin and Mikhail Gorbachev, and then got sick of politics, took up cooking and now only votes Green."

Bruno fell asleep, thinking that was a wonderful start to any book. He awoke just before nine to the sound of the doorbell and female voices shouting through the keyhole. He let Balzac out into the garden and then opened the front door to see two attractive young women on the doorstep. One was tall and blonde, the other short and dark, and it took Bruno a moment — and the sudden rocketlike gallop of Balzac toward them — to realize they were Mandy and Miko.

"Last night on the radio we heard about Ivan and you standing in for him, so we're taking over the restaurant until Ivan is well enough to come back," said Mandy, hugging him, and then bending down to respond to Balzac's lavish welcome.

"I think you need my miso soup, Bruno," said Miko, pulling his head down to plant a smacking kiss on each cheek. "How happy I am to be back in St. Denis, even if we do have to start with the washing up."

THE LOST BOY

A pleasant business breakfast with an attractive young woman was a delightful way to start a fine day in May, thought Bruno. He was sitting on the terrace of Fauquet's café, overlooking the River Vézère, with Nathalie, a real-estate broker from Bordeaux, who wanted to use a drone to take photos of the château her client was selling. A woman of healthy appetite, she had demolished one of Fauquet's croissants with relish and a little help from Bruno's basset hound, Balzac. Now she was finishing a *chocolatine* as Fauquet brought each of them a second cup of coffee.

After Nathalie had called him the previous day, Bruno had checked with the aviation ministry and learned that his town was in a special corridor through which French military aircraft were entitled to fly at low level while heading for practice bombing zones in the Massif Central. As a result, he was now explaining to Nathalie, drone permits were required and strict height limits applied. He took a copy of her permit and told her that since no low-level flights were planned that day, she could fly her drone up to a height of five hundred meters. And if she felt like taking a practice flight over St. Denis, he and the mayor would enjoy seeing her film of the results over a convivial lunch at which she would be their guest.

"Of course," she said, smiling as she opened the small suitcase in which the drone and its camera lay amid cushions of black felt. "Maybe you could use it to promote tourism in St. Denis."

At that moment, Bruno's phone vibrated; it was Coralie, his counterpart at Les Eyzies, the next commune upstream.

"Bruno, we have a missing child," Coralie began. "Can you get here with your dog? I'm at the riverbank near the turnoff to Le Queylou. A family was on a canoe, and their six-year-old boy wandered away when the parents were preparing a picnic. You'll see my van. It looks like the kid crossed the road and went into the woods."

"On my way," he replied. "And I might bring reinforcements."

He turned to Nathalie. "We're looking for

a missing boy, six years old, just upriver. I think your drone could help."

"Of course, happy to do it," she said. "I don't know how useful the drone will be in all these woods, but I'm ready to try. If that's your police van, I'm parked alongside."

She followed him down the road toward Les Eyzies, past the château of Campagne and along the winding northern bank of the River Vézère. He slowed when he saw Coralie's van, but there was no room for him to pull in, so he drove on around a hairpin bend and parked on the dirt road that led to the snail farm at Le Queylou, leaving space for Nathalie to park ahead. He turned on his flashing blue light and put out a warning triangle on the bend of the road ahead before he and Nathalie headed back to Coralie's van with Balzac at their heels.

"This way," called Coralie, emerging from behind a log pile that had been stacked on the far side of the road. A common sight in the wooded Périgord countryside, the logs were left there for two years after the trees were felled to season before being carried off and cut into the stove-sized lengths that heated most of the rural homes of the region. Coralie had been looking out for him. Bruno introduced Nathalie and explained about the drone. Together with Balzac, they scrambled down the slope where a canoe had been beached and a tearful woman in yellow shorts and a pink T-shirt was seated on a blanket, cuddling a little girl. A picnic basket was open beside her.

"This is Madame Daumier," Coralie explained. "Her husband went off looking for the boy before I got here. His name is Pierre."

"Bonjour, madame," said Bruno. "This is Balzac, the best sniffer dog in the valley. He'll find Pierre. Do you have anything that belongs to the boy so he can absorb the scent?"

Wordlessly but with a grimace that was meant to be a smile, she handed Bruno a small jacket. He gave it to Balzac and asked what the boy was wearing and how long he'd been gone.

"Maybe thirty minutes," Madame Daumier said, pulling herself together but keeping a tight hold of her daughter. "We pulled in and began unloading, and when we looked around, Pierre had disappeared. My husband used his phone to call the *urgences,* and they sent this policewoman. Then he went looking for Pierre."

"What was Pierre wearing?" he repeated.

"Brown shorts, gray sweatshirt," she replied. Bruno gave a reassuring nod, although he'd hoped the boy might be wearing something more visible, like red or bright blue.

"Your *pompiers* are on their way," Coralie told him, watching with interest as Nathalie unpacked the drone. "Will that work in this wooded countryside?"

"We'll see," Bruno said and took the number of Daumier's mobile phone. "I'll follow the dog as it tracks Pierre's scent, and Nathalie here will set her drone searching, up and down the river-bank at first, and then ahead of me into the woods. Could you call your husband and ask him to let us know where he is, or at least get into a clearing and wave when he sees the drone overhead? I'll want him with me so Pierre can see a friendly face. Coralie, we can stay in touch by phone."

Bruno set off after Balzac, who went along the riverbank for a few yards and then scrambled up onto the road where he sniffed around the base of the log pile. Bruno wasn't sure if the dog was on Pierre's track or if he had been distracted by the scent of wild boar. Those ever-hungry omnivores tended to root around these two-meter-high stacks of logs, looking for acorns, while their young used their snouts to dig up grubs and nests of insect larvae. Balzac abandoned the logs, crossed the road and went snuffling into the woods, his head down on the scent. Bruno followed as best he could, his first-aid kit slung over his shoulder. With his phone to his ear, he kept the line open to tell Coralie the rough direction he was heading. His phone had a compass app so he was able to give her clear directions.

The ground here rose quickly toward a steep bluff. It was overgrown and dark from the foliage, so it was hard to see any distance ahead. After perhaps fifty meters, most of it uphill, Balzac paused at a hollow beneath a fallen tree. Perhaps the boy had settled there for a few moments. Then the dog tried to scramble his way over the tree, but his legs were too short. Bruno gave him a push over it, and Balzac began snuffling around, circling to look for the scent again. Farther along the fallen tree, he found it and went off in a new direction. Bruno relayed the new compass bearing to Coralie and began calling the boy's name. When there was no reply, he began shouting for Monsieur Daumier, but without success.

He tried Daumier's phone, but there was no connection. Reception was often tricky here where the woods were thick and the ground uneven, with rocky outcrops and sudden hollows. The recent rains had made the going tough, with last winter's dead leaves piled into a slippery mush in places. Bruno was about to call out again when he remembered that his voice and location would be distorted by the proximity of the cliff.

For the first time he began to worry. He'd assumed that, with Balzac and the drone, finding the boy would be easy. But the terrain was more treacherous and steeper than he'd expected. And there were abundant signs of wild boar in these woods. He'd seen several places where the earth had been plowed up around the trees where they'd hunted for truffles, and areas of flattened undergrowth where the pack had slept, ringed with their scat. He bent down to poke at the scat with a stick to see how fresh it was. At least two or three days old, he thought. The scent of wild boar was unmistakable, a pungent mixture of the familiar and the feral with that sourness that comes from omnivores. And they could be ferocious if they sensed that their young were endangered. He hoped that Pierre had the sense to avoid them.

Bruno paused as he tried to draw on his

mental map of the neighborhood. On either side of the rocky bluff were wooded valleys. The one nearest Les Eyzies led to the snail farm and the small hamlet at Le Queylou. The other valley, closer to Campagne, led to another hamlet, a commune that sometimes organized a music festival on Midsummer Eve. But there was a lot of dense woodland between them where the drone would be useless. Bruno sighed. Finding the boy would be up to Balzac and his nose.

He plunged on after his dog, and the sound of his breathing and his feet dragging through the undergrowth filled his ears until he had to stop to help Balzac scramble up another outcrop. Pierre must be a fit and determined lad, Bruno thought. This was no gentle stroll through the woods. They moved on and suddenly broke out into a clearing where Bruno could hear the whirring of the drone somewhere above him. He looked up, waving and turning the flashlight on his phone on and off, thinking the drone might spot the bursts of light. Maybe it had helped, he thought, as he saw the drone descend toward him. He noticed his phone had a connection again and called Coralie.

"We can see you on the drone," she replied. "And we just heard from Monsieur Daumier, although we can't see him. He's hurt, thinks he might have broken his ankle in a fall. And there's no sign of the boy."

"*Merde.* Does the father have any idea where he is?"

"No, he says he's lost." She kept her voice flat. "The father's wearing green and brown, so you'll need a stroke of luck to spot him. He says he fell in a ravine, and he's now trying to crawl to a clearing where the drone might see him. I've asked him to start waving once he hears it overhead. And the *pompiers* say they'll be here in ten minutes."

"If he's got a phone, tell him to use the flashlight app; the drone seemed to pick up mine," Bruno said.

Suddenly Balzac gave a long howl that meant his quarry was close if not yet in sight. Hoping that Balzac's cry would at least keep the wild boar away, he asked Coralie to make sure the drone followed him. Bruno kept his eyes on the flash of white at the tip of Balzac's tail that the dog always carried high when tracking. Suddenly Bruno heard a distant shout, as though someone else was responding to Balzac's cry.

"Monsieur Daumier," he called in a voice that had carried across some of the French army's largest parade grounds.

"*Allô,*" came the faint reply.

Bruno checked the compass reading of the

voice and reported back to Coralie that the man was within earshot at about forty degrees to the northeast. Moments later, the drone swooped in that direction.

"We've found the father," Coralie said, "or at least the drone has, about a hundred meters from your present location. He's in a small ravine, sitting on a ledge and waving at us."

"We're coming to you, Monsieur Daumier," Bruno shouted. "Please stay where you are."

Bruno plunged back into the woods, following Balzac, who was also going in the direction of the compass bearing, when Bruno suddenly felt his feet slide from beneath him and he dropped his phone. He grabbed for a tree to prevent himself from shooting feetfirst down a greasy slope, made slick by a steady stream of water. Luckily the tree, little more than a sapling, held his weight, and he scrambled back to level ground and retrieved his phone. Balzac had been standing over it. Coralie asked if he was okay.

"I slipped, but I'm fine now," he said. "I think we're close."

At the sight of his master, Balzac had turned, climbed to avoid a small spring, then plunged through another belt of trees, mainly hornbeam and hazel. Bruno followed him carefully downhill until he saw that Balzac stood immobile, one front paw raised and the hackles rising on his back. Bruno stopped in turn and caught the boar scent that had alerted Balzac.

As quietly as he could, making sure one foot landed soundlessly before moving the other, Bruno crept forward, feeling the breeze in his face. He came to a patch of drier ground that sloped downhill to a small stream, where two young boar were drinking. Their elders would be close, but upwind, alert to the smell of any threat before it came close.

He edged sideways, trying to look upstream, but the undergrowth around the banks was too thick. He shifted slowly to look downstream, and his heart jumped as he saw a small boy, oblivious to the animals, playing with pebbles at the side of the water. Bruno glanced down at Balzac, still immobile but waiting for instructions.

Bruno knew that boar preferred to avoid trouble if they could, and that they were wary of men with dogs. But the presence of their young made this dangerous. He put out his arm, hand down, and moved it forward, giving Balzac the signal to advance slowly to the edge of the slope, from where he could see the young boar. Balzac glanced at him, Bruno nodded, and Balzac tossed his head back and unleashed the long, powerful bay of a confident hunting dog. Suddenly Bruno saw a huge boar, at least two hundred kilos, lumber down to the stream and stand guard as the two young scuttled to shelter behind him. Bruno watched with his heart in his mouth as the adult boar scanned the banks for danger. At last, it turned and followed his youngsters away. Bruno breathed a huge sigh of relief.

"Pierre, stay where you are. Don't move," he called out as he saw the boy rise and stare after the vanishing boar. Balzac gave a short, sharp bark of success and scrambled down toward Pierre. A few moments later, Bruno reached the bank and greeted the small crouching boy, who grinned widely when he saw the basset hound.

"I have the boy in sight, by a stream, making friends with Balzac and looking fine," Bruno said into his phone and joined Pierre, who seemed to have been trying to build a small dam of pebbles in the stream. The boy smiled and waved at Bruno before making friends with Balzac, appearing not in the least concerned. Bruno glanced up at the thick canopy of trees above the stream. No wonder the drone hadn't spotted the boy.

"If Daumier has a broken ankle, we'll need the *pompiers* to bring him out," Bruno told Coralie over the phone. He looked back upstream to be sure the boar had gone. "I'll bring the boy back, but I'll also reassure the father."

"Is this your dog, monsieur?" the boy asked.

"Yes, Pierre, and his name is Balzac. I see you've made friends with him already. He found you by sniffing after your trail. Your mother asked us to come and find you. She was getting worried. Your dad went out looking for you too."

"I'm fine. It's nice here in the woods. But I haven't found the cave yet. I reached the big rock where I saw it, but I couldn't climb up that high. Papa is taking us to a cave later today that has very old paintings in it. He says the caves are very special in the Périgord."

"Your papa is right about that, but he and your mother are worried about you. They thought you'd gotten lost."

"I wasn't lost. I told Maman I was going to the cave." He took in Bruno's uniform. "Are you a policeman?"

"That's right. Can you stay there a few minutes with Balzac? I want to see if I can catch up with your dad, who went in the

45

other direction."

"I think I saw a deer," Pierre said. "And there were some little *sangliers* by the stream, like the ones in the Astérix books."

"Yes, there are lots of them in these woods. You just stay here and don't move, okay?"

Remembering the boy's father might have a broken ankle, Bruno soaked a bandage in the cold stream and then followed the compass bearing across the water, up another slope and through more woods. He found Monsieur Daumier a few minutes later, the drone hovering above the small ravine in which he lay. He had taken off one of his shoes, revealing a very swollen ankle. Bruno waved at the drone.

"Sorry," the man said. "You must think I'm a real fool."

"No, monsieur," Bruno said. "I think you are a concerned and courageous father. These woods can be daunting if you don't know them. But Pierre is fine. My dog is with him, and I'll just strap up your ankle and then take Pierre back to his mother. The *pompiers* will be here shortly to take you back to the medical center. The drone and I both know where you are, and your wife has been told that you and Pierre are okay."

Bruno probed gently at the ankle but couldn't tell if it was broken or just badly sprained. He wrapped it loosely in the wet bandage to reduce the swelling and gave the man an aspirin from his first-aid kit.

"How the hell do I get the canoe back?" Daumier asked.

"Don't worry about that. Where did you rent it? Les Eyzies?"

Monsieur Daumier nodded.

"That's fine, I'll tell them to pick it up, and I can give your wife a lift back to your car while the *pompiers* take you to the clinic in St. Denis. You stay here for the moment. I'll take your son back, and the drone will guide the *pompiers* to you."

He walked back through the woods, hand in hand with Pierre, but the boy was obviously getting tired, so Bruno picked him up and carried him in one arm, keeping the other free to make sure of his balance, clutching at the saplings on the slopes. Soon the road came into view. As soon as Bruno saw Philippe Delaron's 4×4, with its PRESSE sticker on the windshield, pull in behind the fire engine, he knew this was likely to turn into a media circus.

Nathalie and her drone were Philippe's first target, even ahead of the lost boy. Once he'd taken photos of her, and then of Pierre

47

alone, of Pierre reunited with his mother and sister, of Pierre with his rescuer Balzac and finally of Pierre in the canoe, Philippe took some shots of Coralie, always photogenic in her police uniform, before he turned to Bruno.

"Don't you have enough shots of me?" Bruno asked. He'd been telling Madame Daumier about her son's attempt to find a cave.

"Not looking so muddy," Philippe said as he held down the button on his camera and clicked off a burst of shots that reminded Bruno of a silenced machine gun. Then he pulled out his phone to record a quick interview with Bruno for France Bleu Périgord, the local radio station. From Madame Daumier, Philippe took her husband's full name and their hometown, which Bruno learned was Chatou, a comfortable suburb just outside Paris. Finally, Philippe wanted more photos of Nathalie with her drone as it came back to land. It was a sight that transfixed young Pierre, even more when he could see himself on Nathalie's control screen, filmed by the drone as it descended slowly to the riverbank and finally came in to land.

"Those drones could be useful for you and the *pompiers*," Philippe called out to

Bruno. "Would you like one?"

"That will be up to the council," Bruno replied. "They don't come cheap."

"Will you recommend buying one to the mayor?"

"Perhaps," Bruno replied, wondering how his cautious reply would be spun. "It was certainly helpful in this instance because the boy's father was lost and injured. The drone spotted the father, but in this dense undergrowth it couldn't find the boy. Balzac did that, tracking him all the way."

"So you deployed the old methods along with the new technology," said Philippe. "That makes a nice story."

When the *pompiers* finally returned with Monsieur Daumier on a stretcher, Bruno shook his hand and had to pose for another burst of photos. Nathalie went off to the château her clients were selling. Bruno drove Madame Daumier and her children to their car, which was parked at the canoe rentals office in Les Eyzies. He offered to lead her to the St. Denis clinic, but she said she knew how to get there, since they were staying at a hotel near Campagne, which was on the way.

"We had a booking to visit Lascaux later this morning, but we can't make it with my husband at the clinic," Madame Daumier went on. "Pierre will be so disappointed. And we're leaving tomorrow."

"Perhaps another time," Bruno said, and went into the rentals office to tell them where to find their missing canoe. Then France Bleu Périgord called Bruno, wanting him to describe the rescue live on air. Finally, he waved goodbye to Coralie, and he and Balzac got into his van to drive a few hundred meters beyond Les Eyzies to stop at the Font de Gaume cave.

"We just heard you on the radio, Bruno, about finding that little boy," said Marianne, the wife of a hunting club friend, as he approached the counter.

"The boy was looking for a cave," Bruno explained. "They were planning to go to Lascaux this afternoon, but then he got lost, and they missed their slot. I was wondering if there was any way you could squeeze the boy and his mother and sister in tomorrow morning. They have to drive home at lunchtime, and he'll never get to see a painted cave otherwise."

Marianne took their names and said if they turned up with Bruno at nine in the morning, thirty minutes before the cave opened, she'd take them in herself. He thanked her and drove back to their hotel to leave a message for Pierre's family.

The next morning, Bruno led the way to Font de Gaume, Madame Daumier following in her car. When they arrived, Pierre and his sister seemed far more interested in Balzac than they were in the cave, but Bruno promised them they would see evidence that children like them had been in the cave tens of thousands of years ago.

Marianne, who was waiting for them, greeted Pierre by name and led the way up the steep path that clung to the side of the great limestone cliff. Almost four hundred meters long, it was too much for Pierre's young sister, so Bruno picked her up and carried her until they emerged onto a flat area where two large, circular cave mouths appeared in view, almost like a pair of eyes, sheltered by a great overhang.

"Which cave do you want to see, Pierre?" Marianne asked, then clapped her hands in delight when he pointed to the one on the right. "How did you know that's the important one?"

"Because I'm right-handed," he replied. Marianne asked Bruno if he minded leaving Balzac outside, then she led them into the cave. As they filed in, Pierre turned to give a farewell wave to Balzac, who sat patiently just outside the entrance.

Bruno approved of the brisk way she

showed them around the cave, ignoring the first bison they came across as it required too much imagination to see their shapes emerge through the faded paints and bumps in the rock. Instead, she led them through two very narrow passages to the great chamber, twelve meters high, with a great row of bison on the right and one of the most famous images of prehistory on the left, the two "kissing reindeer." One reindeer was sunk on its knees, its head lowered, while the one standing above had its neck extended to lick the head of the one below.

The curves of the haunches were echoed by the majestic sweep of two sets of antlers, which seemed to flow into each other in a perfect and almost interlocking balance. But beyond the grace of these horns and the way they joined and balanced the images of the kneeling and standing beasts, the power of the painting lay in the unmistakable sense of tenderness and affection the two animals embodied.

"Can you see the mouths?" Marianne asked the two children. "The taller reindeer with the biggest antlers is licking the head of the one below, and you can see his tongue. Do you see the little bump of rock on the wall that the artist used to represent the tongue? And the one below, perhaps his mate, do you see how her mouth is formed from a natural crack in the wall. Don't you think that the artist first saw that crack and that bump in the rock and then imagined the whole scene from that moment?"

Marianne did not test the children's patience by trying to point out the engravings and the faded mammoths lurking behind the bison, but she did show them briefly where their imaginations could help them see the lone wolf and the ancient oxen and also the strange tent-shaped signs over which academic debate still continued.

"Some say they look like little houses or maybe giant traps for animals," Marianne explained. "But other people think they are signs for the names of different families, because at this time the people didn't have writing. We think that some of these signs are eighteen thousand years old, more than five hundred generations of people between them and us."

She showed them the patches of color on a ledge where the artists had made their paints, explaining that they had baked different kinds of clay in fire until the lumps hardened and then ground them into dust once they had dried. The iron oxides produced various shades of red and brown depending on how long the clay had been baked, and the manganese oxides produced black.

"There is so much iron ore in the ground here that there used to be lots of blacksmiths in this valley making swords and armor for the knights in the Middle Ages. And you know cannons, the big guns that were used on sailing ships?"

"Like pirates?" asked Pierre.

"Yes, like pirates, and also navy ships," Marianne replied. "Many of the cannons were made near here at St. Denis and then shipped down the river to the big warships at Bordeaux. A lot of their gunpowder was also made around here.

"The important thing about this cave is that it's one of the last of the painted caves still open to the public. The others, like Lascaux, have entrance restricted because of all the breathing of the visitors and the bacteria they bring in on their shoes. The other caves were sealed off for thousands of years. But this cave has always been open, protected by the long entranceway to reach the main paintings, which is why they have been preserved."

Some of this went over the children's heads, but their mother was totally absorbed. Bruno had heard all this many times before.

Finally, Marianne took the children to the small ledge just below an image of a pair of bison facing each other and told them to bend down and squirm into the cavity. Then she shone her flashlight so they could see the stenciled handprints where people had held their open hands against the wall and then put black paint into their mouths and sprayed it, so that the shape emerged as an eerie white hand.

"Don't touch, but do you think your hand would fit inside? Could they be children's hands, who were here while Mommy and Daddy painted?" she asked.

"My hand fits!" said Pierre's sister, with a squeal of delight.

When Marianne led them out into the sunlight, the grown-ups and the children alike all blinked against the unaccustomed brightness. Pierre, looking up from his embrace of Balzac, said that he wanted to be a cave painter when he grew up, and his sister at once said that she did too as she knelt down beside her brother to make friends with the dog. Bruno was surprised that thirty minutes had passed; he had thought they had been inside for less than half that time. He thanked Marianne for doing such an excellent job.

"That was wonderful, thank you," said

Madame Daumier. "It's made our trip."

"And we'll have to come back so Daddy can see it next time," said Pierre. Marianne refused Madame Daumier's attempt to tip her, but she did allow her to pay for a coloring book of the cave for each of the children.

"Let me know if you come back to the Périgord," Bruno said. "We'll look forward to seeing you all again. Especially you, Pierre, but no wandering off on your own next time. If you want to find a cave, just ask me and Balzac."

"Can we use the drone again when we come, please," Pierre asked.

THE BIRTHDAY LUNCH

Bruno Courrèges, the town policeman of St. Denis, awoke when his cockerel saluted the first glow of a sun that was about to rise. He remembered falling asleep to the sound of heavy rain. He rose, pulled back the curtain and saw the puddles in the yard, drops still falling from the barn roof, but at last the sky was clear and the downpour had ended. He smiled to himself, thinking that his friends would be able to have their lunch outdoors today. His usual morning run through the woods would be sodden underfoot, so he decided to take the route along the ridge, which would be well drained. He felt excited by the prospect of the way the land would look after the storm, as if all the earth and the air had been washed clean and he could see forever.

Twenty minutes later and nearly two kilometers from his home, with his dog, Balzac, trotting tirelessly beside him and not another soul to be seen, Bruno felt privileged, as if this place he knew so well, where the ridge widened into a plateau, had somehow been re-created overnight just for him. The air had never been clearer, the river never such a perfect silver, and the thin grass of the plateau had become a lush green overnight. Even the hardy shrubs looked almost festive, and he enjoyed the freshness in his mouth and throat. It seemed to be pure oxygen he was breathing.

Bruno almost laughed aloud with the pleasure of it when suddenly he stumbled, his ankle turning a little. He slowed and then stopped, looking back at the stone on which he'd lost his footing. One side of it was smooth enough to shine in the slanting rays of the early morning sun. Bending down to look, Bruno thought of his friend Horst, the German archaeologist, telling him of the prehistoric flint tools he sometimes found emerging from the upland soils after rain. He knelt to examine the stone more closely, pushing away Balzac, who had come back to see what interested his master.

The top of the stone was gray and rounded, but what caught his eye was the smoothness below. He put out a finger to feel it. It could almost have been glass, or polished metal. He gripped the rounded top and began trying to rock it loose from the earth. It resisted at first but then gave a little. He persevered until, with a slight sucking sound, it came free.

The stone was not quite as long as his outstretched hand but nearly as wide. The roundness fit comfortably into his palm, and he wet his finger to wipe free some of the soil that clung to the smooth face that had caught the sun. The other side of the stone was rough, and the smooth face narrowed slowly into something too blunt to be called a point. Only toward this blunt end did the side of the stone sharpen into edges. One edge seemed to have lost a chip, and maybe that was why it had been discarded. But the other was still sharp enough to shave the hairs from his forearm. He weighed it in his hand and reckoned it was close to half a kilo. He mimed using it as a hammer, but it felt more like a weapon than a tool. He'd have to ask Horst, but Bruno knew enough of prehistoric tools from his visits to the local museum to think it might have been a hand ax.

The term "Mousterian" came into his head, the flint tools of the Neanderthals who had lived and hunted in this region forty thousand years earlier, and probably for a hundred thousand years before that.

Such items were not rare in the Périgord, where the Vézère Valley contained more prehistoric sites and painted caves than anywhere else on earth. Horst had once called it the Champs-Élysées of our ancestors, a unique concentration of early humans, Neanderthal and their Cro-Magnon successors alike, so stone tools such as this were not hard to find. Souvenir shops sold such items — hand axes, blades and scrapers — for a few euros. And there were professional flint walkers, people who made a modest living from tramping the land after rains with trowels and looking for likely finds. Bruno thought the one in his hand was an unusually fine example.

He peered into the hole in the earth that the flint had left, wondering if the broken piece from the edge might still be there. It looked empty, but a little water had begun to gather at the bottom of the hole. He put a hand in and felt gingerly around, but there was nothing more. He stood up and made a few more passes with his hand ax, thinking it could do a lot of damage, certainly able to stun a horse or an ox, kill a deer or even a man. He wondered what deeds this ax had done in the hands of other men and women tens of thousands of years ago on this same ridge above the same river. Bruno felt himself almost shiver at the thought as he turned and began to run back, the ax in his hand. It was not especially heavy, but carrying it made him feel slightly unbalanced, as though he ought to have another weapon in his other hand, perhaps a spear.

Once at home, he rinsed the stone clean in the sink and set it out to dry in the sun before putting it with some other small finds — some fossils, an arrowhead and a flint scraper — that he kept on the bookcase in his living room. He fed his chickens, showered and, with Balzac beside him on the front seat of his elderly Land Rover, Bruno headed for Pamela's riding school to join the morning ritual of exercising the horses.

"What are you getting Florence for her birthday?" Pamela asked as they rubbed down the horses after the ride. "Or are you just giving her the birthday lunch?"

"I found a decent wine carafe at the last *vide-grenier,*" Bruno replied. He seldom missed one of these local flea markets. The term meant "empty attic," and over the years he'd found them a useful source of tableware, linen sheets and wineglasses. "I'll wrap it up so Florence and the kids can have the fun of opening it. How about you?"

"I got her a couple of DVDs of Jane Austen films. You know she started reading the novels to improve her English, and now she's hooked."

"I'm glad you can join us," he said. "I was worried that you would have to run things here."

"Miranda can take care of the riding school and the *gîtes* for a day, and I wouldn't miss Florence's birthday lunch. What are you cooking?"

"It's a surprise," he said, and kissed her *au revoir*. He put on his uniform jacket and képi before driving back into St. Denis. There he parked behind the medical center and stood beside the big plastic recycling boxes where he waited for people to bring their old newspapers. He didn't have to wait long.

"Good for wrapping presents," he explained as he stored the papers in his Land Rover. Then he performed his customary patrol of the Saturday morning market. It was too early in the day for tourists, so he greeted the regular stallholders before treating himself to a coffee and croissant at Fauquet's, skimming the headlines in *Sud Ouest* and giving Balzac his expected treat of a mouthful of croissant. He strolled out to his favorite fishmonger and scanned the stall.

"Bonjour, Gervaise. Could you fillet me eight of those red mullets but leave the tails on?" Bruno asked, knowing that his fish were always fresh. "If I'm back to pick them up in thirty minutes, will that be all right?"

"No problem. These were trucked up from Marseille overnight," Gervaise replied. "How do you plan to serve them?"

"I thought I'd simply grill them and serve them with zucchini and a tapenade."

"Sounds good, you might want to add a sprig of thyme when you grill them. See you in thirty minutes."

Bruno stopped at Marcel's stall for a bag of lemons and two hundred grams of fat black olives. At Stéphane's cheese stall he bought a pot of double cream and another of crème fraîche, some aged Comté cheese and half a dozen *crottins* of goat cheese. Then he paused at the stall of Vietnamese food where he saw his friend Gilles waiting while Madame Vinh heated his *nem* in her deep fryer.

"You want one, Bruno?" she called. "You can share the sauce."

"You know I can't resist them. Bonjour, Gilles. I don't think one *nem* will spoil our lunch."

Gilles embraced him and bent to stroke Balzac while Madame Vinh poured some of her secret sauce into a small plastic cup. She wrapped the two *nem* in a paper napkin, picked out a two-euro coin from the change Gilles offered and waved away the other money.

"Special price for regulars," she said.

"How's your son?" Bruno asked. "Still enjoying university?"

"Big arguments. We want him to be an accountant, but he wants to study winemaking."

"I thought he wanted to be an archaeologist," Bruno said.

"That was last year. Now it's wine." She shook her head, muttering "Kids these days . . ." before turning to serve another customer.

Bruno and Gilles took turns dipping their hot *nem* into the sauce. Between bites, Bruno asked, "How's Fabiola?"

"She's great, and she's taking Florence to that new hammam at Les Glycines as a birthday present, so they'll both be sparkling clean and relaxed when they turn up for lunch."

Gilles took his final bite and tossed the napkin into the bin beside the stall. "Talking of lunch, shouldn't you be cooking?"

Bruno stopped at the *boulangerie* for a large, round *tourte* of bread. Once back home, he took a pot of chicken stock he'd made earlier from the fridge. He changed into jeans and gardening boots, put on a pair of rubber gloves and took a bucket and a pair of pruning shears to the patch of young nettles that grew around the chicken coop. He snipped off all the young shoots and the youngest leaves and tossed the rest to his chickens before taking a dozen new-laid eggs. Then he picked the two best-looking lettuces, cut ten zucchini and dug up a carrot and some new potatoes. He snipped half a dozen sprigs of basil and some chives and went back to the kitchen where he tuned his radio to France Musique. He liked cooking to music.

He peeled and chopped a large onion and the carrot and washed the vegetables, herbs and salad. He squeezed the juice from four lemons and used a fine cheese grater to scrape some zest from the skin, then broke four eggs plus four more yolks into a bowl, saving the four separated egg whites.

He beat the yolks and eggs together with a hundred and fifty grams of sugar until they were creamy. Then he added the lemon juice and zest and a half teaspoon of salt and began to stir until the mixture was smooth. He put it onto medium heat, stirring steadily and enjoying the fresh tang of the lemon that rose as he worked. When the mixture began to thicken, he pushed it through a large strainer into a bowl. He put this curd to one side to cool before the next step.

He whisked the egg whites until stiff peaks formed, then stirred in a hundred grams of sugar. Next, he began gently to fold the curd into the stiffened egg whites. Once they were mixed, he whisked a hundred and fifty grams of double cream with a teaspoon of vanilla extract and folded this into the lemon mousse. He spooned it into eight serving glasses and put them in the fridge.

Next came the tapenade. He took an anchovy from the jar he kept in the fridge, washed it under the tap and removed the bones. He took the pits from the black olives before tossing olives and anchovy into his blender with a tablespoon of capers, blitzed them and began gradually adding olive oil until he had a smooth but slightly lumpy paste. He put the tapenade into the fridge.

Now for the soup. He scooped a generous spoonful of duck fat into a large saucepan and set it onto a low heat. When it was melted, he tossed in the chopped onion to soften, stirring from time to time. He took a large potato from his pantry, peeled it and cut it into small cubes. This would bulk out the soup. Once the onion was ready, he poured in stock and added the cubes of potato, the chopped carrot and nettles. He seasoned the soup with salt and pepper and brought it all to a simmer. The nettle soup would need fifteen minutes to cook. This gave him time to prepare and take a tray with cutlery, soup bowls, plates and glasses to the outdoor table. He brushed the table clean and wiped it before placing the large sheet he used as a tablecloth. Then he washed the carafe he was giving to Florence and left it upside down to drain.

The soup was ready. He took the handheld blender that the mayor had given him for Christmas from the cupboard and puréed the soup. It looked a little thick, but he could always add some water later. He dried the carafe and wrapped it first in tissue paper left over from Christmas, and then in layer after layer of newspaper until it was swollen to twice its actual size. He recalled from the last Christmas party how much the children had delighted in endless layers of wrapping paper. Then he put it into a cardboard box, sealed it with adhesive tape and took from his box of recycled Christmas wrappings a large square of red paper that looked not quite large enough. No matter. He took a second square of yellow paper and taped them together to wrap the box.

Then Bruno paused. What about the

children? He should have thought of getting something for them, and there was no time now to go back to town. He pondered a moment while Balzac sat at his feet and looked meaningfully at Bruno's bookcase. Bruno nodded. He should have thought of that. From the bookcase he took an arrowhead for Daniel and a flint scraper for Dora and wrapped them both, shiny gold paper for Dora and shiny silver for Daniel. Thinking again, he went back to his bookcase, picked up the hand ax he'd found that morning and wrapped it first in tinfoil and then in white tissue paper.

He set the outdoor table and erected his large parasol while Balzac, realizing that all these preparations heralded the visit of friends, went to the driveway to watch for their arrival. Bruno checked that he had sufficient white wine in the fridge and some apple juice for the children. He prepared the cheese board and covered it with a cloth, cut the *tourte* in half and carved off eight thick slices. He put six coffee cups onto a tray with a bowl of sugar lumps and then washed up the dirty dishes to have a clean kitchen for the final steps. When he heard Balzac baying, Bruno put the soup tureen into hot water to keep warm, turned off the radio and went out to welcome his guests.

Pamela was driving the secondhand Range Rover she had bought for the riding school, with Fabiola beside her and Gilles in the back. Behind her came the baron in his stately old Citroën DS bringing Florence and her two children, who exploded from the rear door to greet Balzac.

"Fresh from the hammam, you look wonderful," said Bruno, embracing Florence. "And happy birthday."

"It was my first time there, but it won't be the last," she said, kissing him on both cheeks. "I feel utterly, completely clean. Fabiola used this rough glove to scrape me down, and I tingle all over. I can't think when I felt so completely relaxed. And I think I could eat two lunches, not just one."

The baron handed Bruno a bottle of cold champagne; Gilles was carrying another and Pamela a third.

"We can't drink all that, at least not today," Bruno said, handing the bottle to the baron to be opened. Then he bent down to give Dora and Daniel a hug. "*Bonjour, les petits*. Does Maman think that apple juice is okay for you two?"

"One glass, and water after that," Florence said as they strolled to the table.

"Just like me," said Fabiola. "I'm prescribing myself one very small glass of champagne, and then it's water."

A child on each knee as he sat at the head of his table, surrounded by his friends and with the sun on his face, Bruno felt content. He asked Florence what time she had been awoken that morning.

"They clambered into bed with me soon after dawn," she said fondly. "They brought me a bowl of yogurt and a glass of orange juice, saying I deserved breakfast in bed for my birthday."

"Can we go and see the chickens with Balzac?" Dora asked.

The children scampered off with the basset hound, and Bruno was able to enjoy a sip of champagne and hear all about the hammam. Then the baron recounted his morning of babysitting. He had taken Florence's children out in his canoe, safely tied into their life jackets, in the hope of catching some fish.

"I'd forgotten how kids of that age are never silent," he said. "They scared away all the fish for miles. But at least they didn't fall in. And it's given me an appetite. What are we eating, Bruno?"

"I'll announce each dish as it comes to the table," he replied. "Give me a minute to bring out the first course."

In the kitchen, he turned on the heat beneath the soup and did the same for the new potatoes he'd prepared. Then he took out to the table a bowl of crème fraîche, the bread and a cold bottle of a favorite local white wine, a Cuvée Mirabelle from Château de la Jaubertie. He asked Gilles to open it while the baron poured out the rest of the champagne. Florence called her children to the table as Bruno emerged with the soup tureen.

"*Soupe aux orties,*" he announced. "Nettles picked fresh this morning."

"Will they sting?" Dora asked nervously as Bruno dropped a spoonful of crème fraîche into each helping. As this began to melt, he added some finely chopped chives.

"Not now that they've been cooked, but if you don't like it, Balzac will."

"Oh no, this is mine," Dora said firmly and began to eat with appetite.

The bowls were emptied quickly, as was the tureen. Bruno excused himself and took the dirty dishes into the kitchen and set the dinner plates onto the rack above the grill to warm. He turned on the grill, took the tapenade from the fridge and began to slice the zucchini thinly lengthwise. Then he remembered Gervaise's advice and went out

71

to pick some sprigs of thyme from the herb garden.

He salted and peppered the flesh sides of the mullets, laid them all on a baking tray skin side up and broke a small spring of thyme onto each one before sliding them beneath the grill. He sautéed the slender strips of zucchini in his largest frying pan in a little olive oil before adding salt and pepper, crushed basil leaves and two large tablespoons of tapenade, stirring it all gently for a few seconds. Finally, he began to arrange the zucchini onto the warmed plates.

The new potatoes were cooked, and he placed them in a deep dish with slivers of butter over the top. Now the eight mullets were ready. He removed the baking tray and placed a mullet on top of the zucchini on each plate, gave a final twirl of his pepper mill and began taking the fish out to the table. He served the children first so that Florence could help them with the bones. Last, he brought out the new potatoes and another bottle of white wine.

A happy silence fell as his friends applied themselves energetically to their food, and the children slipped bits of potato to Balzac, until Florence lifted her glass and called for a toast to the cook. The others raised their glasses and Bruno grinned at them all with pleasure and raised his own glass in thanks. The baron asked Pamela how the season looked, and she replied that her *gîtes* were all booked up for the summer. Fabiola was watching the children fondly, her right hand gently clasping Gilles's left where it rested on the table.

"There are no second helpings of the fish, I'm afraid," said Bruno, clearing the plates. "But there's cheese and salad to come. And dessert."

Pamela helped him clear the table. In the kitchen she piled the plates in the sink and asked when he was going to give Florence her presents. After the dessert, with the coffee, he replied, knowing that she had to be back at the riding school at four to check in the new tenants for her *gîtes*. She nodded and took out the cheese board while Bruno tossed the salad in vegetable oil and a splash of balsamic vinegar, adding a final dash of walnut oil for flavor, and brought it to the table, where he heard Florence explaining her latest plan for her pupils at the *collège*. She had already launched a computer club, a kitchen garden club, and now she was planning an archaeology club, where the schoolchildren could attend lectures at the local prehistory museum and help on its local digs in the summer.

73

Her energy was extraordinary, Bruno thought. But he was even more impressed by the way she used her role as a teacher to broaden the horizons of her pupils far beyond the curriculum she taught. He'd never had teachers like Florence when he was at school. And she was raising two delightful children as a single mother. Proposing that Florence apply for the job as science teacher at the *collège* may have been the most useful contribution he'd made to the town of St. Denis.

He took away the dirty plates and brought out not the tray of desserts his friends had expected but a large wrapped box, with three smaller wrapped items on top. Without a word, he went back to the kitchen and brought out the glasses of lemon mousse on a tray. Pamela realized what he planned and brought out another wrapped gift from her bag and placed it with the others. The baron went to his car and returned with what had to be a framed painting of some kind, wrapped in paper covered with snowmen, clearly left over from Christmas. Gilles followed suit and brought back what seemed to be a book, also wrapped.

"I suspect you have something planned, but I love lemon mousse and I intend to eat it right now," said Florence, smiling widely and shushing her children when they asked if they could start opening her presents. She gave each of them a spoonful of the lemon mousse instead, which successfully distracted them.

Once the mousse was appreciated and devoured, Florence scanned the gifts and asked Dora to choose one to open.

The little girl picked out Pamela's present, ripped open the paper and cried, "DVDs, Maman." But then she paused and made a face. "Is this French?" she asked.

"They have French subtitles," said Pamela. "And I know you're learning to read, Dora."

Florence rose to kiss Pamela and promised that they would all watch the Jane Austen films together. Then it was Daniel's turn, and he opened Gilles's book, a copy of the latest Prix Goncourt winner.

"Just what I wanted," Florence declared, embracing Gilles.

"Now it's your turn to open something," said the baron, handing her the painting. "It's something I found at an exhibition of local painters."

Florence unwrapped it to reveal a framed watercolor of the bridge and waterfront of St. Denis, framed by willow fronds trailing at one side of the painting and a family of ducks at the other.

"It's charming," Florence said, hugging the old man. "This is a wonderful birthday. I can't think when I've had a better one — breakfast in bed, hammam, gifts and lunch with dear friends."

"I think you might need both Daniel and Dora to help you open this," said Bruno, handing her the box.

Florence removed the outer layer of paper, then used her cheese knife to slit the tape and open the box. The children began stripping off the newspaper wrappings one by one, groaning theatrically each time they saw that there was yet more paper, until at last the carafe emerged.

"It's lovely, Bruno," Florence said, kissing him. "But you're too generous. You've already given me this great lunch with our friends. And what are these three wrapped items still on the table?"

"I thought Dora and Daniel worked so hard, they deserved to have a small gift too," he said. But before handing them their presents, he said, "You have to wait and open them at the same time as Maman opens her last gift because these are three things that go together like a family. Now all of you sit down, and when I count to three, each of you open your gift and I'll explain them. One, two, three . . ."

The arrowhead, the flint scraper and the hand ax were unwrapped, and three sets of eyes stared at him, confused.

"Daniel, that's an arrowhead made by people who lived here thousands and thousands of years ago, used for hunting so they could feed themselves," he explained. "And Dora, your gift is a scraper from the same people. When they hunted a deer, they removed the skin and used scrapers like this to remove the fat and prepare the skin to be a cloak to keep them warm, or a blanket to sleep under. Without scrapers like that one in your hand, there would've been no clothing in winter.

"Florence, yours is a Mousterian hand ax, one of the earliest handmade human tools, at least forty thousand years old. Now that you're starting the archaeology club, you'll need to know about these things."

"But weren't these treasures yours?" Florence asked. "Not the hand ax but the arrowhead and scraper — I've seen them on your bookcase. That's your personal collection."

Bruno shook his head. "My real archaeological specimen is sitting under the table. I read an article in the latest *Archéologie* magazine about the skeleton of a dog being found in a cave in Belgium with some human remains dating from thirty thousand years ago. And there's a nineteen-thousand-year-old painting of a dog just down the road from here at the Font de Gaume cave.

"Some historians think that one of the key moments in human history was when our ancestors learned to domesticate dogs," Bruno went on. "This wasn't only because dogs were useful for hunting but because it was only after dogs that humans learned how to domesticate other animals as well — sheep, goats and cattle and eventually horses. That was the great shift that transformed our ancestors from hunter-gatherers into farmers. That's how important dogs have been to us."

"So Florence and her children now each have their own little piece of the prehistory of our region," said the baron.

"And I have mine, in Balzac," Bruno said. "Happy birthday, Florence. And happy history, to us all."

THE CHOCOLATE WAR

The prosperity of St. Denis had rested for seven centuries upon its weekly market, the oldest and largest in the region. Its continued success and security were therefore a priority for Bruno Courrèges. He was usually to be seen patrolling the town's two main squares and the long street that joined them shortly after seven each Tuesday morning when the merchants began setting up their stalls.

Bruno always enjoyed watching as the stalls were loaded with cheeses and salamis, fruits and vegetables, ducks and geese, fish, oysters, mushrooms, chickens, wines and so much more. Some measured the changes in French as well as tourist tastes. Only one still offered the traditional aprons and housecoats that once clad the farmers' wives. But several sold comic T-shirts, miniskirts and the kind of metal-studded high-heeled boots that once were associated with particular tastes. More and more of them offered organic soaps and obscure teas that Bruno had never heard of, hand-carved wooden toys, used books and garish covers for mobile phones.

Bruno knew most of the stallholders well, and his patrol was punctuated by handshakes with the men, and the *bise* of greeting to women of all ages. And the stallholders usually bent down to stroke Bruno's basset hound, Balzac, or offer the dog some tiny treat from their stalls. Sometimes in summer when the usual ranks of regulars were swollen by new merchants, there were arguments that Bruno had to manage over whose stall should go where, or challenges to the accuracy of Fat Jeanne's tape measure. A woman of almost spherical shape with a booming laugh, she even referred to herself by the nickname by which everyone knew her.

Jeanne was *la mère du marché,* the town employee who collected five euros for each meter of frontage for every stall. She stashed the money in an ancient leather bag that she carried securely across her ample body. Two centimeters over the meter was acceptable but no more. Bruno recalled with a smile one salesman offering discount tools who used one of his own saws to carve off an excess sliver of wood no wider than his finger to avoid paying an extra five euros. Among Bruno's various duties was to escort Jeanne to the bank just before it closed at noon and deposit the cash in the town's account. On the busy days of the tourist season she would bank over a thousand euros. In the depths of winter, it fell to two or three hundred.

Bruno kept a watchful eye on Jeanne and her cash and on any strangers around the market. One morning in November he spotted an unfamiliar African youngster loading a trolley from a van he recognized. Bruno stopped, greeted the youth and shook hands.

"Where's Léopold?" he asked.

"He's already at the stall," came the reply. "I'm his nephew, Cali. I'm down from Paris so my uncle can help me learn the market trade."

Léopold usually sold cheap T-shirts and sunglasses, leather belts and bolts of African cloth, but Bruno could see that Cali was unloading square metal tins and boxes of small plastic cups.

"What are you selling?" Bruno asked.

"African coffees and chocolate," Cali replied with a friendly smile. "It was my idea to try something new. Uncle Léo sells almost nothing this time of year. No tourists in November."

Bruno nodded. Léopold usually stayed until the last market before Christmas and then flew home to Senegal for two or three months, visiting family and buying new stock for the next season. Bruno wished Cali luck and walked on to complete his circuit before seeking out Léopold's stall, where an electric kettle was steaming behind the counter, plugged in to one of the sockets that St. Denis provided — for an extra fee.

Léopold was an old friend, a regular at the market years before Bruno's arrival, and he'd once helped Bruno make an arrest during a brief period of trouble between Chinese vendors and the traditional Vietnamese food stalls they were trying to replace. The big Senegalese in his flowing robes opened his arms to hug Bruno, and the two men brushed cheeks. Bruno could see that several cans of coffee plus three *cafetières,* plastic cups and sachets of sugar now took up a third of Léopold's two-meter-wide stall. Labels on the cans indicated that the coffee inside came from all over Africa: Kenya, Tanzania, Rwanda, Ivory Coast, Cameroon, Ghana. Against each can stood a block of dark chocolate from that country. A hand-lettered sign announced that the coffee was one euro a cup, which was cheaper than the one euro thirty cents most cafés charged.

"None of your coffee comes from Senegal," said Bruno.

"People have just started growing it there, but I hope we'll have some next month," said Léopold. "Try a cup of one of the other brands."

Bruno chose the coffee from Ivory Coast, since he'd been stationed there for several months while in the French army. He still remembered the taste of the coarse local coffee, the robusta version that he and most French people had grown up drinking before the finer arabica coffee began to take over the market.

"On the house," said Cali, who had joined them.

Bruno grinned and shook his head, placing a single euro coin on one of the tins. "You know you have to give Jeanne an extra two euros if you're using electricity," he said. "And what do you do for water?"

Cali pointed to a large plastic *bidon* holding twenty liters that was stashed behind the stall. "And I'll rinse out the *cafetières* at the public fountain. We have it all figured out."

The coffee was very good, strong and rich,

just as he remembered it. He closed his eyes and recalled the bustle of the street markets in Abidjan, the African heat, the pungent smells and tastes. With that, he then recalled another drink that was popular there.

"Do you do that *mélange* they used to sell in Abidjan?" he asked. "You know, that mix of coffee with crumbled chocolate."

"I hadn't thought of that," said Cali, looking at the blocks of dark chocolate. He pulled out one of the blocks, unwrapped it and used one of the penknives Léopold sold to begin shaving very thin slices into a bowl. He poured in some boiling water from the kettle, stirred it to melt the chocolate and then added some coffee. He poured the result into two cups, took one for himself and handed the other to Bruno. "Next week, I'll have some properly crumbled chocolate, or maybe I'll try raw cocoa."

"It's not quite right yet, but it's getting there," said Bruno, smacking his lips. "Maybe it needs a bit of honey and a pinch or two of cinnamon."

Then he looked at the price list and his eyes widened. The chocolate blocks were two euros each, which was what he'd expect to pay for chocolate much less exotic than this. But the Kenyan and Tanzanian coffees were twelve and fourteen euros a kilo.

Bruno usually paid a couple of euros at the local supermarket. Even the Ivory Coast brand was six euros.

"I don't think you'll sell much at those prices," he said.

"We'll see," said Cali. "People like something special from time to time. What if you're inviting that special someone to have coffee at your place? Or if you're holding a big dinner party? And we can sell the green coffee beans more cheaply so you can roast your own."

"Good luck," said Bruno and continued his patrol, noting on his next round that several people were gathered in front of Léopold's stall and that Cali was already tying up a large garbage sack full of used cups. He pursed his lips. At one euro a cup, the stallholders were coming to Cali rather than heading for Fauquet's café. Bruno recalled Fauquet saying that he did almost half his weekly business on market day. He glanced across the square and saw Fauquet standing on the steps of his café, arms akimbo, scowling at Léopold's stall.

Bruno believed that preventing trouble was always preferable to dealing with its aftermath. He strolled across to Fauquet's place, sat down at one of the outside tables and asked for a croissant and coffee. Fauquet brought them out and then stood by Bruno's table, glaring across at his new competition.

"It's not right," he said. "I have taxes to pay and social charges for my staff, which damn near doubles the cost of my payroll. I'll go broke if this goes on. What are you going to do about it?"

"What did you have in mind?" Bruno took a bite of his croissant, still warm from the oven, and gave Balzac his usual treat of the other pointed end.

"Tell them to stop undercutting me."

"It's new, people want to try it out," said Bruno. "They aren't really competitors. They don't sell croissants, let alone ones as good as yours. They don't make cakes or special chocolates like you do. They don't bake bread or make ice cream, and they don't do your full breakfasts of fruit juice and *tartines* and homemade jams. You can't sit down and chat with friends at their stall, or arrange to meet as your customers can here. They don't do teas and they don't have a bar or an alcohol license. Above all, you make a point of having all the local gossip. Half of what I need to know in this town I learn from you."

"It's the coffee that brings them in on market day," Fauquet said. "I usually sell forty or fifty cups to the stallholders even on a bad day, a couple of hundred in high season. Guess how many I've sold today."

"Twenty?" Bruno ventured. He glanced into the café where just two elderly women were sitting and chatting. Usually on market day the place was full.

"Six."

"Still, it's a great croissant," Bruno said after a silence.

Fauquet ignored the remark. "Well, if you won't do your duty of helping local taxpayers against unfair competition, Bruno, I'll have to see the mayor."

"What's unfair about it?"

"I bet Léopold's not paying his assistant the minimum wage, nor paying his social insurance," Fauquet said grimly. "Did he have to face an annual health inspection like me? I haven't seen him give receipts like I do or have all his income counted on the cash register for the taxman."

"It's Léopold's nephew, and you know the rules are different for family members. I bet you don't pay your wife the minimum wage."

"Whose damn side are you on, Bruno?" Fauquet slammed his fist down on the table so that Bruno's croissant bounced on its plate and coffee slopped over into the saucer. Without a word of apology he stomped back into his almost empty café. Bruno sighed, put down two euros fifty and climbed the spiral stone steps of the *mairie* to lay the problem before the wisest man he knew.

But the mayor was just as stymied as Bruno, and he faced the added complication that Fauquet was an influential member of the town council who had — so far — always voted with him.

"What do you think Fauquet will do now?" the mayor asked.

"I think he'll make a complaint to the health inspectors, which will most likely go nowhere," Bruno replied. "But he'll probably make another to the tax authorities, and that could be more serious, and not just for Léopold."

The mayor nodded. "If word circulates that the tax inspectors are looking at the market in St. Denis, we're likely to see a lot of stallholders suddenly disappear. And that would be a disaster for the town. *Merde,* Bruno. You're in charge of the market — you'll have to think of something."

"Might there be something in the original market charter that forbids the sale of hot drinks?" Bruno was referring to the royal decree signed by King Philip the Tall in 1319.

The mayor shook his head. "It forbids nothing. When I was a boy, there used to be regular sales of livestock — pigs, sheep and cattle. And we let people sell wine and offer free tastings, and hot drinks in winter. How good a trade is Léopold doing?"

"Enough to fill a garbage sack with disposable plastic cups before nine o'clock," Bruno replied. "But we don't charge stallholders for disposing of their garbage."

"Aha," said the mayor. "Under the new environmental rules, this week's council meeting can pass a resolution banning the use of disposable plastic cups."

"They'll just shift to paper ones," said Bruno.

"You may be right," said the mayor, with a sigh. "But even if it doesn't work, it should keep Fauquet quiet."

"It won't stop them for long. What do we do when Léopold buys a job lot of fifty pottery cups?" Bruno asked. He shook his head. This didn't feel right to him. They should be praising Cali's initiative rather than plotting ways to frustrate the young man. And Léopold was a good man, always generous to local charities and raising two fine sons who were natural athletes, assets to Bruno's junior tennis and rugby teams.

"He'll have to wash the cups after each use," said the mayor. "We can ban the use of detergent at the town fountain."

"We can't ban soap — the fountain used to be the public laundry."

"We'll tackle that problem when it arises. Meantime, you go and tell Léopold no more plastic cups from next week."

Bruno did as he was told, feeling shame-faced as he apologized to Léopold and Cali while passing on the mayor's message. The two Africans seemed worried at first, but then Cali turned to Léopold and said, "Remember cousin Wollo? The one who works at the porcelain factory in Limoges."

Cali pulled out a cell phone, punched in a number and explained his request. He listened briefly, and then his face lit up with an enormous smile as he told his uncle and Bruno, "He can let us have sixty rejects for free."

When the town council came to vote, there was an unexpected objection from Albert, head of the local volunteer fire brigade. They used plastic cups at their fundraising stall in the market, selling iced tea and mulled wine and lemonade, according to the season. Would the ban apply to them too? Another councillor wanted to know if the ban applied to the little plastic cups that the Vinh family used at their Vietnamese food stall for the spicy sauce that went with their hot *nem.* Then Fauquet himself demanded that an exception be made for the disposable cups he used in summer to sell ice cream and frozen yogurt to people who didn't want one of the usual edible cones.

"You can't have it both ways," snapped the mayor, saying that charitable causes like the firemen could use glasses from the *mairie,* so long as they washed them afterward. But Fauquet would have to come up with another solution for his ice cream.

"We must all do our bit for the environment," the mayor said piously as Fauquet grumbled.

"Plastic Wars in St. Denis" ran the headline in the next morning's *Sud Ouest.* This was swiftly followed by a call-in program on France Bleu Périgord, the radio station that most of St. Denis listened to. Those damn Greens were going too far, said some callers. The planet was being overrun by plastic, said others. Did the listeners know that every fish now contained micro-beads of plastic, that eight million tons of plastic went into the oceans each year, that France recycled less than a third of the million tons of plastic it threw away each year?

The public debate was still raging on the next market day when Léopold and Cali arrived with racks of white pottery cups, some of them a little oddly shaped or missing their handles but serviceable enough. They also brought big electric urns, one for water and the other for milk, and a sack full of ground-up Ivory Coast chocolate. A large jar of honey and another filled with cinnamon sticks stood beside them. A big sign hung from the giant parasol that protected their stall.

TRY OUR *MÉLANGE,* THE AFRICAN CHOCOLATE DELICACY THAT BRUNO LOVES, it read. SPECIAL INTRODUCTORY PRICE TODAY — JUST TWO EUROS.

The rush began at eight as all the stallholders lined up to try it. Then at nine it began again as the mothers walked up from dropping off their children at the nursery school. At ten-thirty, half the students at the local *collège* sprinted up to the market during their break to try the new drink, and by eleven the sack of chocolate was empty and Cali's hands were chapped from all the washing of cups he had done at the fountain.

"Next time I'll wear rubber gloves," he said with a beaming smile.

Reminded by Bruno that his taxes had

better be in order, Léopold was assiduously marking down each sale in a new notebook. Cali had registered himself as a self-employed *auto-entrepreneur,* Léopold confided, and was now planning to take his coffee and chocolate to the markets in St. Cyprien, Lalinde, Le Buisson and Sarlat.

"That's just the beginning," said Cali. "I have a brother, a sister, cousins. We can franchise this idea, expand even faster."

"Careful," warned Bruno. "Right now you're riding on Léopold's coattails. He's a long-established figure in the local markets with the right to a good spot. You'll find it harder to come in as an unknown, because I suspect Fauquet is spreading the word that you're a threat to all the other local cafés. They may not keep you out, but they have enough influence to ensure that your stall will be placed behind a gas station, or they'll block you from rinsing out your cups."

"That's not fair," Cali protested.

"He says your competition is unfair because he has to pay taxes, social charges, minimum wage," said Bruno.

"But all the shopkeepers could say that about the competition from the markets," Cali protested.

"And have you noticed how many of the small groceries and clothes shops have closed down in these country towns?" Bruno countered. "The café owners don't want to be next."

Léopold gave Bruno a thoughtful look. "Do you have something in mind, Bruno?"

"I think it's time to see if you can reach some kind of agreement with Fauquet and get him on your side. Otherwise this could turn nasty." Bruno handed over a twenty-euro note for a kilo of Tanzanian coffee and a bar of Ivory Coast chocolate.

He strolled back with his purchases to Fauquet's empty café, where he ordered a hot chocolate and an espresso while standing at the bar and asked for an empty mug. Fauquet gave him a puzzled look but complied. Bruno poured both the coffee and the chocolate into the mug and took a sip.

"That's good," he said. "It's different, but it's as good in its way as the one Léopold is selling. How much would you charge for it?"

"One euro thirty for the coffee, one-fifty for the hot chocolate. So I'd have to price it at two euros eighty," Fauquet replied.

"It's two euros in the market. Can you match that?"

"Not if I want to make a profit. If things go on like this, I'll have to put the place up for sale while I still have a balance sheet that looks healthy."

"Have a piece of this chocolate he's selling for two euros a block and tell me what you think."

Fauquet raised his eyebrows. "I've been a master chocolatier for thirty years, Bruno. I know my chocolate a damn sight better than Léopold's nephew." He broke off a small square and popped it in his mouth, then nodded slowly.

"It's good, very good. I couldn't even buy it through a wholesaler for two euros, let alone sell it for that. I presume they're getting a special price from some relatives in Africa. And they're importing the stuff in a way which is probably illegal. I tried to get the chamber of commerce to help, but when we called the customs office in Bordeaux they just laughed at us."

"Try making two cups of his coffee in your espresso machine, one for each of us," Bruno said, handing over the bag he'd bought. "Tell me what you think. You might be able to reach an agreement with Léopold to buy his coffee cheaply. He's a reasonable man."

Fauquet looked grumpy, but he poured some of the Ivory Coast coffee into the steel pan and pressed the button that triggered the steam pressure. And again he nodded approval when he tasted the coffee that resulted.

"It's not the quality I'm complaining about, Bruno. And it's not just me. The other café in town has been hit even harder because they don't have my cakes and croissants. When they bought that place they paid a fortune because it had a tobacco license, and you know what's happened to that business. This is probably the last straw for them. Word is spreading to other towns, and there's been some angry talk."

"What sort of angry talk?"

"You know, young hotheads."

"You mean café owners? Or people who don't like immigrants."

Fauquet shrugged. "A bit of both."

At that point, Bruno heard a crash followed by angry shouts and the roar of a high-revving engine coming from the market. He went outside and was almost knocked down by Cali, who was racing past in a vain attempt to catch a fleeing motorbike. Two men in black leather and helmets were racing away down the rue de la République. Bruno just had time to note that the rear mudguard was bright blue and looked new.

Cali stopped, saw Bruno standing in the café doorway, Fauquet peering over his shoulder. Cali glared furiously at them.

"I might have guessed you'd be on his side, Bruno." He almost spat the words out. "You whites all stick together."

Bruno ignored him, already walking quickly to the market stall where Léopold was trying to rescue bolts of cloth and other goods from the flood of hot milk and water that spilled from the two overturned urns. Cans of coffee were scattered on the ground along with several broken cups. Some of the cans had burst open, and hot milk from the soaked stall was dripping into the mess.

"What happened?" he asked Léopold.

"A motorbike came up the side street behind, stopped with the motor running, both guys in helmets," he answered dully. "One of them waited until Cali went off to wash the cups, then came around the side, pushed over the urns, knocked over the tins of coffee and the cups, then ran back to the bike and drove off."

Other stallholders and shoppers were crowding around, all trying to learn what had happened.

"You're supposed to protect the market," said Cali. He brushed past Bruno and bent down to pick up the unbroken cans of coffee.

"Did you get the license number?" Bruno

asked. He was addressing Léopold but spoke loudly so he could be heard by everyone. At that point the mayor arrived on the scene to find out what had happened. A dozen people began to speak at once, and Bruno used his parade-ground voice to shout out, "Silence!"

"We know what happened, but what I want now is information that can be useful," he said. "Did anybody get the license plate number of the motorbike? Or recognize it? Or recognize the driver or his passenger?"

Nobody spoke at first. Then a boy of about eight whom Bruno knew from his tennis classes said, "It was a blue Suzuki four-fifty."

"Thanks, Maurice, that could be very useful," Bruno said, the boy's name leaping from his memory just when it was needed. He turned to the mayor. "I think that Léopold, Cali and Fauquet should join us in your office. It's time for a serious talk."

"I agree, but not all of us," said Léopold, in a quiet but determined voice that brooked no opposition. "You stay here, Cali, clean up and look after the stall and leave this meeting to me." Cali looked mutinous but obeyed.

Once in his office, the mayor avoided his

desk, sat each of them around a small, round table and said, "I'd like to start with a little history. Monsieur Fauquet, why not tell us all how you and I met and how your café got started in St. Denis."

Fauquet looked embarrassed and began haltingly, looking at the table rather than at any of the other three sitting around it.

"We met in Paris thirty years ago at the Maison d'Aquitaine, a place where people from this region could get together, read local newspapers, attend talks by politicians. I was doing my apprenticeship to become a *maître chocolatier,* and you were working in the office of Jacques Chirac, who'd just been elected mayor of Paris. You came to my graduation ceremony and you helped me get my first job as *chef pâtissier* in Chirac's Hôtel de Ville. Then you told me there was a café coming up for sale in St. Denis, and you helped me negotiate the price and get a loan from the bank. I've been here ever since."

Fauquet paused, and then added, "And you were one of the witnesses at my wedding."

Well, well, thought Bruno, to whom all this came as news. Not that Bruno was greatly surprised to learn that he was not the only young man whom the mayor had found and helped to become an established citizen of St. Denis.

"Thank you, old friend, and may I say you and your chocolates and your croissants have more than fulfilled my faith in you," the mayor said. "And now it's your turn, Léopold. How did you and I meet?"

"Through my aunt, who was working as a cleaner at the Hôtel de Ville in Paris, but she was short of money so you hired her to do some extra cleaning at your apartment," Léopold said, looking the mayor squarely in the eye. "My father had died and you helped her bring me to Paris from Senegal and got me into a school where I did not do well. You knew another Senegalese who had a stall in the Marché de la Bastille and owed you a favor, so he agreed to take me on and teach me the trade. Then you loaned me some money to start my own stall in St. Denis. And you let me use the car you kept at your father's place here while you were in Paris so I could go to the markets in St. Cyprien and Lalinde. And mine was one of the first marriages you performed when you became mayor."

"And you repaid my small loan ahead of time," said the mayor, smiling at him with affection. "And now Bruno here not only helps you unload your van, but he's also teaching your sons to play tennis and rugby. And you, Léopold, are not just the best bass voice our town choir ever had, but you're also helping another young man to make his own start in life. What do you think of that, Fauquet?"

"I take your point," the café owner replied. "You're saying we all have a duty to help the next generation get on. And I agree, but I have a payroll to meet — a baker who has a young family, an apprentice *chocolatier,* and three part-time waitresses. I'm paying more than two thousand euros a month in social charges alone, and Cali's coffee has really put a hole in my takings. The supermarkets are a big enough problem, selling four crappy croissants for the price I have to charge for a good one that I'm up at five every morning to make."

"And yet most of us would rather have one of your croissants, despite the price," said the mayor. He turned to Bruno. "What do you think we might do about all this, Bruno?"

"I'm wondering whether there might be room for cooperation," Bruno replied. "Maybe Cali could sell Fauquet's croissants on commission at the other markets. And since he seems to be getting his African coffees and chocolates at a lower price than you're paying the wholesaler, Fauquet, maybe you could start buying from him."

Fauquet pursed his lips, looked at the mayor and blew out a long sigh before saying, "It might be worth trying."

"When does your current apprentice get his qualification?" the mayor asked Fauquet.

"June of next year."

"Would you then be looking for a new apprentice?"

"Possibly," Fauquet said cautiously.

"Might that interest Cali as a career?" the mayor asked Léopold.

"I don't know, but it's an idea worth exploring," he replied and turned to Fauquet. "I really don't want to put you out of business, so perhaps you and I could discuss an agreement on pricing."

"Good," said the mayor, standing up. "I think you two and Cali have the basis for some further discussions among yourselves and we all need to get back to work. I'm sure Bruno will want to track down the thugs who attacked your stall."

They all shook hands and left the mayor's office, and as they went down the spiral stone staircase Bruno heard Fauquet and Léopold arranging to meet after the market closed. Back in his own office, Bruno logged on to the police computer and began checking new registrations for motorbikes. There were several Suzukis, but mostly they were trail bikes. The one Bruno had seen looked like a more conventional model. There were two 450s: one in Montpon, in the far western corner of the *département;* the other was in Sarlat and the registered address was a café. Bruno called a friend in the Sarlat municipal police and asked about the café. It was a bikers' place, he was told, less a café than a bar with an unsavory reputation.

"You can't miss it," Bruno was told. "It's still got the Front National posters up from the last election."

Sarlat was out of Bruno's jurisdiction, so he called his friend Jean-Jacques, chief detective for the *département* and known to all as J-J, and explained the situation. Bruno added that he had seen the bike as it drove off and had another witness.

"I suppose we could charge them with criminal damage, but they'd probably get off with a fine. I doubt whether the *procureur* would think it was worthwhile bringing charges," J-J said. "Still, I'll have a word with some colleagues. We've been having some trouble in Sarlat with drugs lately. The local cops might welcome the chance to look the place over, ask a few questions.

Leave it with me."

The next morning, with Balzac at his heels, Bruno went into Fauquet's for his usual croissant and coffee. Taped to the front of the cash register was a small poster, printed out on a computer.

TRY OUR NEW CHOCO-COFFEE *MÉLANGE.* INTRODUCTORY PRICE THIS WEEK ONLY TWO EUROS, it said.

Fauquet pushed one across the bar to him and slid a still warm croissant onto a plate.

"You can pay for the croissant, but this *mélange* is on the house," he said.

"Thanks, I appreciate it. I didn't know that history between you and the mayor."

"And I didn't know the history of him and Léopold," said Fauquet. "He's a good man."

"We're lucky to have him," Bruno said, giving Balzac his share of croissant. He sipped the *mélange* as Fauquet watched, his nervous look turning into a grin when Bruno told him it was excellent.

"Remember when you told me that word was spreading to other café owners about your problems with Cali?" asked Bruno. "I'm hoping that you weren't the one who spread it to a certain bikers' café in Sarlat."

Fauquet looked him in the eye as if willing Bruno to believe him. "Not me, Bruno. I only spoke about it to a friend in St. Cyprien and to the guy who runs the café and *pâtisserie* section at the chamber of commerce in Périgueux. He came back to me and said there'd been some ugly talk after the radio show."

Bruno nodded, thinking that made sense. "This *mélange* is really very good. I think it's even better than the one Cali makes."

"That's because I use the high-cream milk from Stéphane's cows that he uses to make his cheeses," Fauquet said. "Oh, and by the way, that reminds me. Philippe Delaron from *Sud Ouest* was in here just before you and tried the *mélange*. I told him he had a new story after that headline about the war of plastics in St. Denis."

"What's the new story?"

"That the chocolate war is over."

THE GREEN ARMY

As Bruno Courrèges patrolled the St. Denis market one Tuesday morning, his eye was caught by a lovely young woman examining a stall filled with ducks, *magrets* and foie gras. It belonged to friends of Bruno from the nearby farm of Lac Noir. The knowledgeable way she examined the products on offer suggested she was a Périgord girl but not one that Bruno knew. Then the young man with her turned, and Bruno called out, "Pierre."

"Bruno," cried the young man, and they met in a warm embrace, slapping each other on the back and then standing back as Bruno said, "*Mon Dieu,* you've grown!"

Bruno had taught Pierre to play tennis and helped him obtain his first hunting license. Bruno had last seen him four years earlier at the funeral of Pierre's father, shortly before Pierre went off to university in Bordeaux.

"And you haven't changed a bit, Bruno," Pierre said, laughing and turning to the young woman to introduce them. "Marielle, this is our town policeman and the guy who helped me grow up. Bruno, meet my fiancée, Marielle. She's from a wine family in Montravel. She studied at Dijon, but we met in California, working on adjoining properties in the Napa Valley on our vineyard year, and we'll be making wine here again once we're married."

Bruno knew that Pierre was heir to a decent local vineyard of a dozen hectares, occupying one end of the long slope which was at the heart of the town's wine cooperative, founded since Pierre's father's death. It was a stretch of land Julien Dubard, owner of the Domaine de la Vézère hotel and winery, and Hubert de Montignac, owner of the famous local wineshop, had long coveted to expand the town's increasingly prosperous wine cooperative, in which Bruno was a shareholder.

"Don't worry, Bruno," Pierre said, grinning at the suddenly conflicted expression on Bruno's face. "I already went to see Hubert. There won't be a problem. Marielle and I want to run our own show, make our own wine, but we'll happily work with the cooperative for bottling and administration.

Hubert is working out the details and he's happy that we want to make our wine fully organic. I always did, you'll remember. That's why our land has been left fallow for the last four years."

"We've already qualified for the leaf logo on all the wines from the town vineyard," Bruno replied, referring to the image of a green leaf on labels of wine from grapes that had been certified as organic under European Union rules.

"That's good, but we want to do better," said Marielle. She had splendid dark eyes, light brown hair that fell to her shoulders, a fine smile and a soft voice that was almost musical. But there was a hint of firmness, almost determination, when she added, "We're applying to Demeter for certification as fully biodynamic wines."

Bruno raised his eyebrows. Biodynamic was the highest level of organic farming, committed to the ecological self-sufficiency of plants and soils and insects, treating them as cohesive and interconnected living systems. He could understand the principle but in practice thought that some of its ways with organic compost smacked of alchemy, even witchcraft.

"Burying yarrow plants in cows' horns at midnight under a full moon?" he said, instantly regretting his mocking tone as he saw the young woman bridle.

"If you understand that the moon's gravitational pull causes the sea's tides to rise and fall, why would you not think it might have some effect on plants?" she asked him coolly.

"Sorry," he answered quickly. "I didn't mean to be rude. I've drunk some of Franck Pascal's biodynamic wine from Le Jonc Blanc and thought that the Malbec he calls Pure M was terrific, like the wines from Terroir Feely. I drank a red wine of theirs called Grâce that I thought was wonderful. Those are the only biodynamic ones I know around here, and whatever the alchemy involved, there's no arguing with the quality of the wines they make. And I hear that Château Monestier La Tour is going the same way. I really was joking — I use the lunar calendar in my own garden."

"Well, we agree about Pascal's wines," she said, smiling again, but with a wariness in her eyes. "I worked with Pascal on school vacations. And there may be a touch of magic in what he does, but I think he's a real pioneer."

"We're used to being teased about it, and even I find some of the rules a bit strange," said Pierre. "But I've no doubt it's the future, no chemicals, no fungicides, no pesticides. And it makes sense, working with the life in the soil rather than wiping it out."

"We certainly agree on that," Bruno replied. "And if you're going biodynamic, there could hardly be more of a contrast with your neighbor. Cazenau believes in chemicals and fertilizers to get as much wine from his vineyard as he can. He even dropped out of the *vin de pays* system because of all the rules about what grapes he could plant and how much wine he produced per hectare. Now he's complaining that the rules are getting to be just as strict for *vins de France.*"

The French system for classifying wines began with the *appellation contrôlée* for wines of recognized and historic quality. It defined where a wine was from, how much could be produced per hectare of land, which grape varieties were permitted, how much alcohol it contained. Rules were less rigorous for established wines; so in Burgundy in a cool year when the grapes produced less than 10.5 percent alcohol, the vineyards could add sugar to boost the alcohol level. Elsewhere, vineyards had lost their appellation status if they dared to protect their vines during rainstorms with plastic sheeting. It was a rigid and bureaucratic system jealously guarded by the well-established wines within it and not easy for outsiders to enter.

So they could choose to be a lesser status, a *vin de pays,* a country wine from a specific region such as the Périgord, where the rules were a little more flexible, but they were still limited to the types of grape they could use. Or they could choose to be a *vin de France,* where the rules were even more lax. So some of the great vineyards of the region chose, like Château de la Jaubertie, to produce a *vin de pays* because it was the only legal way they could make a wine of Chardonnay grapes.

Bruno had his own troubles with the French passion for bureaucracy, having to spend almost a full day each week filling out forms about the working hours and activities of the other members of his team since his promotion to chief of police for the whole Vézère Valley. And everybody in the region knew of the complaints of the winemakers. The customers wanted lighter and paler rosé wines, but the *appellation contrôlée* system rules required that Bergerac rosé had to be darker. The rigid rules on the varieties of grape that could be planted and the yields that could be harvested required endless paperwork and

111

made the system a real headache for the vineyards.

"We'll cross that bridge with Cazenau when we come to it," said Pierre. "Right now, we're spending all our time working on getting the house back in order, and then we'll start on the *chai,*" he said, referring to the barnlike building where the wines were made, stored and bottled. "The *gîtes* are in good shape, but they have to be. We'll need that rental income to live on until we can start selling our wine."

Bruno wished them luck and left them to their shopping, and then strolled from the square in front of the *mairie* along the rue de Paris where the stalls stretched all the way to fill the old parade ground which faced the gendarmerie. There were more stalls erected in front of the cemetery, mainly selling belts, sandals and T-shirts. The longest stall of all sold secondhand clothes, and customers thronged around it. The recession had been hard on St. Denis.

Beside it was a stall selling Cazenau's wines. Some were sold by the bottle and the five-liter box but also *en vrac* from a barrel on the back of a truck for those who brought their own jugs. At one and a half euros a liter, it was the same price Hubert charged at his shop for the cheapest *vin ordinaire* that was the mainstay of poorer households. A large poster read: VIN DE FRANCE FROM YOUR OWN PÉRIGORD NEIGHBORHOOD. Cazenau also offered a more expensive wine at five euros a bottle; a tray with tiny plastic glasses of this was available for tasting. But the stallholder had an experienced eye for those who were interested in trying it and might buy a bottle, rather than those who simply wanted a free drink.

"Ah, Bruno, come to try some decent wine rather than that fancy stuff you seem to like?" came a loud and mocking voice from some distance behind Bruno. "We're obviously paying you too much if you can afford Hubert's prices."

It was Cazenau, at least thirty meters away, raising his voice like a military man. He enjoyed the way his gibes made people look at Bruno oddly. But Bruno had been a sergeant in the army and knew how to raise his own voice and how to respond to Cazenau.

"I'd rather pay Hubert's prices than pay the doctor's fees after drinking that cheap rotgut you call wine, Jacques," he called back, laughing to make a joke of it. The two men shook hands in apparent amity, enough for the bystanders to turn away, shaking their heads and grinning.

In his sixtieth year Jacques Cazenau stood just short of two meters in height and weighed only a couple of kilos more than he had thirty years earlier when he had been a redoubtable forward for the St. Denis rugby team. He was a keen and astute hunter and a volunteer firefighter, all of which should have made him a natural and close friend for Bruno.

But they were no more than superficially amiable acquaintances. Bruno had several reasons for this. The first was that Jacques drank too much of the wine he made, and he was not a happy drunk, becoming morose and on rare occasions even violent. More than once at rugby club dinners Bruno had been obliged to restrain him and help get him home to sleep it off. The second was that Cazenau had a wretchedly unhappy family. His wife was intimidated, shy and retiring with no close female friends. Bruno had tried to get her into his classes at the local tennis club, but she had pleaded the need to work in the family vineyard. Their only child, Yves, who now lived happily with his gay partner in Paris, was estranged from them. Bruno had made a point of meeting Yves for coffee when he was in the capital, and later discreetly let Yves's mother know that her son was happy and doing well as an electrician in the film industry.

Bruno also refused to drink the wines from Cazenau's vineyard. His forefathers had provided *pinard,* rough reds for the French army conscripts, from the distant days of the First World War when each soldier in the trenches was entitled to a liter a day and was free to buy more. Those days were long over. Drunken soldiers may be able to charge with a bayonet, but they cannot operate sophisticated equipment.

Cazenau sold his wine himself and through a network of self-employed sellers who set up their stalls in the markets throughout the region, like the one Bruno visited that day. He sold it to them either in bulk or in bottles, twenty euros for a case of twelve. They then sold the bottles for anything upward of three euros. He marketed it as *vin de France* from the Périgord, which was true as far as it went, but it frustrated the more ambitious local wine-makers who believed the name deserved a better wine than Cazenau's product.

Cazenau's ten hectares of vines were farmed intensively to produce between eighty and ninety thousand liters a year. This brought him something over a hundred thousand euros a year, from which he had to pay his staff, and provide the bottles, labels and cases. He also had to pay for the pesticides, the fungicides and the sprayers, whose machines were a regular sight in his vineyards, along with the machines he used to harvest the grapes. Human harvesting was expensive, but at least it didn't add the odd mouse and lizard and even the occasional rabbit to the wine.

Bruno was dismayed by the old-fashioned way Cazenau made his wine. He continued like his father to use those large amounts of pesticides and fertilizers that had characterized the years after the great frost of 1956, when most of the Bergerac vines froze. Across much of France, new vines were planted, and chemistry came to the rescue, just in time to provide lots of wine for the new shopping craze of supermarkets, which were more attentive to price than quality.

A TV documentary titled *Pesticides: Our Children at Risk* had found that children at over a hundred schools in the Bordeaux region were affected by the spraying. French law was finally recognizing the damage that had been done, allowing cancer victims among winemakers to claim workers' compensation. Employees in the Bergerac had finally won legal compensation for the illnesses they claimed had come from the chemicals they used. Families in the past, convinced that the cancers of their late fathers and grandfathers came from the chemicals added to the wine, were not so lucky. But the Bergerac wine appellation was now the most organic in France, and French law now required steady reductions in the use of pesticides and fertilizers. But this rule was less easy to enforce in areas outside the formal appellation regions, where wines had to be individually tested.

When St. Denis had created its own cooperative vineyard, Bruno had invested his modest savings in the venture. It brought together land owned by Julien and Hubert de Montignac along with several other, smaller parcels. At the time, Bruno had hoped that Cazenau would join the group. But he had bluntly refused, saying he wanted to remain his own boss. Hubert had been relieved, telling Bruno that Cazenau's land would need years to recover from the chemical holocaust he'd inflicted upon it in order to force the production of far more hectoliters of wine than the land could hope to sustain. He also thought that Cazenau's name would undermine the reputation of the town vineyard.

"I see your neighbor is back, or at least his son with his fiancée," Bruno said to Cazenau. Civility required a little conversation. "It will be good to see the Delluc vineyard at work again."

Cazenau shrugged. "Yeah, he dropped by to say hello and tell me he wanted to make organic wine, just like Julien and Hubert. I told him I knew his land as well as my own, and he'd have to forget these fashionable green ideas if he wanted to make a living from that land. On the upper slope he might do better growing walnut trees. Still, that girl with him is a real peach."

"They make a handsome couple," said Bruno. "It's good to see some of the young ones coming back home to make their lives."

The moment the words left his mouth he knew Cazenau would reckon the remark was aimed at him and his absent son. Sure enough, the man's eyes turned cold and he turned on his heel and walked away. Bruno sighed. That was the second time this morning that he'd spoken without thinking.

Twenty minutes later he was in the back room of Hubert's wineshop, enjoying a glass of the town vineyard's new Chardonnay with the owner. As well as the desk with its two computer screens, Hubert's office contained a couple of armchairs, a coffee table and an antique chaise longue.

"I like it," Bruno said, holding up the glass

against the light filtering through the Venetian blinds. "It's not flinty like a Chablis, softer, a bit like a white Burgundy."

"That's what I wanted to make, so I made sure it had the *malo,* the secondary malolactic fermentation that we normally do only for red wines. But I thought this had the character for it," said Hubert. "If Julien agrees, we might even try keeping a barrel in oak for a few months, see if we can get that buttery flavor of the American Chardonnays."

"I'll be interested to try that," said Bruno. "But I really came by to talk to you about young Pierre Delluc. I ran into him at the market and he said he'd seen you."

"Yes, Pierre came with that lovely girl he's engaged to," Hubert said, refilling their glasses and then relaxing back into his leather armchair. It went well with the image of an English gentleman that Hubert affected in his dress: cavalry twills over well-polished brogue shoes, checked shirts and tweed sports jackets with a silk handkerchief tucked into the breast pocket.

"I know his professor in Bordeaux who speaks very highly of him," Hubert said. "Pierre seems pretty clear about what he wants to do, the kind of wine he wants to make. He doesn't want to join the town vineyard, but he'll work with us, using our bottling and marketing systems. I think we're sufficiently well established now that a prestige organic wine would fit usefully into our structure. It could do very well in the hotel trade where the price points are less important. People will happily pay thirty euros for a bottle over dinner that they'd resist buying from me for twelve."

"What about Cazenau?" Bruno asked.

"That could be a problem. There's just a narrow track and a couple of hedges between their lands, so the crap that Cazenau sprays is only too likely to drift onto Pierre's vines and ruin his hopes of a biodynamic certification. And we know that Cazenau is not a man who will listen to reason easily."

Bruno waited. He knew Hubert would never have given Pierre encouragement if he hadn't thought of a way to solve the Cazenau problem.

"I don't know if you saw that stall in the market this morning," Hubert said.

Bruno nodded. "Offering *vin de France* from the Périgord."

"Exactly, and technically that's an offense. He's passing off a *vin de France* as if it were a *vin de pays,* where the rules are much stricter. And I suspect he's in breach of even the looser rules on spraying that are now

120

required for a *vin de France.* Do you know I stopped selling his wines last year?"

"You mean that stuff you sell *en vrac* as *vin ordinaire* for a euro and a half a liter?"

Hubert nodded. "Cazenau's wine used to be just about okay at that price but the last lot . . ." Hubert shook his head. "I'm getting it now from a vintner near Lalinde, just outside the Bergerac appellation; it's a much better wine than Cazenau makes. I think Cazenau is in trouble, boosting his yield up to a hundred and more hectoliters per hectare to make up in volume what he can't make in price. But where is that extra volume going? I used to buy a couple of thousand liters from him and I hear that some of the other *caves* around here have stopped buying his stuff as well."

"So where's he selling it?" asked Bruno.

"That's the question and finding out may be more your line of work than mine. But do you remember that American movie *Sideways,* all about wine? The hero preferred Burgundy-style wines to Bordeaux and waxed lyrical about the Pinot Noir grape compared to our Merlot. Since the film was a big hit, Merlot sales in America plunged by a third, and the demand for Pinot Noir soared far beyond the supply. So some smart guys in the Languedoc blended

Merlot and Syrah and exported over a million euros' worth to the United States as Pinot. They were too greedy, planning to send vast quantities worth six million euros. Even the local bank manager was involved. Some went to prison and there were hefty fines. But they were only caught because of the sheer volume involved that could not be hidden from the standard checks. I remember thinking at the time that if they had bought smaller quantities of wine from more vineyards, they might have gotten away with it."

Bruno nodded, recalling the scandal. "And you suspect that Cazenau might be involved in a less ambitious version of that?"

"Yes, but I think this time the wine is going to China. They are the world's biggest consumer of wine now. They bought a hundred and fifty-five million cases last year; that's nearly two billion bottles. And you know how the Chinese have been buying Bordeaux vineyards. Easy enough for him to send a truck or two with ten or fifteen thousand liters and mix his stuff with theirs."

"How do you prove it?" Bruno asked.

"Cazenau sells wine to lots of middlemen who then sell it for cash at their market stalls. Any one of them could be doing this, rather than Cazenau. It might be easier to catch him on his taxes, since he's working so much in cash."

"I've been thinking about this," said Hubert. "The fraud guys have the manpower to follow his delivery trucks, but they'll need more evidence than just my suspicions. The same with the tax authorities. I think we might get him on the chemicals, but that would mean somebody checking on every supplier and sprayer. So I paid for a laboratory check on the last batch of his wine I bought, and then got a friend to buy some of his latest wines and had that checked as well. His new wine is well above the European limit of a hundred and fifty milligrams of sulfites per liter. And I've never seen such high concentrations of pyrimethanil — that's a fungicide against grape rot that is suspected to be a carcinogen. We don't use it and we're getting good results with an organic alternative called Mevalone. My own samples of Cazenau's wines would not be accepted as evidence. But if you were to buy your own samples, they would be."

"How many would you need?"

"Six should be enough, each bought from a separate seller in different markets."

"And what would happen to Cazenau if

your suspicions turn out to be right?"

"Stiff fines, at least ten thousand euros and possibly double that, but more important his wines would be tightly controlled in the future. Given his business model, that could close him down and might provoke a backlash against us. That's why I'm not going to the DGCCRF," Hubert said, referring to France's powerful Directorate General for Competition Policy, Consumer Affairs and Fraud Control. "I'd much rather use this as a lever to persuade him to put his land into the town vineyard. We'd pay him a reasonable fee for a lease but not much at first, since it would take four or five years for his land to recover."

"So how would he make a living?" Bruno asked.

"We'd stop the use of chemicals from day one, so he'd still get some wine to sell but a much lower yield, and we could pay for the use of his *chai* and his bottling plant. He'd take a big hit, but the alternative for Cazenau is worse. And the guy is sixty years old, so retirement looms anyway. And by the time he's sixty-five he'd have a decent income from the lease because by then the land will have recovered and we can use it to make good organic wine."

"Let me run this past the mayor," Bruno

said. Hubert gave him a couple of bottles of the Chardonnay to lubricate the conversation that then took place in the mayor's office. Bruno laid out Hubert's scheme, adding, "This keeps the entire affair among ourselves as a local solution and I always prefer an arrangement that has something in it for everybody."

"And it means we won't have the fraud or tax authorities sniffing around St. Denis," the mayor agreed. "Voters hate that. But won't the lab people have to alert the authorities if they find illegal readings?"

"Hubert thought of that," Bruno replied. "One of the main lab technicians is an old friend. He's promised to do the analysis himself and report to us first."

"In that case, let's try it," said the mayor.

Over the next two days, Bruno and his two colleagues in the Police Municipale, Juliette in Les Eyzies and Louis in Montignac, bought six samples of Cazenau's *en vrac* wine in different markets, and Bruno himself drove the wine samples to the wine laboratory in Bordeaux to preserve the chain of evidence in case the matter went to the courts. Within the week, they had the results. Cazenau's wine contained nearly three hundred milliliters of sulfites and the highest levels of pyrimethanil the lab had ever recorded.

But by then, and while Bruno and Hubert were assessing the results from the Bordeaux lab, the affair had taken a new turn. Marielle and Pierre had taken some time off from cleaning and repainting the family home and taken a long stroll together through the vineyard to see the effect on the land of four years lying fallow. The good news was that they had been delighted by the wildlife, the bees and butterflies, voles and hedgehogs. The bad news was that the closer they walked to the boundary with Cazenau's land, the less wildlife they saw and the more bizarre the vegetation appeared. Huge brambles were scattered amid almost dead patches of earth and the occasional sprouting of giant new grape shoots. Pierre called Bruno to come and see for himself.

"It's like the landscape of some alien planet," said Marielle as they stood in the lane between the two vineyards. To one side, Cazenau's vines stretched like well-drilled soldiers, not a shred of vegetation between the neatly ordered rows. To the other, Pierre's landscape looked not only wild but almost sinister in the bizarre contrast between plants that had fed on the fertilizers and others that had been killed by the herbicide.

"There'll be no question of our having children if we have to live next door to this," said Marielle. "I shudder to think what it would do to a fetus. Is anybody keeping watch on the number of miscarriages and cancers among this bastard's employees? He's a public menace."

"And we have the Demeter people coming to check on our land the day after tomorrow," said Pierre. "We're counting on that to get our biodynamic certification. They'll take one look at this stretch of land and laugh in our faces. It looks as if something close to a quarter of our vineyard is affected, maybe more."

"What happens if we bring in a bulldozer and clear away all the vegetation that's affected, and maybe the topsoil?" Bruno asked. "Would that help?"

"Probably, and it would certainly look a whole lot better," said Pierre, putting his arm around Marielle. "But it doesn't solve the problem. As long as Cazenau keeps spraying we can't hope to grow organic wine here. We'll have to give up and go somewhere else."

"Give me a day and I'll tackle this," said Bruno, taking out his phone to call the mayor as he walked back to his van. With the mayor's approval, Bruno called Michel, who ran the commune's public works department, and within the hour the bulldozer was slowly descending from the truck that had brought it to the land between the two vineyards. Ten minutes later, it had started clearing Pierre's land. And then with the mayor in tow, Bruno arrived on Cazenau's doorstep.

"He's not well, Bruno," Cazenau's wife said as she answered the door. "*Monsieur le Maire, bonjour.* I'm afraid Jacques is having one of his turns."

"Do you mean he's drunk again?" the mayor asked, his tone so calm and polite it was almost menacing. "Or is he really ill? If so, we'll return at once with a doctor."

"He gets these headaches," she said. "And then he drinks. You won't get much sense out of him in this state. I never can."

"Make coffee, pour it into him, douse his head in cold water, do whatever you need to do, but get him up. In the meantime, we'll wait, with your permission, of course, madame. And please tell your husband we're here in an attempt to keep him out of prison."

She led them indoors without saying a word. Cazenau was insensible on a couch in his office. Wet sponges, coffee and even Bruno sliding ice cubes down the back of

128

his neck and into his underpants had not the slightest effect.

"Tell him we'll be back in the morning," said the mayor. That meant the very day that the Demeter experts would be visiting the Delluc vineyard. Time was running out for young Delluc, Bruno thought to himself, but also for Cazenau.

When Bruno and the mayor arrived at eight the next morning, Cazenau had already left in his truck, telling his wife he would be away all day on business. He had also told her to be sure to prepare a decent lunch for the driver of the spraying machine, who was scheduled to start treating his vines that day, from nine in the morning.

"What do we do now?" the mayor asked.

"I'll go to see Michel again," Bruno said, "and you get every employee in the *mairie* to call every household in the commune and ask them if they own a leaf blower. If they do, the *mairie* needs to borrow it. Get as many volunteers as you can to meet me here as soon after nine as they can. Get Hubert to do the same with all the shareholders in the town vineyard who live in other communes nearby."

By the time the clock on the *mairie* struck nine, the spraying machine was at work on the far side of Cazenau's vineyard, a huge machine that could spray four rows at a time. By ten-thirty it was only twenty rows of vines from the border with Delluc's land.

Bruno's defenses were ready. Every member of the public works department was there and each of the volunteer firemen, except for Cazenau. All the employees of the *mairie* and most of the members of the tennis and rugby clubs had turned up along with the *collège* students. The employees of the Crédit Agricole bank and the amusement park and several occupants of the retirement home were there too. And so were all the friends of Bruno, including Father Sentout and his housekeeper and sacristan, as well as Pamela, Miranda and Jack Crimson.

Every one of them, man, woman and youth, was lined up at Delluc's hedge, each of them with a handkerchief over their mouth and nose while Philippe Delaron of *Sud Ouest* stood by to take photos and report what he would call in the newspaper "The Battle of the Greens of St. Denis."

"Ready," called Bruno as the spraying machine turned into a row just eight vine rows removed from the hedge, while a light breeze from the west began carrying the chemicals toward Delluc's land.

"*Allez,*" Bruno shouted as the machine

130

turned into the next row.

And like so many archers in the medieval wars, each member of the public works department, each *pompier* and every one of Bruno's friends and volunteers, raised their individual leaf blowers and the sound of a great mechanical wind filled the air to send the spray blowing backward onto Cazenau's land.

Better still, it blinded the driver of the spraying machine, who was already wearing goggles and a face mask. He almost disappeared in the storm of dust and moisture particles that swept over his windshield and sent his machine careering into and then getting stuck in one of Cazenau's rows of vines. But the motor kept running and the spray kept on spraying.

Under cover of this blowback, Bruno advanced toward the sprayer, his face covered in a mask and a kilo bag of sugar in his gloved hands. He approached the sprayer from the rear, opened the cap to the fuel tank and poured in the sugar before running back to Delluc's land. By the time he reached it, the machine's engine had stalled.

That was the end of the spraying. By the end of the day, Pierre Delluc had his certificate from Demeter. A sober Cazenau, confronted by the mayor with the threat to publish the lab results from Bruno's samples, had glumly accepted Hubert's deal. And all the volunteers and their wives and families gathered at the town vineyard to celebrate and cheer as the mayor made a victory speech that hailed them all as the green army of St. Denis. And that was the headline in *Sud Ouest* the next day, with a photo of Marielle holding her leaf blower.

Nobody ever said a word in public about Bruno's bag of sugar. But he and the mayor had a quiet word with the town's insurance agent. He in turn talked to the insurance agent for the company that owned the spraying machine, which soon found itself awarded the contract for spraying the town vineyard, but only with organic products.

A MARKET TALE

Like so many events in St. Denis, deep in the gastronomic heartland of France, this story begins in the market. On a Tuesday morning in early summer, Kati, a young woman with short, fair hair and a little redness on her bare arms from her first exposure to the sun, was staring entranced at a wider selection of strawberries than she had ever known to exist. Her eyes darted eagerly among the four varieties she could distinguish, from deep crimsons to plump reds, and from orange fruit to the purple ones that looked so moist she could almost imagine the juice seeping through.

"Try one of each," the stallholder called out cheerfully. As he came from the other end of his stall, where he had been placing oranges in a careful pyramid, she noticed his lively dark eyes and tumble of curly hair before she realized that he limped. "See which one you want."

With the deliberation of a woman used to watching her pennies, Kati tried the cheapest first, the plump, red Gariguette, which would have tasted as she expected a strawberry to taste, except this was her first of the year. And since it had been picked just after dawn that morning, it was much fresher than any fruit she had ever sampled. The taste seemed to explode in her mouth, and without thinking she closed her eyes, feeling the flavor intensify until she felt that she was eating the very essence of summer.

"Try this one," the stallholder said, and held out to her a small berry of deepest red, impaled on a cocktail stick. "It's my favorite, Mara des Bois."

Nothing in her life had prepared her for the detonation of flavor that now filled her mouth. It was like tasting perfume, a sweetness that was intense without being sickly, and with a sparkling zest that seemed both full of energy and deeply comforting. She closed her eyes again and thought to herself, This is why I came to France.

"Mmm," she said, opening her eyes and seeing his friendly face beaming at her. "That one."

"Eat them today," he advised, offering her a small plastic box that seemed to hold more than she could possibly eat.

"That is too many. Do you have a smaller box?" she asked in the careful French she had learned at school.

"Not usually," he said, but he shook half of the *panier* into a paper bag and added one strawberry from each of the other varieties. "Where are you from?"

"Switzerland," she said. "How much is that, please."

"Call it a euro. You here on holiday? What's your name?"

"Yes, holiday. I am called Kati."

And so it had begun. Kati came from Schaffhausen, a town in northern Switzerland famous for its watches and for the Rheinfall, the majestic waterfall of the River Rhine. Its tumbling roar, she thought, had hitherto been the soporific soundtrack of her uneventful life. She had earlier that year celebrated her twenty-eighth birthday with the suitable young man she was expected to marry. Over a glass of champagne in what he called "our" restaurant, he had presented Kati with a small box that contained a ring. At that moment several thoughts that had long lain almost dormant suddenly thrust themselves simultaneously upon her.

The first was that she did not enjoy her job as a junior official in the prosecutor's office. The second was that she was bored by the young man, whose name was Dieter, and who not only worked in the same office but spoke of little else, except for sports. The next thought came with a growing sense of dismay, that there should be more to her life than this. So far it had passed without drama or excitement. She owed herself some adventure, something unpredictable, Kati said to herself, something that was truly her own. She rose from the restaurant table, apologized to Dieter while explaining that she would not marry him after all and walked briskly home to her studio apartment. With a sense of liberation that was as thrilling as it was alarming, Kati then began to pack her suitcase.

And now, as she strolled through the market of St. Denis, buying a small disk of goat's cheese and trying to choose among the array of different pâtés at the charcuterie stall, a friendly looking policeman with a loaf of bread under his arm smiled at her and touched his cap. At each stall, Kati noticed, he stopped to shake hands with the men and kiss the cheeks of the women. He would sample a slice of *saucisson* here and a sliver of melon there as he headed for the small table between a cheese stall and the one where she had bought her strawberries. Already, two of the stools at the table were occupied, one by the man who had been selling wicker baskets who was uncorking a bottle of wine, and the other by a man who sold olives and who was opening an unlabeled can of pâté. Perhaps, she thought with pleasure, it was homemade.

"Bonjour à tous," said the policeman, laying the large baguette, still warm from the oven, on the table. He was greeted by a chorus of "Bonjour, Bruno." Hands were shaken, places taken, bread torn into chunks and cheese and pâté spread upon them. Wine was poured, glasses chinked together to jolly cries of *Santé,* and the ritual of the *casse-croûte* was under way.

Kati paused before the giant *rôtisserie* in which quails, pigeons and chickens were turning on spits as their juices dripped down onto the potatoes roasting in the tray below, and asked herself why these men were embarking at nine in the morning upon the very meal she would be having for her lunch some three hours later. Even as she formed the thought in her mind, the answer came that these were men who rose at dawn to prepare their stalls, to drive to the market, to unload and prepare for the rush of locals who would come between eight and nine. They would then sit to enjoy their breakfast before the tourists arrived sometime after ten and the second rush of locals arrived to buy food for their own lunches. Lingering nearby, she eavesdropped discreetly on their merry chatter.

They looked like men who met this way regularly. The man with the limp who had sold her strawberries was called Marcel, she learned, and the man with the cheese stall was Stéphane. The basket seller was Raoul, and he also staffed an adjoining stall that sold Bergerac wines, as she discovered when he was summoned from the table to offer a free tasting to a customer. When Raoul returned they were joined by Jean-Paul from the *rôtisserie,* who brought a freshly roasted chicken and a vast dish of roast potatoes.

When she noticed that Marcel was watching her as she hovered nearby, Kati turned away to examine a stall of colorful African cloths and leather belts and T-shirts manned by a tall, dark-skinned man in flowing robes and a skullcap. He grinned at her, muttered something she did not catch, pointed to the table with the other men as if to say she could find him there and headed across to buy a plate of shrimps from the fishmonger before joining the others.

From his place at the table, Bruno had noticed the exchange of glances between Marcel and the stranger, and asked quietly,

"Who's the new girl?"

"A Swiss tourist. Her name is Kati," Marcel replied, pouring a glass for Bruno and another for himself. "She likes my strawberries."

Bruno, who had not previously seen his friend noticing another woman since the car crash that had taken Marcel's leg and made him a widower, glanced discreetly at Kati, who was now examining the honey stall with its beeswax candles. He saw a young woman in her twenties, he guessed. She was without makeup and wore a sleeveless white dress and red sandals. The dress was belted with a red scarf, revealing a waist that looked almost too trim for her sturdy figure. Bruno guessed she would play a powerful game of tennis. A canvas shopping bag was slung across her shoulder, and she strolled over to the terrace outside Fauquet's café and sat, taking the strawberries from her bag. Suddenly, as if aware she was being watched, she glanced across to see Bruno and Marcel still looking at her. She gave a hesitant smile and turned away to order a coffee from the waitress.

On an impulse, and with a daring that Bruno was tempted to applaud, Marcel excused himself to his friends and limped across to the terrace to join her. She welcomed him with a shy smile. A second coffee was ordered, the strawberries were shared, and then a *pain au chocolat,* and still they lingered. Alerted by Bruno, Jeanne, the woman who collected the market fees, happily replaced Marcel at his stall, although most of the locals simply placed the money for their fruits and vegetables in the small basket he used for change.

So it had begun. And it continued over dinner that evening at Ivan's bistro, where the *plat du jour* was *gigot à la bretonne,* a leg of roast young lamb that had been studded with slivers of garlic and sprigs of thyme and served with *haricots blancs.* Unlike that evening in Schaffhausen that she remembered so vividly and with such a sense of pride at her own daring, this was a restaurant that Kati had no wish to leave. The glass of chilled Bergerac Sec that Ivan offered her as an *apéritif* delighted her more than the champagne of that earlier evening. Kati was even more pleased by the house Pécharmant red wine that was served with the lamb, and Kati and Marcel both took it as an omen that Ivan's dessert that evening was Mara des Bois strawberries. Marcel was charmed to hear, in Kati's stilted French, that she had come to St. Denis because of a postcard a school friend had sent her years earlier of the prehistoric cave paintings of Lascaux, and she had resolved to visit them.

The one moment that could have been difficult came when Marcel asked if he could walk her back to the hotel, and Kati knew she must not look down at his lame leg nor offend him by mentioning it. But Marcel had been thinking of this all evening and had resolved on bold measures. He rose, raised his leg to rest it on an adjoining chair and lifted his trouser leg to show the prosthetic limb, and rapped on it firmly with his knuckles.

"I worked hard to get used to this," he said with a touch of pride. "At first, just a couple of meters each day, but after a week a hundred meters, and after a month I tried for my first kilometer. Now I walk ten kilometers every weekend and can still totter up and down the rugby field as a linesman."

The hotel, the most modest in St. Denis, was a short stroll from the bistro. It being very early in the season, Kati had booked a week at a special low rate and had resolved to hire a bicycle to visit the caves. Lascaux might be a little far for cycling, unless you are in training for the Tour de France, Marcel said with a smile. He added that he had no market on Thursday, his day off, and would be delighted to take her there. He had not seen the caves since he was a schoolboy and had always promised himself to go again.

Bruno later heard from Mauricette, the wife of the hotel owner, that they had parted on the hotel steps with a polite exchange of kisses on the cheek. Then the girl had stood awhile in the darkness of the lobby, looking after Marcel as he limped away along the street, whistling. And Bruno, being a romantic soul, wondered to himself what tune had come into Marcel's head, and what thoughts and fantasies the two people had entertained as they made their way to their separate beds.

Marcel's thought, Bruno learned the next day, had been very practical. Kati had said the previous evening that she was also using the week to see if she could find work and spend the summer in the Périgord while thinking what she might do next, now that she had resigned from her tedious but secure job in Schaffhausen. Marcel called the *mairie* to ask if Bruno knew of anything. And naturally he did, since not much happened in St. Denis and the broader commune around it, from love affairs to business ventures, family scandals to political plots, without Bruno learning of them. So on the morning of the trip to Lascaux, while Marcel waited in his car outside, Kati went into the offices of Delightful Dordogne, a rental agency for dozens of local *gîtes* and holiday villas, hoping to get a job as a cleaner.

Dougal, the Scottish owner, had been happy to learn that she spoke German and English as well as serviceable French and Italian. Kati explained that her mother was from Yorkshire, and the sound Swiss education system had equipped her with French and Italian. Dougal hired her on the spot as a troubleshooter to take care of any concerns or problems his foreign clients might have. The job came with a room in one of the staff houses Dougal maintained, and with a battered but serviceable Citroën *deux-chevaux* that was older than she was.

Bruno learned later from Marcel that the day had only improved, and that in the sudden darkness in the cave of Lascaux when the guide had turned off the entrance lights, Kati had clutched at his hand. And their hands had stayed entwined as the different lights came on to illuminate the great bulls that soared over the white chalk walls and ceilings around them. And when Kati had looked up to marvel at the tumult of painted life on the ceilings, where horses and bulls and deer seemed to dance together, she had leaned back against him and rested her head against his shoulder.

Bruno took great pleasure in the love stories of his friends, in part because he was of a generous disposition and enjoyed seeing people he knew fall in love, and also because their affairs always seemed so much simpler than his own complicated romantic life. He felt a special happiness at this great good fortune that had fallen upon his friend Marcel, who had been dealt such a hard blow by fate. Bruno had still been playing rugby for the town team when Marcel had returned to St. Denis, equipped with a new diploma as a specialist teacher in physical education. He joined the rugby team and taught the sport so well that the *collège* team became champions of the *département.* He also taught tennis and basketball, and took the older children on skiing trips to the Pyrenees and to the Basque coast in summer for surfing. He was the fittest young man in St. Denis, and once he married his childhood sweetheart Yvonne and they settled in one of the subsidized apartments the *collège* made available for its teachers, he was probably the happiest.

The idyll lasted for three years, until the night of the annual dinner for the *départe-*

ment tennis clubs. Yvonne had been driving, since she seldom drank at all, and somehow on the steep, twisting road from Montignac the car had gone over the cliff. And Marcel had lost his wife, his leg and his profession.

With great determination, he learned to walk again and took over the fruit-and-vegetable stall in the market that his uncle had run, supplied mainly by the vast extended family of cousins and half cousins in the surrounding communes. But that was not quite enough for Marcel, who had resolved to have the finest stall not only in St. Denis but in the whole of the Périgord. He selected only the best items, washed them carefully and displayed them with style. In summer, he was at different markets six days a week, and five days in winter. On his day off he visited every restaurant in the region, offering his produce but also asking them what they might like but could not easily obtain. Armed with this knowledge, Marcel set off for Rungis, the giant wholesale food market near Orly Airport outside Paris, to see what might be available and, more important, what might be possible in the way of exotic fruits and vegetables that other stalls would not have.

By chance, on his first visit, Marcel

learned that one of the players on the Rungis rugby team had been with him at the physical education college where Marcel had earned his diploma, and they had played on the same team. A reunion was arranged, his limp explained and within the day Marcel had been introduced to the importers and distributors of the finest products that the planet, and not just the fertile fields of France, had to offer. The trucks that left Rungis market at dawn each day for deliveries to Bordeaux and Périgueux henceforth kept a special corner for Marcel of St. Denis. Marcel made a good living and had the satisfaction of pride in his work and the food that he sold, along with the deep respect of his market colleagues and his friends like Bruno for the way he had rebuilt his shattered life.

And now, Bruno reflected, his friend was showing interest in a woman again, for the first time since Marcel had lost his wife. And the woman in question seemed wise enough to have looked beyond Marcel's limp to the qualities of the man beneath, which was to her credit. Bruno's one slight concern was Marcel's family, or at least one crucial member of it, Marcel's big sister Nadette. It was short for Bernadette, but since her days as a schoolroom bully nobody had ever thought she deserved the name of the saint.

The very name Nadette, a sound that was hard, blunt and to the point, seemed to sum her up. She was big, bigger than Marcel, and as tall as Bruno and probably weighed a few kilos more than he did. Had there been a rugby club for girls when Nadette was at school, she would doubtless have been its star. She had been married, briefly, to an older man who had lost his job with the closure of the Lorraine coalfields. He left after two years, saying he only stayed that long for her cooking, leaving her with a young son who had since joined the navy. Nadette was not much liked in St. Denis. She worked at the Trésor Public, the town's tax collection office, and was said to take a sadistic pleasure in tracking down late payers and making surreptitious visits to houses that were not paying the TV tax, to see if they were illegally watching.

Nadette also had a reputation as a malicious gossip, and while Bruno did not reveal this to others, Bruno knew her to be the source of many anonymous letters to the authorities, accusing unemployed neighbors of taking odd jobs without paying taxes and social insurance. Since he was the one who had to follow up on these accusations, which might have been justified but took little account of the economic realities of the recession, Bruno found her both tiresome and damaging to the town's social fabric. He usually managed to resolve matters with a friendly warning and a pamphlet on the useful system of *chèque emploi service,* under which an employer paid for temporary work with a check that deducted from his or her bank account a modest amount for social insurance. This protected both employer and employee in case of accidents. To Bruno it seemed a very sensible French compromise, to civilize the underground economy without stifling it.

Marcel, who had been the baby of the family, an unexpected child when his mother was past forty and his big sister was already a teenager, was unusually patient with Nadette. When their parents had died, he had allowed her to take the family house, a handsome old stone building on the outskirts of St. Denis. The three-story home, with its large garden and a barn which she rented to a local farmer, was worth considerably more than Marcel's share, the land on which the family kept the market garden that provided fruits and vegetables for his market stall. When he married, Marcel had built a small, cheap house on a corner of his land, and after his wife's death, Nadette had campaigned tirelessly for it to be sold and for Marcel to move in with her.

"She says we'd both save money and families should stick together," Marcel explained to Bruno over a beer at the rugby club bar one evening. "But I need to keep an eye on the garden and I want my own space. It's hard to make her understand when she's trying to be so kind."

Nadette used her key to get into Marcel's house and clean it on Sunday mornings when he was at the market in St. Cyprien. She'd empty his laundry basket and wash and iron his clothes. She left meals for the week in his freezer and insisted that he join her for family supper on Sunday evenings.

"It's not really my business, but doesn't she understand you need a life of your own?" Bruno had asked. Marcel had just shrugged. "What happens if you meet a new woman, if you want to marry again?" Bruno had asked. He remembered some of the shouting matches between Nadette and Marcel's wife before her death. On a couple of occasions, he'd had to stand between them in the market, convinced the two women were about to hurl themselves upon each other, fists and nails flying. At the funeral, Nadette had been dry eyed, probably reflecting that Marcel without a wife would be Marcel without direct heirs, so the family property would pass to her and her son. Such matters of land and inheritance had frequently stoked family feuds in France.

"Not much chance of a new woman for me," Marcel had replied, tapping his prosthetic leg. Bruno was not so sure. The family genes had played a cruel trick on Nadette and her brother. She had the stolid, almost lumpish shape of a once athletic man whose muscles had gone to seed, and her skin was pale and blotched easily in the sun. By contrast, Marcel was slim and lithe, with an olive complexion and flashing dark eyes.

Bruno knew instinctively that Nadette would be shaken by the prospect of her brother embarking on a new affair. At first, she appeared unconcerned, believing it was no more than a holiday fling that would end once Kati left town. It was when Bruno heard that Kati would be working for Dougal's rental agency that he braced himself for trouble. He did not have long to wait. An anonymous letter claiming that Dougal was improperly hiring foreigners arrived at the *mairie.* Bruno checked the regulations and found that the Swiss had the same rights as European Union citizens to live and work in France, just as the French did in Switzerland. He ignored the letter, but next time he was in the Trésor Public he commented on the boost the foreign residents, including the Swiss, brought to the town taxes. Nadette's next ploy was to claim Kati was not paying tax on the TV in her staff house. Bruno sighed. The TV was in the communal sitting room and the tax was paid by Dougal. He wondered what Nadette would try next.

But Nadette seemed to back off, or at least to assume that the holiday romance would end when the tourist season passed and Kati's job went with it. Bruno kept a wary eye on the *mairie's* postbox and tipped off Sergeant Jules at the gendarmerie that Nadette could be on the warpath. Perhaps because her own brief courtship and marriage had been so unhappy, Nadette seemed to miss the signs that were becoming evident to everyone in St. Denis. Kati and Marcel were becoming a couple. They giggled together as they tasted the different vintages at the town's wine fair, shopped together in the flea market that raised money for the Red Cross and strolled hand in hand along the riverbank to watch the sunset from the bridge. They even watched the final of the tennis tournament together, although most of it was spent staring dreamily into each other's eyes.

It was impossible to see them and not to feel better about the human condition, thought Bruno. Old men and young sportsmen, teenagers and matrons, shopkeepers and tourists in the market: all their faces broke into indulgent and tender smiles. Some were perhaps a little wistful, a little regretful that those days had passed, or were yet to come. But one reason that Bruno on the whole liked the human race was the way that most of its members tend to be inspired into a generosity of spirit by the sight of young people in love.

However much in love she might be, Kati was a practical young woman. She knew that her job would end with the summer and had been thinking what she might do then. She could have helped Marcel at the market stall, but she thought it best to keep a measure of independence. So she looked carefully at the St. Denis market and asked herself what was missing. She visited other markets in the region, including the big ones at Sarlat and Périgueux, and thought about markets she had seen in Germany and at home in Switzerland. She toyed briefly with the idea of a stall selling Christmas items, but that would be no use after December. And one day in Eymet, a town with many British residents, she saw a van in the market that was flying a Union Jack and selling hot pies.

Instantly, Kati was transported back to the Schaffhausen kitchen of her childhood and the scents that came when her mother pulled out the Cornish pasties, the cheese-and-onion tarts and the steak and Stilton pies, the sausage rolls and bacon sandwiches of her native land. Kati bought a Cornish pasty, the golden pastry with its filling of meat, turnip, potato and onion in warm gravy. The woman in the van handed her a square brown bottle with a blue label that she remembered, HP Sauce, with the picture of the Houses of Parliament in London.

At once, Kati had her solution. The only other people selling hot food in the markets were the Vietnamese with their *nem* and Jean-Paul with his *rôtisserie.* There would be no competition. And after the end of summer hot food would become increasingly popular.

"Takes you back, does it, love?" the woman in the van asked Kati, in English. She looked older than Kati's mother. "Lots of people miss their home food."

"My mother's English, but my dad's

Swiss, and that's where we were brought up," she explained. "Where did you find this van?"

"On the website leboncoin," came the reply. "But if you're interested, this one's for sale. I'm getting too old for this lark, up at five to start baking every day, then there's all the cleaning up, both the van and my kitchen at home. It's no picnic, my girl."

The woman, whose name was Ethel and who came from Rotherham, not far from Kati's mother's birthplace in Leeds, put on the kettle and made them both a cup of tea. Then Kati took over the stall for ten minutes while Ethel did her market shopping. Then when the market closed they had lunch together, sharing an unsold cheese-and-onion pie and some sausage rolls with the harsh yellow English mustard.

"HP Sauce, and good, strong chutney and Colman's mustard, dear," Ethel confided. "If you've got those, the English will be your faithful customers. For the French, I've got different sauces, that Thai sweet chili, and there's one I make with *vin de noix* and honey that's very popular. And there's always ketchup."

Over another cup of tea, they agreed that Kati would join Ethel on Saturday mornings, getting up before dawn to help her bake and then learning the ways of the market. Kati was already thinking of Swiss pastries she knew how to make, from honey-walnut tart to apple strudel, *Mailaenderli* cookies and *Spitzbuben,* and there was *Zopf* bread. The possibilities expanded brightly before her.

There was, however, one very large obstacle. Kati wondered how to raise the issue and decided to explain her problem honestly. There would be no point in starting to learn the trade with Ethel if the English-woman wanted eventually to be paid in cash.

"I don't have the money to buy your van outright," Kati said. "Could we arrange a leasing deal, in which I pay you out of my earnings? Or maybe I could rent the stall from you."

Ethel put down her teacup and eyed her solemnly. "Let's see how it goes," she said. "If your sales are good, the bank might be prepared to make you a loan."

"It sounds as if you need the money," Kati said, crestfallen.

"I do, but not right away. Besides, once you see how much work it is you might change your mind."

But Kati did not change her mind, not about Marcel, nor about St. Denis, nor

155

about selling pastries from the market stall. And when the summer season came to an end and Dougal began paying off his cleaners and hinted that he'd be renting out the house he used for his employees, Kati moved in with Marcel. Bruno learned of this the day after it happened, when Marcel invited him and some other friends to dinner at his home to celebrate the new arrangement. Kati would cook, he said.

The weather was still warm enough for them to eat outside on Marcel's terrace, looking over his carefully tended vegetable garden. Kati's hair had grown out during the summer, and she had piled it in a fetching way on top of her head, revealing a shapely neck. Bruno had always thought that the back of a woman's neck was one of the most beguiling of the endlessly enchanting features of the female anatomy. It was set off by a collarless blouse of white linen, with which she wore a long cotton skirt of a blue he had only seen on the stall of Léopold, the Senegalese in the market. The skirt had been well cut and fitted perfectly, so he assumed that either Kati had made it herself or had been sufficiently thoughtful to find her way to Marie-Josette, the town's dressmaker. Bruno guessed the latter; Kati seemed instinctively to understand that a new merchant in the market would do well to spread her euros among the established businesses.

They were nine at a table set for ten, and Bruno realized with a touch of foreboding that Nadette had been invited but had failed to attend. The food quickly improved his mood, but he kept an ear cocked for a telephone call from Nadette pleading some sudden illness or emergency, and he resolved that he would insist on handling the matter rather than Marcel. Nadette must not be allowed to spoil Kati's evening.

The first course was a chilled gazpacho, made from peppers and cucumbers that Kati had picked from the garden that day. Then came a pâté she had made from trout that the fishmonger had smoked for her; she had blended just the right touch of horseradish. For the main course, she explained shyly, she was serving the same roast lamb that had been the first meal she and Marcel had shared. Bruno's smile became a little fixed. He liked his lamb pink, but Pamela, his partner that evening, preferred hers well done. When they dined together, she had the outer slices and he had the inner. But to his relief, Kati's lamb somehow contrived to suit all tastes. When Pamela came back from the kitchen, having insisted on helping clear away the plates, she whispered to Bruno, "She cooked it very slowly at a low temperature. That's the secret."

Kati had accompanied the lamb with a carrot mousse that Bruno found delightful and a *tarte aux tomates* which had somehow preserved the crispness of its pastry. Bruno, whose own pies and quiches tended toward a dismaying sogginess that greatly frustrated him, understood he was in the presence of a cook of rare quality. And that, he suspected, would make Nadette's animosity all the sharper.

Nadette did not call that evening. She was waiting for bigger game. And she did not have long to wait. The day that the van that had been renamed Kati's Kitchen appeared at the market in St. Denis, the *casse-croûte* club loyally skipped their usual fare and breakfasted with sincere and growing appreciation on cheese-and-onion tart, bacon sandwiches in whole wheat buns that Kati had made herself and sausage rolls that Kati had blended with sage and a little grated ginger.

"I could get used to this," said Stéphane, washing down the last of a cheese-and-onion tart with a glass of Bergerac red from the town vineyard. "I wonder if she'd like to experiment with some of my cheeses."

"She'd love to do that," said Marcel, who was looking sleeker and more contented than Bruno could remember. "And I don't think she's finished with us yet."

As he spoke, Kati appeared carrying one of Raoul's baskets, its contents covered in a tea towel. She put it on the table, whipped off the cloth with a cheerful "Tra-la!" and revealed a heaped pile of *Spitzbuben* cookies. She was dressed like a classic bistro waitress, black blouse and skirt and a freshly starched long white apron. But something was missing. Bruno went quickly into the *mairie* and picked a handful of the thin evidence gloves from the box by his desk and came down to give them to Kati.

"Just in case we get a surprise inspection," he confided as he slipped them to her. With Nadette's malignance in mind, Bruno had already studied the various regulations on serving food in the market, and while no stallholder had ever in his memory observed the rule about wearing gloves to handle food, he thought it a useful precaution. He had already verified that the oven and refrigerator in Kati's van were in compliance and that the paper plates and napkins and the plastic utensils she offered were officially approved. He had also checked

Kati's insurance and he thought he had covered every eventuality.

He was wrong. Nadette's strike was unexpected. She had filed her complaint neither to him nor to the gendarmes in St. Denis but directly to the *motards,* the gendarmes who enforced the traffic rules. And rather than calling the *motards* down upon St. Denis, which could have put most of her neighbors and even her brother at risk, she chose Marcel's day of rest when Kati's Kitchen was selling pies and pasties in Lalinde.

Kati was one of three stallholders who had vans equipped to sell their wares, but Kati was the only one whose van had not passed its *contrôle technique,* the road-worthiness and emissions test required for all vehicles every two years. She was fined on the spot and told her van would have to be towed to an inspection station. At least the *motards* did not stop her selling food, and even bought some of her pasties. But the fine and the towing fee came to four hundred and fifteen euros, a sum she could barely afford. It amounted to her profits for a week, and she lost another day of business waiting for the van to pass its inspection.

Bruno went back to the regulations governing markets, poring over the small print to see what vulnerabilities might remain. He could find nothing, but to be sure he called on the Vinhs, the Vietnamese couple who sold *nem* and other Asian delicacies, to ask whether there were any hygiene rules that had to be followed. Not as far as he knew, said Vinh. Kati had a sink to wash her hands, which was the important thing. Then Bruno asked Jean-Paul from the *rôtisserie* if he could think of anything, and Jean-Paul came up with a list of requirements that Bruno had already covered, and added, "As long as she's done her food-handling course, she'll be all right."

"That's not in the market rules," Bruno said.

"It's a new one, a food-hygiene directive from Brussels. But unless you can show you've been in business for three years already or worked in a restaurant, you have to go through the course if you're selling cooked food for immediate consumption. It only takes three days and you have to pay for it, but the fine can be stiff if you don't take the course and they can confiscate your equipment. Talk to Marie-Claire, since she does the lunches for the kids at the *collège,* and she's a qualified instructor. That's where my son got his certificate."

Marie-Claire was helpful. She prepared

the school lunches in the mornings and ran her courses in the afternoons. The *collège* courses were free, but they lasted five days. Kati could join the next one on Monday afternoon. Kati said she would comply when Bruno explained, but there were tears in her eyes as she told him that after the previous fine, she couldn't afford to give up a week of selling at the markets in the mornings. She would have to take the risk.

"But please don't tell Marcel," she added. "I don't want to turn this into a family row between him and Nadette. I can't stand the thought of that hanging over us."

Bruno checked the hygiene regulations. Only one person at the stall needed to have the certificate, and they could have an unqualified helper. And so with Madame Vinh and Jean-Paul's son and Ethel from Yorkshire, who had been running the stall for more than the three years required, Bruno and Kati between them arranged for her to be covered for the five mornings.

It was on the fourth day, once again at Lalinde, that the hygiene inspectors arrived. As a courtesy, Bruno had called his various counterparts in the markets to explain the problem, and with Guillaume Quatremer, the town policeman in Lalinde, he had a stroke of luck. Guillaume, an ex-serviceman like Bruno, had developed a taste for Kati's sausage rolls and was eager to help. And he had some useful news: a friend in the sub-prefecture had emailed him a copy of the anonymous letter they had received complaining that the writer had suffered food poisoning after buying a pasty at Kati's Kitchen at the Lalinde market.

So Bruno, in civilian clothes, was enjoying a *citron pressé* at a discreet table in the café by the small canal when the inspectors swooped. Fortunately, Jean-Paul's son was in Kati's van, wearing plastic gloves and equipped with his certificate. The inspectors checked that all the equipment conformed to the rules and took away with them a sample of each of the products on sale for testing. Bruno was at the counter paying for his drink when a familiar figure came into the café, sat down, brusquely demanded service and ordered a café-cognac. Nadette had evidently taken time off from the Trésor Public to witness the downfall of her rival.

Bruno slipped out through a side door and called Laurent, the director of the Trésor Public in St. Denis, and asked him if Nadette was at work that day. No, he was told; she had called in sick. How odd, Bruno told him with a feeling that poetic justice was being served, that she was at that very moment drinking café-cognac in the Lalinde market. Bruno then asked if Nadette had complained of food poisoning, or any other ailment, in the previous three weeks. Not at all, Laurent replied, but Nadette would certainly have some explaining to do when she returned to work. Bruno closed his phone and looked through the café window to see a second glass of cognac being placed on Nadette's table. Aha, Bruno thought and went in search of Nadette's blue Renault Clio, a vehicle he knew from the Trésor Public parking area. When he found it, he called Guillaume, told him where to find the car and suggested that a Breathalyzer test might be in order.

"We got her," Guillaume reported when Bruno was back in his office at the St. Denis *mairie.* "She failed the breath test, so we got the doc to take a blood sample and we impounded the car until she was sober. I took her to the bus stop, but she'll have a couple of hours to wait."

Bruno checked his watch and then the bus timetable. He thanked Guillaume and walked down to the *collège,* where he saw Kati's van parked and peeked through the kitchen window to see Kati sitting in a row with three young women and taking notes

164

while Marie-Claire was writing on the blackboard. One more day and Kati would have her certificate. He walked back to the Trésor Public and told Laurent he'd be just in time to meet his supposedly sick employee at the bus stop by the bank. They walked there together and waited inside the bank until the bus drew up and Nadette climbed out.

"In my office at eight-thirty tomorrow morning, Nadette, to explain why you're too sick to work but healthy enough to take jaunts around the countryside," Laurent told her grimly before marching off. After a moment the red-faced Nadette followed him across the bridge at a discreet distance and took the road to her home. Bruno gave her some time to collect herself, and about an hour later he knocked at her door. She was wearing an apron and the smell of baking wafted enticingly from within as she glared fiercely at him.

"Nadette, it's time you and I had a serious talk," he said. "I know it's been a rough day, but it can get a lot rougher if we have to talk about certain anonymous letters, trumped-up denunciations and false claims of food poisoning."

Her jaw fell open in surprise, and she made no objection as Bruno walked in and went straight to the kitchen, where a quiche Lorraine, fresh from the oven, was cooling on the counter beside the stove. It smelled wonderful and reminded him that he hadn't eaten since breakfast. He took a seat at the kitchen table, removed his képi and said, "I'm starving, Nadette, and that smells wonderful."

"I made it this morning and just warmed it through," she said, and brought out two plates, knives and forks and a couple of glasses. Even a woman as mean-spirited as Nadette could hardly ignore the Périgord tradition of hospitality. She took from the fridge an already opened bottle of Bergerac Sec, handed it to Bruno for him to pour and then sliced the quiche into quarters and served them.

"So you're behind all this, Bruno," she said. "I should have known."

"No, Nadette," he replied. "You are. You brought all this on yourself, including those café-cognacs in Lalinde where you were expecting to watch the success of your ploy against Kati."

He took a forkful of the quiche and suddenly felt a sense of contentment stealing over him, dispelling the quiet anger that had been building up against Nadette throughout the day.

"Mon Dieu," he said in surprise. "This is the best quiche I ever tasted."

"Better than hers, you mean," she said sharply, but she looked pleased and began to eat. Bruno poured out the wine, and they ate in silence for a few moments.

"Are you going to try to get me fired?" she asked when her plate was cleared.

Bruno shook his head; his mouth was full with the final taste of the food, the pastry that seemed lighter than air but crisper than biscuit, its butter merging richly with the cream in the filling and the touch of salt on the slivers of ham.

"This is France," he said, after a final, regretful smacking of his lips and a hopeful glance at the remaining half of the quiche. "You won't get fired for stealing a sick day. If we fired everybody who did that, there'd hardly be anyone left to work. But if you can bake like that, I don't know why you don't set up a business. You'd make a fortune. I'd be your first customer."

Nadette's face seemed to soften, and she cut the remaining quiche into two large portions and served one to each of them. Then she refilled their glasses. It was at that moment that the idea came to Bruno, the goal he had in mind, the means to bring it about, the way he could best prepare the ground.

167

"That's not your real problem," he said. "It's the false accusation of food poisoning. Once an official dossier gets opened, that's serious, particularly when we trace the paper and printer and show you wrote it on Trésor Public equipment. Your fingerprints will be on it. That could get you fired, and open to criminal charges, and then Kati would have quite a lawsuit against you."

Nadette stopped eating. Bruno continued in almost casual tones, "And I doubt whether Marcel would ever speak to you again. I know you're devoted to him, but you must see how happy Kati is making him. Put yourself in Marcel's shoes, Nadette. Don't you think he deserves a bit of happiness, after all he's been through?"

He finished his quiche, emptied his glass and picked up his hat. "That quiche was so good, I'd love another one. I'll come here and pick it up Saturday morning after the market opens, about nine. Don't worry, I'll happily pay for it. Your cooking is worth its weight in gold. Thank you for the meal, and I'll see myself out. Until Saturday, then."

On the next afternoon at four, he and Marcel, along with Stéphane, Raoul and Jean-Paul from the market, were in the *collège* kitchen waiting to applaud when Marie-Claire handed the certificates of

168

course completion to Kati and the school-girls. When their applause died down, Marie-Claire told her pupils that their formal attestations from the prefecture would follow in due course, but they were now qualified and entitled to work as food handlers for sale to the public. When Kati turned, waving her certificate, to embrace Marcel, Bruno remembered how Nadette had stayed immobile at the table when he left her kitchen, tears spilling down her cheeks.

Marie-Claire, who had been warned what to expect, was opening the cupboard and bringing out wineglasses as Bruno took the bottles of champagne he had placed earlier in the big refrigerator. When all the glasses were filled, and the young girls warned that one glass each was their limit, they drank a toast to the success of Kati's Kitchen, another to Swiss-French relations and a final one to the happy couple. And before the two lovers left, hand in hand, Bruno drew them to one side and told them of his plan for the following day. So intent were Kati and Marcel upon each other, he wasn't sure they had fully appreciated the scheme, but he could take care of that in the morning.

So just after nine on a lovely day in early

autumn, with the trees along the riverbank just turning to a rich gold and the ducks waddling with all the fatness they had stored in summer to fuel their long migration flights, Bruno presented himself at Nadette's door. She offered him coffee, which he accepted, and she served a fresh, hot brioche she had made along with some of her own apricot jam. They were delicious but could hardly compete with the scent of the quiche, wrapped in a dishcloth, that awaited him. Nadette shrugged when he asked what he owed her and then said, "Call it two euros." Bruno put down the coin, asked her to remain in the house until his return, and left for the market, the quiche held carefully in both hands.

Within thirty minutes he was back, and without explanation asked Nadette to accompany him. He knew from Laurent that Nadette had been given a formal reprimand and written warning the previous day and doubtless now she was wondering what new torment to expect. He led her in silence to the market, past the fishmonger and Stéphane's cheese stall so they could avoid Marcel and stopped in front of Kati's Kitchen.

In pride of place on the counter stood the dish she had sold to Bruno that morning, and a hand-lettered sign behind it read NADETTE'S QUICHE, 6 EUROS. Underneath, in slightly smaller letters, were the words: "The best I ever tasted," and signed Chef de Police Bruno.

"It's already sold," said Bruno. "I bought it and here's your share of the profit." He took a two-euro piece from Kati and pressed it into Nadette's hand.

"She's going to be family, Nadette, and I think you have here the makings of a good family business," he murmured as Marcel came around the corner from his stall to take Kati's hand as she descended from her van. They all admired Nadette's quiche and the poster in the brief moment before Stéphane called them all to join him and his friends for the *casse-croûte*. And as Marcel led his sister and his lover to their table, Bruno took the quiche from the counter and carried it across to the *casse-croûte* table.

"To Nadette and her wonderful quiche," said Kati, raising her glass. And as the others joined in the toast, Bruno grinned widely at the happy young woman from Schaffhausen and saw her give him a conspiratorial wink.

"This quiche is great," said Stéphane, "but there's not much to go round all of us."

"I've got two more I made ready," said Nadette. "Give me a minute and I'll go and bring them."

DANGEROUS VACATION

The connection between the two mobile phones was very bad. Although Pauline's voice sounded surprisingly calm, the only words that Bruno heard clearly were "crash" and "Vitrolle." Racing with his phone to his ear down the stairs of the St. Denis *mairie,* Bruno Courrèges kept asking if anyone was hurt. But suddenly the call dropped completely. He tried calling Pauline back as he bundled himself into his official police van and set off, siren howling and blue light flashing, for the Domaine de la Vitrolle. He couldn't even get a busy signal from her phone as he sped along the road toward Limeuil. He called the *pompiers* instead, the town's volunteer fire brigade which doubled as the medical emergency team, telling them to get to the Domaine's entrance gates.

Bruno spotted the crashed minibus about five hundred meters beyond the *domaine* entrance, close to the twelfth-century Chapelle St. Martin. The minibus was facing him, leaning to one side with two wheels in the ditch. A forlorn bunch of stunned American tourists huddled together on the grass verge, and the driver was sitting at the roadside, a cigarette between his lips and his head in his hands. A young woman in jeans and a bright red sweater was standing in the middle of the road to wave him down, a mobile phone in her hand. It was Pauline, a relieved smile on her usually impassive face. There was no other vehicle in sight.

"Nobody's hurt," she said quickly. "Just the bus. That's why I called you rather than the *urgences*. And thank you for coming so quickly. The driver's kind of shaken up, along with some of the clients."

Bruno breathed a fervent sigh of thanks when he saw that the tourists all seemed fine and were even starting to talk together. Some began to smile at him and look cheerful, apparently reassured by the sight of Bruno's police uniform with its promise of help being at hand. He touched his cap to them in salute with a confident *"Bonjour, messieurs-dames,"* and assurances that he would soon have them on their way again.

When he drew them aside to ask what had happened, Pauline and the driver agreed.

They had parked to visit the *chapelle,* one of the finest Romanesque churches in the region, where Pauline had shown her clients the medieval frescoes and pointed out the dedication stone, which announced: RICHARD KING OF ENGLAND HOLDS THE DUCHY OF AQUITAINE. As the driver pulled out afterward and made the sharp turn to get back onto the road toward the *domaine,* both wheels on the passenger side just seemed to give way. The minibus had lurched and then veered to the right and into the ditch.

"Both wheels at the same time?" Bruno asked, surprised. He went to look for himself and saw that both tires in the ditch were flat. He saw no sign of cuts or punctures and pulled out his phone to call Lespinasse at the local garage to bring his tow truck, along with some new tires. Then Bruno called the *domaine* to ask Sybille, the receptionist, to send a couple of cars to take Pauline and her group of tourists back for an impromptu wine tasting. He shook hands with each of the Americans when the cars came and wished them *bonne continuation,* and he was pleased to hear their praise of the Périgord and of Pauline as a guide.

Pauline and her tourists had disappeared by the time Lespinasse arrived with his truck a few minutes later. A small, plump man with a twinkle in his eyes, Lespinasse was the best car mechanic in the region. He bent down to look underneath the minibus, tapping and probing, before examining the two flattened tires and scratching his head. Then he got into the ditch and carefully unscrewed the small plastic cap that covered the front tire valve. As the cap began to come free, he cupped his hand beneath it, pulled the cap free, and some tiny pebbles of gravel fell into the palm of his hand. Lespinasse then unscrewed the rear valve cap, and again little bits of gravel trickled out.

"You been making enemies, Boniface?" he asked the bus driver. He turned to Bruno. "This was deliberate. Somebody replaced this cap after putting the gravel in to depress the valve and start a slow leak. Once the vehicle starts moving, the leak gradually speeds up and the tires start to go flat, and then when you make a sharp turn you're in trouble. If you'd done this at speed the bus could have rolled over."

Lespinasse used his winch to pull the minibus out of the ditch, lifted it on his hydraulic jack and changed the tires. He checked the driver's side wheels but found no gravel. He then examined the two flats.

He didn't see any permanent damage, but he'd take them back to the garage, inflate them and check them later. He climbed behind the wheel of the bus and drove it about a hundred yards up the road, turned and drove back. He climbed out, told Boniface the bus was fit to drive and then took Bruno's arm and led him to the front of his truck, out of earshot of the driver.

"This looks more like a case for you than a job for me," Lespinasse said. "I don't know whether somebody is out to get Boniface or Pauline, or the Americans, but you'd better identify the target and put a stop to this before people get hurt."

"You don't think it's just a prank?"

"I doubt it. Kids usually just let the air out of tires, they don't do this kind of thing. Anyway, the wheel joints and axles look fine and there was no wobble when I drove it, so Boniface can carry on with the tour. But I'd keep this minibus locked up overnight until you sort this out, Bruno."

Bruno thanked him and let Boniface drive on to the *domaine* to pick up the passengers and continue their tour for the rest of the day. What he hadn't told Lespinasse was that this was not the first trouble for Pauline's tour. Two days earlier, toothpicks had been jammed into the door locks of the minibus overnight and broken off. Luckily, Boniface carried a small folding toolkit that included some needle-nose pliers, and he'd managed to extract the wood. As he drove back to town, Bruno thought he'd better ask the gendarmes if the minibus could be left in their secure parking lot overnight.

He stopped at the pharmacy opposite the medical center to pick up some of the special toothpaste he liked to use. Still thinking about the minibus problem, he was not really looking where he was going and was almost knocked down on the steps by a young woman dashing out. He was aware of a pungent perfume and an expensive hairstyle with blonde streaks in the second before they collided. The woman's bag fell, spilling open, and a pregnancy-testing kit fell out along with some other toiletries. He apologized and bent down to help her gather them. She was in her midtwenties and vaguely familiar, but not from St. Denis. She was heavily made-up and wearing tight clothes that suggested too much body being squeezed into too little fabric.

The perfume reminded him that he'd seen the woman in the company of Claire, the mayor's secretary, who had a similar taste in clothes, perfumes and exotically decorated fingernails. Claire was a flirt, given to standing too close in elevators and incapable of even saying bonjour to a male colleague in the *mairie* without flirting. Bruno now recalled having seen the two young women together. It was at the town fair, shrieking with laughter in a bumper car as they repeatedly rammed cars containing young men.

Claire was single, but very keen to be married, and since her friend seemed to be her cruising partner, the fact that she thought she might be pregnant would have interested Claire. Bruno wondered if Claire knew. He smiled to himself at the thought that some young man could be in for a surprise and probably a hastily arranged wedding. The old rules were still strong here in the Périgord, and he reflected that many a good marriage had started that way. The young woman mumbled some words of thanks and flashed him a quick smile before rising with her bag. She then darted across the pedestrian crossing to the medical center, barely looking at the traffic, glancing at her watch as she headed up the steps as if worried she'd be late for an appointment.

She stopped again, holding the door just as Fabiola, one of the doctors and a good friend to Bruno, was coming out. The two women exchanged tense words that he could not hear, but their body language was explicit. The blonde was asking something, hands out in appeal, and Fabiola was refusing, her back straight, face grim, one palm held in front of her as if to stop the discussion. Fabiola then shook her head firmly before marching determinedly down the steps to her car. The young woman stared unhappily after her.

Bruno wondered what the story might be behind that little confrontation. Knowing Fabiola's concern for the privacy of her patients, he knew she'd never tell him. He headed across the bridge to his office in the *mairie* and called Yveline, commandant of the local gendarmes. He told of his concerns for the minibus and asked if it could be left in her yard. Of course, she replied, but asked where was it usually parked overnight. In the courtyard at the back of the retirement home, he replied.

"Why not have it parked there and put up a discreet surveillance camera? We might catch whoever is doing this," she replied. "We have reasonable cause and it's a sensible security measure. I'm sure you can persuade the director of the home to agree. You can leave the vehicle in our yard until the camera is installed."

Bruno thought that made sense and sat

180

back to think what might be behind all this. He did not think that Boniface, a jolly man of about sixty with a potbelly and an equally plump wife who also worked at the retirement home as a cleaner, was a likely target. But who would want to sabotage Pauline's fledgling new business as a private tour guide? He couldn't see any of the other guides being responsible, since there was no shortage of tourists and Pauline's tours were unique. Nobody else had ever thought a literary tour of the region could be a success. He leaned back in his chair and gazed out of the window at the canoes drifting down the River Vézère, recalling how Pauline's business had begun.

It had been earlier in the year, just before Easter, and he'd been sitting on the terrace outside Fauquet's café on a sunny morning in springtime, enjoying a croissant still hot from the oven with a fine cup of coffee. A shadow had come between him and the sun. Philippe Delaron was standing there with two coffees on a tray and asking if he might sit down at Bruno's table.

"I brought you a coffee because I want your help," said Philippe, an engaging young man who had helped his mother run the town's photo studio before the popularity of cell phones drove it out of business. Just in time, Philippe had been hired by *Sud Ouest* as a news photographer. He'd then become the paper's correspondent in the Vézère Valley. He and Bruno had an amiable, if slightly wary, relationship, as reporters and cops usually do. But Bruno had played rugby and tennis with Philippe and, during Bruno's first year as the town policeman, he'd managed to prevent Philippe from getting a criminal record for a teenage joyride in a "borrowed" car. Philippe and his friends had to pay for the repairs and furnish the car's owner with firewood for the next winter. It was a solution Bruno had been proud of, one of the incidents that had taught him that a village policeman's job is as much about keeping people out of trouble as making arrests.

"It's about a girl," Philippe went on. Bruno nodded, sighed inwardly and sipped at his coffee. Philippe was a good-looking young man, slim and cheerful with a slightly dashing air. Along with these advantages he had a sweet, gentle smile that had attracted girls up and down the "Valley of Mankind." This was the tourist board's name for the world's richest home of prehistoric people, with their cave paintings, engravings and burial sites. For Philippe, it was more of a happy hunting ground. He seemed to have a girl in every town and village. From the envious tales of Philippe's love life that his friends told in the rugby club bar, Bruno wondered how the man had any time to work, or to sleep, for that matter.

With a company car and his camera, he was free to roam one of the prettiest districts of France with a press card that allowed him to sidle into almost any event or meeting. Philippe had since become a minor local celebrity after his appointment to the team of reporters who did an hour-long weekly review of local news on Radio Bleu Périgord and then another hour interviewing local politicians. Philippe was smart enough always to prepare a joke in advance, and to allow himself just one cheeky question to the local mayor or regional councillor who occupied the hot seat that week.

"Her name is Pauline," Philippe said. They had been at the lycée together, just schoolmates and friends, he insisted, not romantically attached. He looked down shyly, an expression Bruno did not recall seeing on Philippe's face before, when he said he'd always felt there was something special about her. When all the other girls were listening to pop songs, she had turned him on to jazz and classical music.

"She plays guitar really well. It runs in the

family. You know her dad, Loïc, the singer in that band that does all the club dances," he went on. Pauline had the best grades in her class at the lycée, studied languages at the University of Bordeaux and had one summer *stage* in Brussels working in the tourism commission of the European Union. She had spent the last year in New York, with a scholarship that allowed her to work for the Alliance Française. She was now working on a short-term contract at the tourist office in Périgueux and earning her *brevet* as a professional tourist guide.

"But she has this crazy idea of starting her own business and I want you to talk her out of it," Philippe said.

"What's crazy about it?"

"She's always been a reader, never without a book, and she thinks she can make a living as a guide for literary tours here in Périgord. You know, Montaigne and Bertran de Born and a bit of Cyrano de Bergerac, but he was fictional."

"No, he wasn't," said Bruno. "He existed and even wrote one of the first science fiction stories about a voyage to the moon. But he was a Gascon, not from here. The story of the impossibly long nose and his doomed love for Roxane in Bergerac was all made up by Rostand for his play."

"Oh, really?" Philippe said. "You see, you know this stuff. You'll get on with her and she'll listen to you. I mean, how many people want to spend a week being guided around castles of medieval troubadours and flog out all the way to Castillon to see Montaigne's tower?"

"Me, for one," said Bruno. "If her friends at the Alliance Française in New York can help her with clients, it could be an asset to the region. It sounds like exactly the kind of new market that the tourist board is trying to build, so they'll do what they can to help her."

"You think she can make it work?"

"It might take time, but if she's got the right kind of manner and makes the tour friendly as well as literary, she could make a success of it," Bruno said. "I wonder if we can bring St. Denis into this, maybe get a deal with one of our hotels or with renting one of Dougal's big *gîtes*. I presume she plans to drive the visitors around so that means a minibus that can transport maybe a dozen clients at a time. Does she have one?"

"No, she's only got some modest savings. She's living with her parents for the moment and they're paying off the mortgage on a house they bought in Périgueux. That's why I don't want Pauline to lose what little money she has on this crazy idea, because then she says she'd sit the concours to get a permanent job in Brussels." He paused and a blush was rising to his face when he added, "And then I probably wouldn't see much of her again."

Bruno noted that and wondered whether the fabled Romeo of the valley had finally fallen for a woman who was not ready to throw herself into his arms. But he showed no expression as he asked, "So what do you think she should do?"

"Stay here in the Périgord as a professional tour guide, doing the caves and castles, food and wine, the usual circuit. Make money with her guitar in the evenings. She speaks English and German. She could probably get a job as a guide at Lascaux and that would be year-round."

Bruno nodded, thinking that made sense. But he suspected that Pauline would be committed to her own plan. She sounded like an impressive young woman, the kind with the brains and skills and ambition who usually left the Périgord for Paris. It was interesting that she had thought of an unusual way to come back to the district and build her own business at the same time. Could it be that Philippe was the attraction that drew her back?

"I'll be happy to meet her, but I don't think I'd want to talk her out of her idea," Bruno said. "Nor should you — it sends the signal that you don't have much faith in her. Even if she drops the plan, she'll always feel a resentment, musing on what might have been if she'd just given it a try, especially now that we've got the new *auto-entrepreneur* system to help people start their own little company."

"But if it fails?" Philippe asked.

"You're her friend, so help her. You can get her some publicity in your paper and with your contacts you could arrange for some of the retirement homes to hire her to give their people an interesting day out. That would bring in some money in the off-season. If she fails, she could always try for Lascaux next year. And she'd know you always believed in her."

Philippe ran his hands over his face and stood up. "I still think it won't work, but maybe you're right about believing in her. I do. I always did, even at school. So we'll try it your way. Thanks, Bruno."

Pauline came to Bruno's office a couple of hours later and said in a pleasantly low voice that Philippe had told her Bruno had an idea or two that might help her project.

She was wearing a plain dress of blue linen with a red-and-white silk scarf around her neck and shoulders. Her hair was dark blonde, shoulder length, with a soft natural curl. She was a little above medium height and had a perfect, almost glowing complexion. Her face was not beautiful, but the features were even, with high cheekbones and a full mouth over a determined chin. What made her attractive was the liveliness and intelligence in her clear blue eyes. Bruno could understand why Philippe was taken with her.

"Philippe mentioned Montaigne, de La Boétie, Bertran de Born and Cyrano de Bergerac," he said. "Is that it? I was wondering if you knew about Henry Miller staying at Trémolat?"

"Indeed. That's when he wrote that this Périgord will always be a sacred spot for man and for poets," she replied with a smile.

"And when the cities have killed off the poets this will be the refuge and the cradle of the poets to come," Bruno responded, enjoying the company of someone who felt about this region as he did.

Her face took on a serious look as she went on. "Philippe's list is barely the start. I'll have trouble leaving people out. There's Fénelon, tutor to the heir of Louis XIV and author of the eighteenth-century best seller *Telemachus,* on how to raise and educate a good and just king. It was a founding document of the Enlightenment, much of it still relevant today, and he was born in the château just down the river. There's Jean-Paul Sartre, who spent his boyhood vacations at his stepfather's house in Thiviers. There's André Maurois's place at Essendiéras, and Bourdeille, who guarded Mary Queen of Scots and built the Château de Richemont. He was the great chronicler of court life in the sixteenth century. Much of what we know about the royal circle comes from him, and his *Lives of Fair and Gallant Ladies* is still a diverting read. There's even a Maigret novel with a local link — *The Madman of Bergerac* — in which Maigret is shot and wakes up in the hospital, suspected of being a serial killer."

"You obviously know your stuff. Why do you think you can reach and attract enough clients to make it work?"

"I'm making a special tour for the American market, not just Henry Miller but Ezra Pound and Thomas Jefferson. The Alliance Française in New York has already generated enough interest to fill three weeks this summer, six to eight Americans each week. Then for the Germans I'll bring in André

Noël from Périgueux, the personal cook of King Frederick the Great. The king even wrote a poem to him, calling Noël 'the Newton of cuisine.' There's another verse about the way his exquisite dishes have 'bewitched the Prussians and turned them all into Epicureans.' "

Her eyes sparkled with a humor that lit up her face. "I'm told you're a good cook, and I'm not, but it might be fun to re-create some of Noël's dishes. According to Casanova, the king particularly liked Noël's cabbage soup *à la Fouquet,* but I don't know what that is. Then there was *tarte à la romaine* and *poulet à la Pompadour.* Maybe you could help me with those?"

Bruno was aware that he was being teased and at the same time given a marketing pitch by a smart and accomplished young woman. Her style of delivery was amiable and informal. She wore her learning lightly. Her tours were likely to be an entertaining experience.

"You can sign me up for a tour right now," he said. "*Tarte à la romaine* is like a quiche but with eggplant, and *à la Pompadour* is a cream-and-onion sauce with Madeira. I've no idea what *à la Fouquet* means, but we can probably find out. And I'm sure we can find chefs who'd love to re-create the dishes.

Are there any of these writers you can connect directly with St. Denis? If so, we can probably give you some extra help here in town."

"I was going to bring in Jean Rey, your town's great chemist and herbalist," she said. "I need to check if you still have the remnants of the herb garden Rey laid out back in the seventeenth century. Then there's André Malraux, whose secret headquarters for the wartime Resistance is just a stroll down the road at La Vitrolle. He was based there in the spring and summer of 1944. I think *La Condition Humaine* is one of the great French novels of the last century. Beyond that, there's the blind poet Lafon-Labatut. And, of course, the wine tour — the Saint-Exupéry family at Château de Tiregand and the philosopher Maine de Biran, whose tower is still to be seen at the Terre Vielle vineyard in the Pécharmant."

"This is very impressive indeed. I think you can count on the mayor and me being among your first customers." He'd never heard of a blind poet from St. Denis. "But I want to ask you something. Philippe said you were first in your class at the lycée, which means you could have gone to one of the *grandes écoles* in Paris. Why didn't you do that?"

She raised her eyebrows, as if taken by surprise, then her words came out in a rush. "You know what kinds of career they lead to — politics, big business, the civil service," she said. "They didn't appeal to me. I wanted languages, literature, the chance to meet interesting people. I think I'd like people who are interested in books. And I wanted to live in the Périgord."

Bruno nodded. "How much do you plan to charge?"

"I'll need some advice on that. For the Americans, with room and board included, along with the minibus and me as guide, Alliance Française thought I could charge two to three thousand euros for a full week, depending on the season. I would pick them up and take them back to Bordeaux airport. For locals, I like your idea of giving old people a day out from the *maison de retraite* in the off-season. I thought forty euros each for the day, lunch included. But I'll need your help there. I can't cook to save my life, but at that price I can't afford to give them a restaurant meal."

"Could you host it yourself, and get the food from a *traiteur*? I understand you're living with your parents in Périgueux. Could you use their place? That would be central for Montaigne and Bertran de Born's château at Hautefort."

"No, my mother would want to take over and give them a feast." She said this without a smile, and Bruno inferred that her return to the family home had not been smooth.

"I checked prices with the local bus companies before coming to see you," she went on. "The best I could get was two hundred euros a day for an eight-seater with driver, plus the cost of the fuel. The driver and I make two, so only six paying customers. Even with a full bus, I'd lose money."

"Most of the bigger retirement homes, like ours, have their own bus and driver," he said, scribbling down some figures on a pad. "That could be free, but you're stuck with the thirty-five-hour week. And since we raised money for a new bus, we have a spare. So as long as St. Denis is included on the tour, we could make the old minibus available, and I know people who'd happily drive you all day for fifty euros in cash. And if St. Denis is your base, you could give them lunch at the retirement home. The locals would eat free. Others, you might have to pay five or six euros a head."

"Honestly?" She took a deep breath. Her eyes were shining. Bruno got the impression of a prisoner suddenly seeing the open sky. "You really think this can work?"

He nodded slowly. "Yes, but I'd put it differently. I really think *you* can make it work because everything depends on what you put into this. You have the knowledge and the determination. As I said, if we are part of your tour I can promise you some help from St. Denis. I'll talk to the retirement home about using their minibus. Meanwhile, I'd like you to draw up a real business plan so I can take it to the mayor, who is also chairman of the tourism committee on the regional council. He can open a lot of doors for you. You might also want to suggest giving these literary tours to schools in the region. The education committee has a budget for this, and it could bring you some business in the winter months."

She was nodding eagerly as Bruno rose and put out his hand. "Good luck with this. I'm glad Philippe introduced us."

"A lot of people underestimate him, but he's always been a good friend to me," she said. "I never really fitted in at school, but Philippe was always very popular, and he took me under his wing."

A good friend indeed, thought Bruno, and a refreshing side of Philippe that Bruno had not seen before. But Philippe seemed to be seeking a far closer relationship with Pauline than friendship. Bruno doubted whether that was what Pauline had in mind, but that was none of his business. Pauline's literary tourism sounded promising, just the kind of upmarket attraction the region needed as it sought to broaden its biggest industry beyond camping sites and canoe trips. The goal now was to attract wealthier visitors to fill the growing number of fine restaurants and boutique hotels.

The mayor was charmed by Pauline and by her idea and had personally reviewed her business plan. The regional tourist board promoted her tours and so did Atout France, the national tourist office. The larger retirement homes and the education department had responded enthusiastically to her proposal, and the future looked bright, until this sudden burst of sabotage that threatened to ruin Pauline's business at its very outset. Bruno would not let that happen. Perhaps setting a trap was the best way to find the culprit. He'd have to ask Pauline if she had any idea who it might be.

As well as Boniface, who drove the tourists during the day, Bruno had arranged for another driver to be available for her in the evenings. So he started his inquiries with him, a retired postman named Didier. Bruno found him playing *boules* near the cemetery and asked if he'd had any trouble with the minibus. None at all, Didier said, adding that the Americans had given him some nice tips, so he was doing better from the work than he'd expected. Boniface had told him about the toothpicks, but they'd assumed that was kids. He grew concerned when Bruno recounted the latest incident.

"If it helps, I could drive it home in the evening, park it in my own yard and return it first thing in the morning," Didier suggested, clearly determined to defend his new part-time job. He said he'd seen nobody hanging around the minibus at the various restaurants the tourists had visited, and it was usually quiet at the retirement home when he parked the minibus back there. Bruno took a list of the restaurants to which Didier had taken the clients, all of them on the list of recommendations Bruno himself had given to Pauline. This evening, he saw, they would be at Ivan's bistro in St. Denis. Ivan had accepted the challenge of preparing Frederick the Great's menu of *tarte romaine* and chicken *à la Pompadour,*

Bruno went back to the *mairie,* intent on persuading the mayor to install the security camera. When he arrived, Claire said the mayor was on a conference call with other members of the regional council. It was scheduled to end soon, and she offered him a coffee from the mayor's private stock, knowing Bruno could not stand the stuff brewed on the ancient coffee machine in the kitchen.

"I ran into a friend of yours today," he said, recounting the incident outside the *pharmacie*, "A young woman you were with at the fair, riding those bumper cars."

"You mean Denise?" Claire asked. "Yes, she's a good friend and fun to be with. And such a good person. Do you know she volunteers at the church orphanage, helping take care of the little ones? She adores children. We were at secretarial school together. She lives in Bergerac, where her dad runs the big Renault garage on the road to Gardonne. She's his receptionist. I don't see quite so much of her these days, now she's got her eyes on a certain someone."

It never ceased to surprise Bruno how much information about people he gathered just from chatting and the local gossip mill. "Who's she got her eyes on? Anyone I know?"

"That would be telling," said Claire. "But I get the impression it's been getting pretty hot and heavy."

She handed him the coffee just as the red light went out that showed the mayor's phone line was no longer busy. Bruno went in, got the mayor's approval for the camera and bought a cheap model with its own built-in recording tape at the town electrical shop. He went to the retirement home where he and the director watched the handyman install and test it. Bruno was then invited to lunch in the cafeteria, sharing a table with some of the old people. The director was proud of the food on offer and, like him, Bruno took a quiche and salad followed by cheese and an apple, and listened to the elderly residents tell him that St. Denis and France and the local rugby team were not what they used to be. Then they led him outdoors to admire their small patches of vegetable garden.

Afterward, coming back out onto the main street, Bruno was startled to see a small crowd gathered around a large cloud of thick gray smoke. Through the fog, he could dimly make out the shape of a minibus, and then Pauline clambered out, waving the smoke away from her face and guiding her tourists from the rear seats. Boniface, a handkerchief clutched to his mouth and nose, was bending by the exhaust pipe, from which were spouting great plumes of gray smoke.

"I can't figure out what's wrong," Boniface said when Bruno arrived. "The engine temperature is normal and I checked the oil this morning. It doesn't smell like exhaust smoke. Lespinasse said the vehicle was fine when he drove it."

He turned off the engine and opened the hood. He and Bruno stared into the engine compartment, seeing no sign of smoke. Nothing appeared to be wrong. Once again, Bruno called Lespinasse, who came within minutes. He took one sniff of the tailpipe and said, "Castor oil. Somebody's playing games again, squirting some oil into the exhaust pipe."

He turned on the engine, checked the oil and shook his head. "If it wasn't for what happened this morning, I'd have said it was kids. It's annoying, but it's not serious. Just drive on and it will disperse."

"Where were you parked during lunch-time?" Bruno asked Boniface.

"In the main square, in front of the bank. Somebody could have tinkered with the bus then."

"You must have some idea who's behind this," Bruno said to Pauline, who just shook her head blankly. "You realize they're out to destroy your business." She gave him a look of pure despair.

Bruno gathered the tourists together and with some translation help from Pauline explained that some of the local school-children were fond of practical jokes and he'd make sure it didn't happen again. He apologized on behalf of the town for their incident-packed visit and wished them a pleasant afternoon. The minibus drove on, Bruno following in his van at a discreet distance, just in case some officious traffic cop pulled them over. But the smoke thinned, and before they reached Lalinde the castor oil seemed to have burned away. He tooted his horn, waved Boniface to continue and turned back to St. Denis.

He called Philippe and found him in Brantôme, forty minutes away, where he'd been all day, photographing a spring garden show. That ruled him out. Philippe said that he knew of no enemies Pauline might have. Bruno called Pauline's father, the musician, wondering if somebody might be trying to get at him through his daughter. Again he drew a blank. Bruno would have to rely on the surveillance camera. But what if the saboteur wore a hood? Bruno sighed, knowing he'd be spending some cold night hours keeping watch.

The rest of the afternoon passed quietly until it was time to drive to Pamela's riding school and exercise the horses. It was the evening of the weekly dinner at Pamela's house, with her business partner, Miranda, and the usual crew: Fabiola and Gilles; Florence the schoolteacher; Miranda's father, Jack Crimson; and the baron, along with Miranda's and Florence's children. It was not Bruno's turn to cook, which meant that he had to supply some wine. Pamela had texted him she was making fish pie, so he picked up two bottles of Château Montdoyen, a Bergerac Sec white wine that he and the baron both liked.

He was opening the wine as Pamela was mashing the potatoes to spread across the fish that was baking in the oven and Fabiola was at the sink preparing the salad. Over the sound of the table being prepared and the children clattering their way downstairs from their bath he heard Fabiola say, "That persistent young woman was in again today, it's so tiresome. She's constantly badgering me for fertility treatments when there's nothing at all wrong with her. I checked her out twice and told her nature would take its course, but after reading up on it on the Internet she's become convinced she needs this expensive procedure because she desperately wants to have a baby. The Internet's becoming a real problem for us at the clinic, half the patients now think they know more than we do."

A young woman, fertility treatments, badgering Fabiola, buying a pregnancy test, her father a garage owner so she'd know about cars. Suddenly the pieces started falling into place. After dinner, which was excellent and convivial and reminded him how fortunate he was to have such friends, Bruno stopped off at the Bar des Amateurs on the way home and ordered a beer. Run by a couple of veterans from the town rugby team, it was the young people's bar with all the main football and rugby matches on a wide-screen TV. The Girondins from Bordeaux had been playing that evening, so there were still several young men he knew at the bar, and Bruno casually asked one of them if Philippe was seeing any special girl these days.

"None that's going to nail him down," said Édouard, Lespinasse's son. "He plays the field, our Philippe. He said he'd be in Bergerac tonight, that girl from the Renault garage he's been bonking." Édouard grinned. "He calls her his first reserve because he'll go play there when he can't get fixed up elsewhere."

"I think I know who you mean," Bruno replied. "Denise, is that her name?"

"That's the one. Philippe says she's hoping to tie him down, but she'll have a hell of a long wait. No settling down for our Philippe."

That was all Bruno needed to know. He finished his beer and went home. There was no point even checking on the surveillance cameras if Philippe was with the girl that evening. Before he went to bed, he left a text message on Philippe's phone saying he wanted to see him at the café the next morning at eight. And that he should bring a photo of Denise.

"Tell me about Denise," Bruno said when the two men had been served their coffee and croissants. They were sitting at the far end of Fauquet's terrace, against the stone wall overlooking the river out of earshot of anyone else.

"Just a girl," Philippe mumbled, handing over a flattering photo of the young woman Bruno had seen arguing with Fabiola. "She's not important."

"Important enough for you to spend the night with her, and not for the first time," Bruno said. "I hear you call her your first reserve."

"Spying on me, Bruno?"

"Not on you, but I might have to start watching her. You know about these problems Pauline has been having with her minibus. They aren't accidents, and I'm wondering who would have a motive to sabotage her business."

Philippe almost choked on his croissant. "You think Denise . . ."

"Did you know she's trying to get pregnant? Are you using a condom?"

"Condom? No, I hate the things. She assured me she takes care of that."

"Maybe she doesn't, if she's trying that hard to get pregnant. From your attitude, it's clear the girl doesn't mean much to you, but there could be serious repercussions."

"What do you mean," Philippe said, with a touch of his usual bluster. "This isn't the old days. You don't have to marry the girl if she gets in the family way."

"Of course, there's the potential birth of a child who'd have no father to speak of. And then there's the practical point. How much of your newspaper's advertising comes from the Renault garages around here? If it comes down to a choice between keeping you on staff or offending a big advertiser, who knows what happens? And didn't I hear that *Sud Ouest* was cutting staff?"

"That's for the old guys . . . ," Philippe began and then paused. In a different voice, he then said quietly, "I see what you mean."

"Denise seems to come up here quite a lot, is that just to see you?"

204

"No, we usually meet at her place in Bergerac. She has her own apartment. But she has a grandmother in the *maison de retraite* here, so she comes up to see her quite a bit, usually on Tuesday or Thursday evening after work. Denise brings something in and they have a meal together. She's a nice girl in many ways, just a bit too hyper, not the type you'd want to settle down with."

"But good enough to take to bed," Bruno said, shaking his head sadly. "Your generation was supposed to be better than that, not just using girls as if they were so many paper tissues. Denise is a real person with her own dreams. You know that, but you're still prepared to take advantage of her just to get your rocks off. That's really sad. What do you think Pauline would make of your behavior?"

"Jesus, Bruno, what's this about? Denise and I are two grown-ups having fun together. And who are you to talk? We all know you're no saint when it comes to women."

"This isn't about me, Philippe. It's about you and these two women. If I'm right, and I think I am, Denise is the prime suspect in trying to sabotage Pauline's tours, to get her out of the way and have you to herself. Are you seeing Denise tonight? It's a Thurs-

205

day when you say she'll probably be seeing her grandmother."

"Yeah, but I'm not seeing her tonight. I've got an early photo shoot tomorrow morning in Domme for a new tourist train they're launching."

"Well, you'd better go take a nap because I want you on watch with me tonight at the *maison de retraite* from ten o'clock on."

"You want to catch Denise in the act, is that it?"

"Not just that. I want to keep her out of jail. I'll see you at ten in the rear courtyard."

Leaving Philippe, Bruno went looking for Didier and again found him playing *boules*. He confirmed from Philippe's photo that Denise was one of the relatives he saw regularly at the retirement home, that he knew her well enough to say good night if their paths crossed. And yes, he thought he'd seen her leaving her grandmother's room a couple of nights earlier after he'd parked the minibus.

Back in his office, Bruno wanted to reach Denise's father, Robert, but without going through the car showroom's switchboard, which might alert Denise. He called Laurent, a friend in the Bergerac police, and asked him to set up an urgent meeting later that morning at a bar beside the old covered market. When Laurent called back to say he'd spoken discreetly to Robert and the meeting was on, Bruno set off for Bergerac.

"I know you from seeing you play rugby, Bruno," said her father when they had settled down with a beer each. "What's this about?"

After Bruno had explained and suggested that the man should join him at the retirement home that evening, the father ordered two cognacs and downed his in one. Bruno pushed back the cognac meant for him.

"I blame myself," Robert said. "I went through a nasty divorce and I didn't see that much of Denise after she was about twelve or thirteen, until she came to work for me. And then I suppose I spoiled her, bought her an apartment and a car, gave her the job. But my own job didn't leave me much time."

"So now she's trying to create the family life she never had," said Bruno. "But the guy she's chosen isn't the marrying kind, at least not with Denise. She's going to need a lot of support from you in the next few weeks, and I don't mean money."

"I can't believe she'd do that to a minibus. She could have killed somebody, and she's seen enough wrecks brought to our yard after an accident." Robert finished the second cognac and agreed to meet Bruno at the Bar des Amateurs in St. Denis at nine-thirty that evening.

"Will she go to jail?" he asked in parting.

Bruno looked him in the eye and shrugged. "That will probably depend on Pauline, the tour guide whose minibus your daughter has been vandalizing. Pauline would be in her rights to demand we bring charges. Even if the *procureur* declines to prosecute, Pauline could still sue your daughter in civil court for trying to undermine her business, and then it would be all over the newspapers."

"I get the picture," Robert said, and Bruno left him staring blankly over the bar at the shelves of bottles.

Bruno went back to St. Denis, briefed the mayor and called Fabiola at the clinic to invite her to lunch at his home. He'd picked up some spring salad and early strawberries at the Bergerac market, some bread at his preferred *boulangerie* in St. Denis and would open some of the game pâté he'd put into cans that winter. Now he was making mayonnaise in his kitchen to mix with a can of tuna while Fabiola looked at him suspiciously, her glass of Bergerac Sec white wine untouched, as he explained his plan.

"I understand that you saw me arguing

with her after she'd spilled the pregnancy test, but how did you put it all together?"

"When I heard in the bar that Philippe was calling her his first reserve, good enough to sleep with but nothing more. But what's important now is how we handle this when we catch her having another go at the minibus."

"Only if she's stupid enough to try it again after the tricks with the tires and the castor oil didn't work."

"I think she will. Pauline has become an obsession with her. Denise is your patient and I'd like you to be there with us tonight. If she's in your care, we may be able to keep her out of jail."

"You don't leave me much choice, Bruno," Fabiola said. She took a sip of her wine and began to eat.

Bruno had one more call to make that afternoon before he went to the tennis club and spent an hour coaching the junior team, some of them already skilled enough to give him a decent game. Another couple of years and they'd be beating him. With his dog, Balzac, in tow he headed for Pamela's riding school to join her and her stable boy, Félix, on the evening exercise of the horses. Balzac trotted easily along behind, picking up his pace slightly when Bruno put his horse, Hector, into a canter and then into a gallop. Balzac knew he'd catch up later. Telling Pamela that he had a job that evening, he left Balzac to bed down in Hector's stable. Then he went to the Bar des Amateurs for a slice of pizza and a salad while he waited for Denise's father.

Then it all went according to plan, or almost. Denise arrived in the rear courtyard of the retirement home. She took a small tube from her bag and leaned over the front of the minibus to do something with the windshield wipers and then moved to the door. At that point, Bruno walked out of the shadows, illuminating Denise with his flashlight while her father turned on the courtyard lights.

"You're under arrest, Denise," Bruno said, taking her arm. "Criminal damage and malicious damage." He looked at the tube in her hand. It was superglue, and he pulled out an evidence bag to keep Denise's fingerprints fresh. "So you've glued down the wipers and next you were going to glue the locks and doors. You don't give up, do you?"

Denise glared at him and then looked uncertain as her father came out from the rear door to the retirement home to stand beside Bruno. Her face fell as Philippe then came out to join them, followed by Fabiola, and then a final figure who walked slowly out and stood directly facing the stricken woman.

"Why?" Pauline asked. "Why put people's lives at risk? Why try to ruin me? What have I ever done to harm you?"

"Always the best at school, that's why," Denise snapped. "Always teacher's favorite, getting to university and then that scholarship to New York. And now you have him as well." Denise glared at Philippe with something like contempt as he stood stock-still, staring at her. "It's Pauline this and Pauline that with him."

"But you've got it all wrong," said Pauline. "Philippe has always been a good friend, but I'm not interested in him that way. I want to find out more about myself and what I can do before I look seriously at men. Perhaps you should do the same, Denise."

Denise sagged in Bruno's arms as Philippe stared down at his feet and Fabiola came forward to take her pulse and shine a penlight into Denise's eyes. Robert shuffled forward, concern in his eyes for his daughter, but looking helpless as though unsure what to say or do.

"She's all right," Fabiola told him. "Just a bit shocked and emotionally wrung out."

"I'm sorry about this," Robert said to Pauline. "Can we work something out? Some compensation?"

"Don't worry about that," said Pauline, without looking at him. She stared at Philippe, shaking her head sadly, and then looked at the half-crumpled Denise. "I'm not going to press charges. I think with Philippe's help she's already punished herself." She looked at Bruno. "Do you need me anymore? I have to be up early for my clients."

He shook his head and Pauline walked away slowly. Bruno and Philippe turned to watch her leave. Then Bruno heard a sudden roar of *"Merde!"* from Robert, and he swung a roundhouse slap against Philippe's cheek, so hard that it knocked the young man to the ground.

The older man glared down at him and said, "A piece of *merde,* that's what you are. And that's nothing to what I'll do to you if I ever see you near my daughter again."

He turned to Denise, pushed Bruno to one side and embraced her. "Come on, sweetheart, let's get you home."

Then before leading her away he looked at Bruno. "You can tell that other young woman she's going to get a new minibus from me, at no cost. And thanks, Bruno."

Bruno helped Philippe to his feet and said, "You deserved that."

"I know," he said, feeling his jaw and blinking to clear his head. "I think I owe you a drink."

"Men!" said Fabiola, stomping off. "It's like law and order on the damn frontier. Have Denise's father send her to see me at the clinic tomorrow."

Philippe led Bruno to the Bar des Amateurs. Just before they reached it, he put his hand on Bruno's arm. "At least Pauline gets a minibus out of this."

"And you've learned an important lesson," said Bruno. "Never judge a cop by the arrests he makes. Just as important are the people he keeps out of jail."

SUGAR LUMPS

It was a warm evening in May, a quiet time
at the riding school once the horses had
returned from their exercise, been brushed
and given their water. The chickens had followed the mother hen back to the coop,
with Napoleon the cockerel watchfully
bringing up the rear. The dogs, after their
run with the horses, were stretched out
companionably on the grass, watching the
humans. Bruno and his friends were sitting
at the big table in the courtyard as the
charcoal in the barbecue burned slowly
down toward the required glow. They were
enjoying a bottle of white wine from the
town vineyard, a refreshing, unpretentious
blend of Sémillon and Sauvignon Blanc,
while waiting for Florence and Miranda,
Pamela's partner in the riding school, also
English, to bring the children down after
bath time.

The baron, however, decided in his traditional way that he would prefer a glass of absinthe after his labors on the river. He'd caught eight plump trout that had now been gutted and stuffed with slices of lemon and sprigs of fennel, ready for the barbecue. He went to the bar in the big living room for the bottle, put it on a small tray with a jug of water and the silver absinthe spoon he had years earlier given to Pamela, their hostess. He returned with the tray and looked frustrated.

"Sorry, Pamela, but I can't find the sugar cubes."

"Ah," exclaimed Pamela, looking embarrassed. "I'm sorry, but Miranda and the children have decided we should ban sugar from the house and use honey as a sweetener instead. Apparently growing sugarcane or even sugar beets uses vast amounts of water, quite apart from what it does to the teeth."

"So there's not even one sugar cube left to go with my absinthe?" asked the baron.

"Wait a moment, Baron," said Bruno as he headed for the ancient Land Rover he'd inherited from a hunting friend and delved into a storage panel in the door. He returned with a small oblong wrapped in paper. "Two brown-sugar cubes, courtesy of the café at the gas station."

"Thanks," said the baron. "Why do you have that bandage on your forehead, Bruno? Did you walk into a door?"

"Something like that," said Bruno, watching as the baron unwrapped the paper and carefully centered a sugar lump on the slotted spoon that was now balanced on the rim of a glass above a generous portion of absinthe. He began to pour water from the jug onto the lump, drop by drop, so it slowly crumbled the sugar and dripped into the absinthe.

"I thought that stuff had been banned in France since the nineteenth century," said Jack, Miranda's father. "They called it La Fée Verte, the Green Fairy, and claimed it caused alcoholism, crime, incest and insanity. Remember those paintings of absinthe drinkers by Toulouse-Lautrec?"

"Reversing that ban was one of the few good things the European Union ever did," said the baron, still concentrating on his precise dripping of the water as the last of the sugar crumbled through the slots in the spoon into the drink. "They said that it had all been a ridiculous scare tactic by the nineteenth-century press and politicians who said that absinthe caused moral laxity, bohemian habits and undermined the moral fiber of the French nation. Some years ago the EU declared that absinthe contained only minute portions of wormwood and was in no way hallucinogenic."

"I've always preferred honey rather than sugar in my coffee, anyway," said Bruno. "But doesn't everything we eat consume lots of water?"

"The children have downloaded something from the Internet and pasted it onto the fridge door," Pamela replied. "Twenty thousand liters of water to produce a kilo of beefsteak, five thousand liters for a kilo of pork, two thousand for a kilo of coffee or a liter of wine, nearly three hundred for an egg and so on. It makes for very depressing reading."

"I thought all the water eventually gets recycled back into the earth and the sea and comes back again as rain," said Bruno.

"You may be right, but my grandchildren take it all terribly seriously," said Jack. "I almost have to drink my wine in secret, hiding from the little Green thought police."

"And here they come," said Bruno, at the sound of a thundering herd descending the stairs as Florence's twins raced to keep up with Miranda's slightly older boys, who emerged demanding to know what was for dinner.

"Please," said Miranda.

"What's for dinner, please? And is Bruno cooking?"

"We want hamburgers," cried Daniel, Florence's son, swiftly echoed by Dora, his sister, her voice somewhat muffled as she cuddled Bruno's basset hound, Balzac, to her chest.

"A hamburger means three thousand liters of water, each," objected Tom, Miranda's eldest. "Can we have pizza instead?"

"No," said his mother, firmly. "We're having fish from the river, asparagus and salad, then fresh strawberries, all from the garden. Grandpa picked the strawberries for us all so don't forget to thank him — and Bruno has made us his special summer soup."

"And now you're all coming to help me pick the radishes, lettuce and asparagus," said Bruno, marching the children off to grab some buckets and then to the *potager* with the dogs trotting at their heels.

"Dora and Daniel, help me with the asparagus, please. You'll have to hold it straight while I cut it at the base. And Tom, how many heads of lettuce do you think we'll need?"

"Three if they're big enough, Bruno, four if not."

"Okay, you decide and then help your brother pick out some plump radishes. And

Dora, do you know where the broad beans are? That's where we go next."

At the broad-bean patch, Bruno showed the children how to squeeze gently at the fat pods to see if the beans inside were big enough. Daniel pointed out one that seemed perfect, so Bruno picked it, used his thumbnail to open the seam and then invited each of the children to pick out a fresh bean. He took the last one for himself and popped it into his mouth.

"Nothing could be fresher than that," he said. "Try it, they're terrific when they're raw."

A little gingerly the children did as they were told and then smiled and asked for another. Bruno opened two more pods and then gave a bean to Balzac, who invariably ate anything he'd seen Bruno enjoy.

"Now try it with Beau and Bella," he said. And the two sheepdogs, mother and son, who had been rescued and adopted by Pamela after the death of a local farmer, accepted the beans, dropped them, sniffed them, then ate them and looked up for more.

"If we each pick a fat pod, we can let the grown-ups try them while we trim and wash the radishes and lettuce," he said. The children scampered back to the courtyard, bean pods in hand, while Bruno brought up the rear with the filled buckets.

Another bottle of wine had been opened when Bruno sent the children from the kitchen to hand out one bowl of freshly shelled broad beans and another of radishes that had been brushed clean. Jack and the baron had set the table and Pamela was asking why Gilles and Fabiola were so late.

"Because she's on duty at the clinic today," Bruno called out from the kitchen as he began steaming the fresh asparagus before making the salad and then taking from the fridge the two soups he'd made earlier.

One was a vichyssoise, the classic white soup made of potatoes and whites of leek with some chopped onion, cream and chicken stock. The other was *crème d'oseille,* made of fresh sorrel leaves, potato and cream, which was distinctly green. Bruno's party trick was to pour from each jug into the soup bowl at the same time, so that as the two soups met each one retained its own color. The children thought it was magic and loved to swirl the green and the white together.

The toot of a horn signaled the arrival of Fabiola and Gilles in her Renault Zoé. Pamela, meanwhile, was glancing through a notebook while Jack poured another glass of wine for Bruno.

"I've been calculating what we've eaten at our Monday dinners," she said. "As we had to postpone some because of the cookery classes, this is only our eleventh this year. So far we've had wild boar twice, venison three times, duck three times, roast lamb once, Bruno's famous *boeuf périgourdin* and one of Jack's famous mystery stews."

"It was beef," said Jack, looking aggrieved.

"And it has been hunting season, so we've been living off the land like good little *écolos*," added Bruno, who had brought in the venison, ducks and boar. With more than forty thousand road accidents a year in France now involving wildlife, the limits on the numbers of deer and boars that could be shot had been raised in rural *départements* like the Dordogne. Pamela's cooking classes, which she organized in the off-season to fill the *gîtes* she offered for rent, had taught several different ways to cook game, to make venison pâté, wild boar sausages and rillettes of duck.

"Bruno, my hero, how's your head?" called Fabiola from across the courtyard as she climbed from the car and marched determinedly in Bruno's direction. "Put that glass of wine down until I've had a look."

"It's fine, Fabiola, just a scratch. Doesn't hurt a bit."

"Hmmmph," she grunted. "Five stitches isn't a scratch." She took his head in her hands and gazed piercingly into his eyes while addressing her partner. "Gilles, would you pass that candle back and forth in front of Bruno's eyes, please? I need to see how his pupils react."

She grunted again. "Well, you're a lucky man, Bruno. I see no sign of a concussion. Lord knows you deserve some luck after what you did. It's been on the radio, and everybody's talking about it. The good news is that I spoke to the hospital and the grandmother is stable and should recover, both of the kids are fine, and their parents are driving down from Antwerp and should be at the hospital soon."

"What on earth are you talking about, Fabiola? What was on the radio?" asked Pamela.

"You haven't heard what happened this morning?" Fabiola asked. "They even had me and Stéphane and Sylvain on the radio. Gilles and Philippe Delaron have been going crazy trying to get hold of Bruno to interview him, but his phone was switched off."

"What the devil has Bruno done now?"

Jack asked, and Fabiola stared from him to Pamela and then to the baron, shaking her head in disbelief. Gilles laughed, and muttered that they must be the only people in St. Denis who didn't know.

"Bruno saved two children and their grandmother from drowning this morning," Fabiola said. "And there was no way you could have saved the old man, Bruno. I spoke to the doctor who did the postmortem. Apparently the man had a massive stroke and was dead before he hit the water."

"I think it's time we all sat down and began to eat," said Bruno. "The coals in the barbecue look just right and if we put the trout on now . . ."

"I want to hear exactly what happened before we eat," said Pamela, in her schoolmistress voice. "Bruno, what have you been up to this time?"

"It was just a camping car that drove into the river," he said, backing into the kitchen. "I have to look after the asparagus before it gets oversteamed."

"Fabiola," said Pamela. "Kindly explain."

"There was a crash. It was at the camping-car site that's just behind the medical center, and one of the campers drove his vehicle up to the sewage discharge point and instead of stopping seems to have accelerated. The camping car went through the fence, over the bank, landed on its nose and then toppled upside down into the river," Fabiola said.

"Bruno had been having coffee with friends at the café on the other side of the river and saw what happened," Fabiola went on. "He and his friends ran across the bridge and saw the van was teetering on the sandbank and could have floated off downstream at any moment. Bruno used his knife to cut down the lanyard on the flagpole beside the medical center, tied one end to a tree and swam out to tie the other end to the vehicle's tow bar. Then he dived inside the camper while Stéphane called the *pompiers,* Raoul called the medical center and Sylvain and Philippe rounded up some of the other campers to form a human chain from the riverbank into the water, as close to the van as they could get.

"Bruno came out with the two children and handed them to Sylvain," Fabiola said. "Then he dived back into the upside-down camper and brought out the grandmother before going back in to try and get the old man out."

"I just couldn't move him," said Bruno quietly, almost as if speaking to himself.

"His feet were jammed under the pedals."

"The firemen tried to get him out, but even they couldn't free him until they finally managed to winch the van ashore," Fabiola said. "I was down at the riverbank just at the time Bruno got the old lady ashore and started pumping her chest, but he'd cut his head somehow and was bleeding all over her, and the children were screaming."

"At least I was able to get the man's wallet and the van's registration number," Bruno said. "And one of the neighbors at the camping site said it was two grandparents taking their grandkids on a vacation. So Sergeant Jules at the gendarmerie called the Belgian police, who tracked down the parents and then got the grandmother an ambulance. If anybody saved a life it was Fabiola, working on the grandmother."

"Nonsense, Bruno," Fabiola almost snapped at him. "You did it."

"No, Fabiola, everybody played their part," Bruno replied. "Sylvain, Raoul, Philippe and Stéphane, you and the medical team, Sergeant Jules and the *pompiers* and let's not forget Jeanne from the *mairie* who took care of the two children and the people at the hospital in Périgueux. And even Philippe was in the human chain. He didn't pull out his camera and start taking photos for *Sud Ouest* until they were all safe."

Bruno paused, and then said firmly, "If we don't put those trout on the barbecue right now we'll have to make new coals."

"You certainly deserve a drink," said the baron, refilling Bruno's glass.

"Maybe I do, but first I want you and Gilles to put the trout on the barbecue and everyone else to take a seat, and then the children should come up to me one at a time, each with a soup bowl, and watch me pour the magic two-color soup."

Just as he began doing so there came the sound of another car pulling up, and Philippe Delaron climbed down with his tape recorder, saying, "So this is where you've been hiding, Bruno. Tracked you down at last."

FIFTY MILLION BUBBLES

Although Bruno enjoyed champagne, he seldom bought it. Good champagne was too costly for his policeman's salary, while cheap champagne was not to his taste. He preferred the reasonably priced regional variants of sparkling wine and found much better value in the crémants of Burgundy and Alsace. Above all, he relished the *blanquette de Limoux,* a sparkling wine of southwestern France, which he could enjoy for five euros a bottle when even the cheapest supermarket champagnes cost three times as much.

Bruno studied with affectionate care the countless, soaring bubbles that were rising in his glass before raising it to toast his friends and fellow directors of the town vineyard of St. Denis. Making a crémant for this valley of the River Vézère had been Bruno's idea, and he was pleased with the result. Unlike some champagnes, which used Pinot Noir grapes that were pressed gently and quickly before their red skins could color the wine, the Vézère crémant came from Sémillon, Chardonnay and a touch of *muscadelle,* their own white grapes. It had been made in the traditional way, with a little yeast and sugar in the bottles before they were sealed and cellared for eighteen months for the secondary fermentation to work its magic. As with champagne, the pressure of the carbon dioxide inside the bottle would swell to double the amount of pressure inside the tire of a family automobile, giving the festive pop when opened.

"Julien has made ten thousand bottles," said Hubert, owner of the legendary local wine store and chairman of the board. "I propose that we leave six hundred bottles in the cellar for another few years as an experiment. That's how they make vintage champagne, and I'd like to see how our crémant ages."

"We paid out over twelve thousand euros for the bottles and corks and we have yet to sell a single one," said Jacques Touvier, the new manager of the local Crédit Agricole bank, who had been made a director of the vineyard as a courtesy. "I'd be happier if we could recover our investment quickly."

Touvier's predecessor had been born and raised in St. Denis and knew all his customers. He had also been an enthusiastic supporter of the vineyard, investing his own money as well as extending a sizable bank loan. Touvier was of the new breed, sharply dressed, inclined to speak in business-school verbiage and constantly deferential to the head office. And he was from the far north, near the Belgian frontier, where their drink was beer, not wine.

"I had an idea about getting some publicity," said the mayor. "I was talking to a friend who runs the Maison des Vins in Bergerac. You know it's been modernized? They now have a wine bar where they serve light meals, a tasting center and so on. Remember when they put Bruno on the jury to select the best Monbazillac of the year? I think they might agree to host another blind tasting for the best sparkling wine."

"Well, Julien and I are proud of this crémant we've made," said Hubert, with a glance at the mayor that suggested to Bruno the two men had rehearsed this. "It would be a risk, of course, going up against well-known sparkling wines from Alsace, Burgundy and the Loire Valley. But I think we'd do pretty well. We could make a real contest of it."

"If we make a decent showing, even without winning, the publicity would certainly put us on the map," Bruno added. "My guess is that we'd sell all those bottles overnight to people in the Périgord."

"If we invite wines from other European countries to take part, I think the European Union might help with funding for the event," said the mayor.

"But who will be on the jury?" asked a glum-faced Touvier. "That's the question, and also the risk. How can we get to choose the jurors?" He looked even less happy when the others looked shocked at the suggestion and solemnly shook their heads.

Six weeks later, the jury had been chosen by the Maison des Vins and assembled. It included the wine critic of *Sud Ouest,* the regional newspaper; the editor of a German wine magazine who was on a tasting tour of the Bergerac; the sommelier from a three-star Michelin restaurant in Paris; an American wine consultant; the buyer for a major wine importer in Hong Kong; and an expatriate Englishwoman who wrote on food and wine for Anglophone magazines in France. Bruno knew her slightly as an old acquaintance of his dear friend and former lover Pamela.

These six jurors were gathered in the main salon of the Maison des Vins, a large, wooden-floored room with a long bar on the upper floor of a building that also housed the Bergerac tourist office. The tasting room was lined with showcases for dozens of local wines and had an outdoor terrace with a fine view of the Dordogne River. Behind the bar a door led to a kitchen and to offices and laboratories on the upper floors. Another door led back into the late-medieval cloisters and stone steps leading down to the massive cellars.

The jury was told that they would be blind tasting twenty sparkling wines, two from different vineyards in each of the invited regions. No wine cost more than twelve euros, which ruled out champagnes. The wines competing were Prosecco from Italy; a German Sekt; Spanish cava; *blanquette de Limoux* from Languedoc; crémants from Alsace, the Loire, Bordeaux and Burgundy. Finally, the Bergerac offered two sparkling wines, one from the Saussignac and the other from the town vineyard of St. Denis.

The room was big enough for the St. Denis contingent — Bruno and Pamela, Hubert, Julien, the mayor and Touvier — to stand and watch, along with other observers

231

and winemakers from the various competing regions. Two young men and two young women dressed in white shirts and black slacks had lined up the twenty bottles on the bar counter. Each bottle was shrouded in a thick black bag to hide the labels and marked with a number, which was how the tasters would identify them. They were expected to take account of the appearance and bubbles of each wine in the glass, its mouth "feel" and its aftertaste. Above all, they were expected to give marks for gaiety, since everywhere such wines were expected to bring joy and happiness.

The tasters had to confront a wide variety of styles and grapes. The wines from Germany and Alsace were predominantly Riesling, but Burgundy and the Loire preferred Chardonnay. The little-known grape Mauzac was used for the *blanquette de Limoux.* The Proseccos were made from Glera, and the cava from Macabeo, Parellada and Xarel-lo. The Bordeaux and Bergerac wines used Sémillon, Sauvignon Blanc and *muscadelle.* The French wines tended to aim for champagne's reputed fifty million bubbles in a glass, while the Sekt and Prosecco seemed less lively, since their secondary fermentation usually took place in vats.

The French preferred their tradition of

adding sugar and yeast before corking, as Julien had done, so that fermentation could take place in the bottle. That, after all, had been how the Abbey of St. Hilaire had first made sparkling wine in Limoux in 1531. Dom Pérignon himself had learned his craft at St. Hilaire before heading north to introduce his skills to the Champagne region near Reims and Épernay, whose northern wines were in those days thin and flat, bare of even one bubble, let alone fifty million.

The ritual of tasting was solemn and the room largely silent, save for the subdued murmurings of the tasters as they scribbled down notes and scores and exchanged comments. The servers poured and retreated in silence, pausing only to display the number of each wine to the tasters, and they, Bruno noticed, were taking their time over each bottle.

"The tension is making me thirsty," whispered Pamela. Bruno was thinking it strange that the tasting should be so silent and serious when for him sparkling wine was all about fun and festivity.

The members of the jury held each filled glass against the light and sniffed long and deeply before sipping, swirling and then spitting out the wine into the receptacles provided. Between glasses, they nibbled at slices of bread or dry biscuits and sipped from glasses of water before signaling to the servers that they were ready for the next wine. Bruno glanced at his watch; four minutes for them to taste the first wine, three for the second, almost four for the third and fourth, and then an endless five minutes and much muttering for the fifth. The tension mounted steadily, and whispers spread among the crowd as the tasters passed the hour mark with three wines yet to go.

A sigh of relief swept through the room when they finished the last wine, but then silence fell as the tasters called for the second bottle of each of the wines to be brought, as if to refresh their memories. Then they all examined the notes they had taken, added up the points they had given for various characteristics and signaled to the tall, white-haired resident of the Maison des Vins that their work was done. The president, wearing his robe of office as a grand consul of the Vinée of Bergerac, took the final scores from each taster and began to calculate the various totals.

The rules stated that each first-place vote counted for ten points, eight for second place, six for third place, then five points, four, three, two and one for the next-placed wines. The wines judged poorest in each category scored zero points. In the silence that stilled the room as the president tallied the results, and had them checked and double-checked by two aides, Bruno tried to work out what would be a good score. With six tasters the maximum would be sixty points, which would signal a first place from each taster. The minimum would be zero. A mix of second and third places would be around forty points. A wine that each taster had put in fourth place would get thirty. Anything close to forty would be a good result for St. Denis.

Finally, the president gestured to the testers to come and stand behind him on the small stage that had been erected, and as they left their tasting tables Bruno was one of several in the crowd who moved across to take their places for a better view. Some of the new arrivals were slipping off the black coverings from the bottles to see how much of the wine had gone and then began helping themselves to what was left. Not a bad idea, thought Bruno. He found some empty glasses and poured himself a half glass of the one before him, number 8. The bottle turned out to be full. He didn't recognize the wine, but it was very good, although a little warm. When the mayor and Pamela joined him, Bruno poured each of them a glass. The mayor's eyes widened in respect as he sipped, but Pamela looked startled, then sipped again and looked troubled.

The servers came with trays and hastily removed the remaining glasses, the plates and most of the still shrouded bottles from the tables before going back through the door behind the bar. The mayor hung on to the bottle he and Bruno were enjoying. Bruno asked Pamela why she was so pensive, but she gestured him to silence as the president rose, looking nervous as two TV cameras rolled and reporters clustered around him with microphones.

"This was a highly competitive tasting, with no wine winning the maximum number of points, so I congratulate all the wines that participated," he said. "In fifth place, with a very creditable thirty-one points, is the Prosecco. In fourth place, with thirty-five points, is the brut from Château Lestevenie in the Saussignac region of our own Bergerac. In third place, with forty points, is a Riesling-based wine, the Sekt from the Palatinate in Germany."

As he paused, shuffling his papers, Bruno's heart sank. He knew the wine of St.

Denis was good, but third or fourth place had been the best he'd hoped for. Glancing at his companions, they seemed equally depressed.

"There is no second place," the president declared. "That is because the two winners each scored forty-six points, and are the oldest and newest wines here, the *blanquette de Limoux* and the *crémant de la Vézère* from St. Denis, a remarkable result for a new wine in its first competitive tasting. I congratulate them all and invite the two winning winemakers to come forward."

Bruno jumped up and thrust his arms into the air to clap his hands above his head, and then hugged Pamela, lifting her off the ground in delight. Julien from St. Denis went up with his rival from Limoux to receive their prize. The president whispered urgently into the ears of the two winners before they nodded and shook hands.

"We did not expect two winners and prepared only one first prize, so our two champions have kindly agreed to share it, holding it for six months each," the president announced. Telling the two victors to put their hands together, he gave them simultaneously the elaborate modern sculpture of a silver vine set into an onyx plinth. Julien and the vintner from Limoux smiled dutifully for the cameras and mobile phones that most people in the room were holding above their heads to record the scene. Touvier the banker, Bruno noticed, was not among them. Instead he was hunched over, phone to one ear and his spare hand covering the other ear as if trying to block out the noise in the room. He was probably assuring his bosses that the loan to the vineyard looked safe, Bruno thought.

Pamela put her hand on Bruno's shoulder and pulled him close. "We have a problem," she murmured. With the mayor watching intently, she slipped down the black covering on the bottle he was holding, and Bruno recognized the label as the wine from St. Denis. But his mouth told him that could not be right. "Let's follow the servers," the mayor said, and he, Pamela and Bruno moved quietly through the door into the kitchen where the waiters themselves were enjoying some of the remaining wine.

"Who served the table with bottle number eight?" Bruno asked. Nobody replied, but two of the girls glanced at a slim, dark-haired youth of about twenty who was looking down at his feet. Bruno went up to him, showed his police ID and said, "What went on here? That wasn't the right wine that you served."

The mayor searched through the various bottles for the other bottle of number 8, found a clean glass and poured out what little remained.

"That's the St. Denis, sure enough," he said, handing the glass to Pamela, who sipped and nodded her agreement. Bruno sipped in turn. The mayor was right. "Go and get the others from St. Denis," he told the mayor. "I'll stay here with this server."

He eyed the young man. "Two bottles marked number eight but two different wines," Bruno said. "What are you up to?"

"I don't know what you're talking about."

"Let's see your ID card," Bruno said. "Are you a regular server here?" The youth said nothing but handed over his card. René Coustance, born in Bergerac, aged nineteen.

"We're all volunteers, from the vocational school, doing the wine course," one of the girls said.

Bruno pulled the black sacks bearing the number 8 from each of the bottles, one empty, the other three-quarters full. The two bottles, he saw at once, had subtly different shapes. The empty one he recognized as the bottle they had chosen for St. Denis, slightly bulbous at the shoulders and then narrowing gracefully a little toward the base. The almost full bottle was the more conventional shape, the one used by big champagne brands like Mumm, Heidsieck and Lanson, descending straight from the shoulder.

"Look at that," Bruno said as the mayor reappeared with Hubert, Julien and Touvier. "Not just different wines but different bottles.

"Would you care to explain?" he asked the worried-looking Coustance. "Or shall I bring in the fingerprint guys to look for your prints on this bottle?"

"Not just a different bottle but an extra label," said the mayor, pointing. Bruno looked down and saw a sliver of a second label hiding beneath the one proclaiming this to be a crémant from St. Denis. He peeled it away a little, realizing it had been freshly applied, and then looked up at Coustance. The young man's head was down, but he was glancing under lowered brows at Touvier. *Putain,* thought Bruno, the damn banker is behind this!

"The rest of you, leave us, please," Bruno said to the other servers. When the St. Denis contingent was alone with Coustance, he turned to Touvier. "Before I arrest this waiter and have him formally questioned at the police station about his accomplices, is there something you might like to tell us?"

"I wanted to be sure we won," said Touvier, almost casually. "The server was supposed to give them the good bottle first. It's a Mumm, bound to be better than the second-rate sparkling stuff."

"You're a fool," Bruno replied. He returned Coustance's ID card and told him to go. When the door closed behind him, Bruno turned back to Touvier. "Those people tasting the wine out there are experts. They can tell a Mumm blindfolded. If they'd had a sniff of it, there would have been a scandal."

"There's no harm done," said Touvier, smoothly. "We won fair and square with our bottle, even without the Mumm."

"No thanks to you," said Bruno. He turned to face the others. "I'm afraid I'd better resign from the board of this company."

Hubert and Julien looked dumbfounded.

"My conscience won't let me sit on the same board as this cheat," Bruno went on, giving Touvier a contemptuous glance.

"Not just Bruno, me too," said the mayor, picking up the offending bottle. He unpeeled half of the top label revealing the Mumm label beneath. He put the bottle into a bag and put it firmly under his arm. "And if I have to resign, I'll make sure the head office of the bank knows why."

241

Bruno, the mayor, Hubert, Pamela and Julien all stared accusingly at Touvier, who shrugged, and said, "Well, no harm done, but if you insist, I'll resign from the board."

"I'll tell you the harm you've done," said Bruno. "These two colleagues of ours have made a magnificent wine that St. Denis could be proud of, and you've just turned that achievement into something about which we'll always feel ashamed."

He turned to Hubert. "Is there some way we could let Limoux have the trophy all year, say that since we are the hosts and they're the guests . . ."

"Sure," Hubert said. Pamela, Julien and the mayor nodded agreement. And the five of them turned and walked out, leaving Touvier alone.

"How did you know?" he asked Pamela as they strolled to his Land Rover, thinking they'd be in time for the evening exercise of the horses at Pamela's riding school.

"I think I've told you before about that dreadful husband I made the mistake of marrying. Mumm was his favorite champagne."

"So you got to know it well," Bruno said.

"Because of him I grew to hate the stuff, even before the divorce," Pamela replied. "But then he was a banker too."

Oystercatcher

It was one of those dead days between Christmas and New Year's. The great bay of Arcachon stretched out endlessly ahead, merging into what might have been the surly waves of the Bay of Biscay or merely the gray sky in this faded light of midwinter. On the huge sand dune of Pilat, nearly three kilometers long and more than a hundred meters high, a couple stood close, braced against the freshening wind. The woman leaned her back against the man, her eyes closed, relishing the comfort of his arms wrapped tightly around her body. His face was buried in the short hair at the back of her neck, and they were content together in their silence.

They weren't new lovers, but long interruptions between their meetings made each reunion all the sweeter. There was no other person in sight. But the boats out in the bay were jolting along the vast rows of oyster beds, stopping every few moments to take aboard more of the cages that carried the oysters that would grace half the tables of France on New Year's Eve.

"We could be the last people left on earth," said Isabelle. "I suppose there are some fishermen on those boats. I'm starting to freeze, but it must be even colder for them out there."

"You'll warm up again on the way down this dune," said Bruno. He felt comfortable enough in the heavy wool of his old army greatcoat and happy just to be holding her close. "Most people end up tripping and rolling all the way to the bottom. The sand is soft enough. The only problem is that the sand gets everywhere."

"Is it true that the dune moves?" she asked.

"They say it creeps back a little toward the land every year," he replied. "There are old maps that show it used to be farther south and a few hundred meters out to sea. The tides here are strong, rising four or five meters every day, and the wind drives the whole Atlantic Ocean against this shore."

"And you'll be out there tonight." He noticed that she made an effort to keep the concern out of her voice.

Bruno was one of thirty policemen

brought in from rural areas so they would not be recognized by the locals, all called in for a major police operation against the recurrent thefts of oysters. Clearing out a whole bed could net the thieves fifty thousand euros or more. The oysters took three years to grow from spawn, and after the recent devastation caused to the beds by the red-tides plankton, supercharged by the runoffs of agricultural fertilizers, few oyster growers could survive a major theft.

That morning, while Bruno was waiting for his on-and-off girlfriend Isabelle to arrive from Paris, he had sat with the rest of the team in the large briefing room at Bordeaux police headquarters as Commissaire Pleven, the man in charge of what he called Operation Dominique, laid out his plan. Pleven had not explained the name, whether it was a random identifier spewed out by some computer, or perhaps the name of his wife. But the resources he had assembled were impressive.

"This time we have at our disposal two navy patrol boats," the commissaire said with pride as he pointed with a long stick to the blown-up map on the wall behind him. "One will be blocking the entrance to the bay, and the other will patrol the sandbank and Île aux Oiseaux, where some of the most valuable oyster beds are found. We have three helicopters equipped with infrared vision and night sights, and full of heavily armed Gendarmes Mobiles in case of trouble. We've even been allotted a squadron of Republican Guards, who are standing by with tracked armored cars, which are highly mobile on the beaches."

Bruno had heard from one of the Bordeaux cops he'd worked with before that the commissaire had even persuaded the local prefect to activate an old nineteenth-century statute to recruit *gardes-jurés,* formally sworn informants among the local oystermen. They might be sworn, Bruno thought to himself, but he had no idea how far they could be trusted. They were still part of a tight-knit local community of seamen, no more than a couple of hundred families who had intermarried for centuries. He'd heard of some families who had worked the oysters of the bay for six or seven generations. They had their own codes, their own rules, and they knew the local waters, the tides and currents, better than any French naval patrol boat could hope to.

"However, we have tried all these techniques before and we failed to catch the culprits," the commissaire said. "The thieves are probably local people who know these waters, know the routes and the back roads, and they probably expect that we are mounting this operation. Just before the New Year is the most lucrative time for the oystermen."

Until this point, Bruno had been paying only spasmodic attention. His thoughts kept straying to Isabelle, hurtling toward him from Paris on the latest high-speed train for another of their snatched, occasional reunions. They were all the more passionate for that, he understood. He'd be working each night, so their time together would be limited to lunches and languid, loving afternoons.

Suddenly Bruno sat up, startled by the commissaire's new, confident tone as he said that this time they had a secret weapon. Working with a new French high-tech company, they had developed artificial oysters that contained a transmitter that could be tracked. Each of the transmitters had a different code, so that they could see at once which of the many sprawling oyster beds was being targeted. Six drones would be flying over the main beds, tracking the movements of the fake oysters. Onshore there were roadblocks to stop each of the big refrigerated trucks that would be waiting to haul up to twenty tons of oysters to the hungry consumers of France.

That sounded interesting, Bruno thought. Against local knowledge the technology could make all the difference.

France was the biggest producer of oysters in Europe and the biggest consumer per head of oysters anywhere in the world, the commissaire explained. The country produced over a hundred and sixty thousand tons of oysters a year in a trade whose annual worth was over six hundred million euros. And almost half of them were sold in December. They had heard from one of the *gardes-jurés* that there was talk in the waterfront bars of a big hit this week. Police sources in Paris, Lyon and Lille had picked up hints at restaurants of cut-price oysters being available for those with the right connections. That was why this Operation Dominique had been mounted.

The role of Bruno and the twenty-nine other rural policemen who had been put under political pressure to join Operation Dominique was relatively modest. They would each patrol different sections of beach throughout the night, using night-vision glasses borrowed from the French army. They had all been equipped with portable sensors to track the radio transmitters, in case the drones failed. The sensors looked like a smartphone. They had to report each truck that arrived on their stretch of beach, note the number of the license plate and check the driver's papers. They had been equipped with mug shots of locals with previous convictions and some snatched photos of other suspects. Bruno reckoned the chance of his recognizing someone at night, probably with a scarf around his face against the cold, would be close to nil.

"These are tough guys, people who know the oyster trade and have the contacts to sell the stuff by the truckload," the commissaire went on. "You are each armed, but the usual rules of engagement apply. Only fire if you have reason to believe that you or an innocent civilian could be in danger. Use your heads. Stay in touch on the radio network so we know if you are stopping a truck and we can have reinforcements with you within minutes by chopper. We have armed gendarme teams standing by."

Bruno had studied the maps before coming down to Bordeaux the previous evening from the Périgord, nearly two hundred kilometers inland. The coastline of the Bay of Arcachon was at least fifty kilometers long, not counting the sprawling beaches to each side of the entrance to the bay. That was close to two kilometers of ground for each of the thirty rural cops to patrol. On the maps Bruno had counted over a hundred roads and tracks leading away from the endless beaches, and locals probably knew of more that weren't shown. There were five sizable towns and dozens of small villages around the bay. And with the huge market of New Year's Eve awaiting them, every one of the five hundred local oystermen would be out in the bay and bringing in his harvest.

Bruno wondered if the commissaire was putting too much faith in his technology and in the sheer number of cops and troops available. If Bruno had planned this operation, he'd have used the thirty extra cops to increase the number of roadblocks. The thieves had to get the oysters to market, and Bruno suspected that would mean getting the trucks onto the autoroutes as quickly as possible. Perhaps with millions of French families on the roads, going to or coming from family reunions, the commissaire had not been allowed to clog the autoroute access points. Could there be another bottleneck somewhere the police might use, Bruno asked himself as the commissaire paused and lowered his voice, apparently coming to the end of his briefing. The man had been word-perfect so far; he'd evidently rehearsed his presentation.

"Seven tons of oysters stolen in Gujon-Mestras, another twenty tons in the Marennes basin, more thefts off the Île de Ré, we are going to stop this surge in oyster thefts and we're going to stop it tonight," the commissaire insisted. "And remember, we are dealing here not only with an important local economy but with the cultural identity of France. As our great poet Léon-Paul Fargue put it, 'To eat an oyster is to kiss the sea on the mouth.' "

He paused, and then asked, "Any questions?"

Another member of the top brass raised a hand. Bruno presumed it would be a prepared question.

"Sir, we know that the oysters have to be sluiced in clean water for a day or two to get the sand out after they are harvested. Presumably we know where all the sluicing points are around the bay. Why not monitor them?"

"Good question," the commissaire replied. "We tried that last year and found that they weren't using any of the ones around the bay. Oysters are raised all along the Atlantic coast up to Bretagne and beyond, so there are hundreds of sluicing points available to them. But that's why we are deploying these fake oysters with their transmitters. If we miss the hijackers on the bay, we'll still be able to track them as they move out. And once we track the trucks, we can follow them all the way to the crooked wholesalers they are using and wrap up the whole operation."

That made sense, Bruno thought. He saw heads nodding in agreement around him as the briefing ended and the meeting broke up. He checked his watch. Isabelle would be arriving in Bordeaux a few minutes after eleven. Then they would take the local train to Arcachon. He'd already bought the tickets, and they would arrive shortly before noon. There would be time for him to take her to lunch and then to spend the afternoon together before reporting for duty. He relished the prospect of a weekend with her in any circumstances, but there was an extra frisson to a tryst in a hotel paid for by the police budget.

Bruno had been surprised when Isabelle had emailed him to invite herself to join him at Arcachon. He knew she stayed in close touch with her old colleagues in the Police Nationale in the region, so he might have guessed she would know of the operation. And she had proposed it in a way that suggested he would be doing her a favor, rescuing her from spending more time than she could stand at a family Christmas with her father and his new wife, whom Isabelle did not like. Bruno had been delighted at the prospect.

He arrived on foot at Bordeaux Saint-Jean station as the clock struck eleven, feeling his skin tingle with anticipation at seeing Isabelle again. He had time to smooth down his hair and slip a mint into his mouth before reaching the Relay newspaper kiosk where they had arranged to meet. He scanned the crowd from Paris, looking for that familiar face, and was surprised when a slim figure, head wrapped in a woolen scarf, slid out of the throng toward him and into his arms.

"I almost didn't recognize you in all that wool," he said, and kissed her. "It's so good to see you."

She returned his kiss with enthusiasm before saying she'd checked the weather forecast and knew it would be cold. Arm in arm, Bruno carrying her overnight bag, they headed for the platform for Arcachon where the train was waiting. They took their seats in an almost empty car facing each other and holding hands, her eyes alight as she slipped off the scarf. Then she turned serious.

"I did some checking around," she began. "You'll have to watch Commissaire Pleven. He's got the reputation of a guy with political ambitions who'd clamber over dead bodies to get ahead. That's why he's called in cops from all over the region. It's not only because he can't afford a failure. You and all the rest of them will start receiving New Year's cards, phone calls on your birthday, invitations to meet for a drink when he's touring the prefectures and the *mairies.* He's a brilliant networker, and he's not just after your vote. He'll try to turn you cops into his local organizers, so long as this operation is a success and his brilliant career continues its ascent. I hear he's on the list for the regional government, probably planning to be deputy head before angling for a ministerial job in Paris. It's up to you whether you back him, but don't get in his way."

This was not how Bruno had expected the first talk of their brief time together to begin. They had met and fallen in love when she was a detective inspector for the Police Nationale in the Périgord. After a delicate but successful operation she had been invited onto the staff of the Minister of the

Interior in Paris, had then been wounded in an otherwise successful operation against a shipload of illegal immigrants and was now on the staff coordinating the antiterrorism efforts of the European Union. If anyone knew about brilliant careers, it was Isabelle. Bruno, who thought of her as the love of his life but felt no temptation to move beyond his native Périgord, knew the personal cost to each of them of Isabelle's own relentless ambition.

But this was no time to think of that as they sat together in the warmth of a waterfront restaurant's glass-fronted terrace, a plate of fresh oysters and a glass of Mouton Cadet Sauvignon Blanc before each of them. Isabelle loosened an oyster from its shell, squeezed on some drops from a slice of lemon and slurped it into her mouth. With her eyes closed, she chewed it once, twice, and finally swallowed with a purr of deep satisfaction. Eyes open again, she nodded her appreciation and reached for her wineglass.

"*Mon Dieu,* that was delicious. There's the merest hint of iodine that makes these the tastiest oysters I know," she said, and reached for another. And then she smiled roguishly at him. "Oysters always make me think of you, and here you are."

She loosened another oyster from its shell and lifted it to his mouth, keeping her eyes on his. When he'd swallowed, she took the almost empty shell back to her lips and raised it to sip the last of the juices before saying, "I'm glad our room is just upstairs."

Two hours later, their desire for each other slaked for the moment, they took a local bus to the huge Dune of Pilat, which she'd never climbed before, looking at the bay below them and turning to survey the vast stretch of the forest of Landes behind. They turned back to the sea again, watching the distant oyster boats, and suddenly Isabelle pulled a pair of binoculars from her bag and seemed to focus on one boat that she thought was behaving differently. She explained that while the others remained in one small area and kept stopping to take in more oysters, this one was sailing slowly but without stopping along each of the lanes between the oyster beds.

"There's one man in the wheelhouse and another on the bow, as if he's a lookout. And he's holding something," she said, and passed Bruno the binoculars. "It's as if he's doing an inspection. But I thought they'd all be hauling in as many oysters as they could for the New Year's market."

Bruno found it hard to focus, but she was

right. The boat was behaving differently, and the deck seemed clear of oysters, while the other boats were piling them aboard as quickly as they could. "I can't see what it is he's holding, but there's something in his hand. It's as if he's looking at his phone to check something on the Internet, but I can't imagine he'd have a connection out there in the bay."

He tried to see if the boat had a name, but he saw only a number, hard to discern. It seemed to dance elusively in the binocular lens.

"I can make out a number, capitals A and C and then three-two-two, but there are more numbers I can't distinguish. Can you try?" He handed her the binoculars.

"I get the A and C and I think there are two nines at the end. The one in the middle could be a seven or a two, even a four or a six. It's a bit faded," she said.

Bruno fumbled in an inside pocket for his notebook and pen and scribbled down the numbers he was sure of and the ones Isabelle had guessed at. When she asked why, he explained about the fake oysters and the sensors they had all been issued, so very like a smartphone.

"It may be one of our guys checking that the transmitters are working, but if not, we could have a problem. We'd better head back. I should call this in."

He pulled out his phone and called the number for the operations room. He gave his name and described what he'd seen and asked if anyone was checking on the sensors and transmitters. He was told to hang up and stand by. They'd get back to him. He and Isabelle managed to scramble down the dune without tripping, and as they walked along the beach, she asked what time he had to report for duty.

"Six," he said as his phone rang. It was a deputy commissioner. When Bruno had repeated what he'd seen, he was asked to report at once to the Arcachon police station. He explained where he was, and they said they would send a car. Bruno suggested they should drop Isabelle at the hotel.

"Are you trying to protect my reputation?" she said, with that impish grin he adored.

"Given what you said about Commissaire Pleven . . ." He stumbled.

"Bruno," she said firmly. "The day I'm not prepared to be proud of the man I'm sleeping with is the day I enter a nunnery. Besides, Pleven and I are of equal rank."

Pleven was not at Arcachon. He was in Bordeaux, at the main operations room with its better communications. He listened to

Bruno's report and did not seem too impressed until Isabelle seized the phone, introduced herself and her rank and said she happened to be on the dune with Bruno and confirmed everything he had said.

"That boat I saw was behaving oddly," she insisted. "Have you checked the numbers and possible owners?"

"The information was kind of vague," he replied smoothly.

"It usually is," she said crisply. "That's the nature of intelligence. But I'm confident you have access to a list of all the boat registrations and will be able to narrow down the owner and make the appropriate inquiries. If somebody knows about your new technology, your entire operation could collapse."

"I understand, but I'm not clear what standing you have in this operation," he replied.

"Why not call the minister of the interior and find out?" she snapped. "In the meantime, may I suggest that you arrange a car to bring me to your operations room, or I'll be drafting my report on what seems like a cavalier attitude to fresh intelligence from a high-ranking source."

The car was arranged, and Isabelle disappeared.

At least the commissaire had thought through the assembly points for all the cops. The local police station at Arcachon was too small and too visible for thirty men to arrive and sort out the various patrol routes they would take. Bruno had been told to report at a local parking lot by six that evening, where an unmarked car would take him and two other cops to their patrol points near Cap Ferret. Other cops were meeting their cars in the parking lots of shopping malls or at the bus and rail stations. They had each been told to wear civilian overcoats on top of their police uniforms. Bruno's old army greatcoat would have to do. He wore one so seldom that he'd never seen the point of buying something new. His hunting jacket and layers of cotton and wool underneath had always kept out the cold.

The colder he got on the deserted beach, the more Bruno wondered why the hell Pleven had summoned thirty cops to what increasingly seemed like a useless mission. The lights of the nearby town had already faded and disappeared in a thickening mist. The only buildings he'd seen nearby were one beach restaurant, little more than a shack and now closed, and a small cottage set back from the beach that seemed dark and empty when Bruno had prowled around it. Like the rest of the rural cops, Bruno did not know the area and wasn't entirely sure what he was supposed to do if a boat full of stolen oysters and a truck turned up. There would be three or four nervous and probably aggressive men facing a lone and frozen policeman with a gun he had been warned not to use. He removed the thick woolen scarf from around his neck and wrapped it around his head and ears.

Stomping up and down in an effort to fend off the cold, Bruno tried to work out the cost to the police budget. Thirty rural cops, each with a rail fare, a hotel for three nights, a per diem for food and overtime pay for night duty. It could not be less than thirty thousand euros, which was more than Bruno's annual salary. Throw in the cost of these fake oysters with their transmitters plus the drones and helicopters — unless the Gendarmes Mobiles and the naval patrol boats were counting this as a training exercise, the overall costs must be running well over a hundred thousand.

His phone rang. It was Isabelle.

"It looks as though the man on the boat we saw is Yves Tallarin. He's had several arrests for brawls when he was young but no convictions," she said. "He's got problems with the tax authorities that could be serious, and his brother-in-law owns a trucking company. I'm trying to find out if there's any connection to the tech firm that produced the fake oysters. There's a nephew who is said to have graduated in computer studies. Tallarin has got a big new house at Andernos-les-Bains, and his own oyster beds are close to where you're patrolling at Cap Ferret. Anything happening near you?"

"Not a thing. Cold and quiet. It sounds like you've been doing good work. Any chance of reinforcements?"

"I'm working on that, but they may have to come by road. The chopper pilots are complaining about the visibility."

"Pleven should have thought of that," Bruno said.

"You're right. It could also have been a problem for the boat, unless Tallarin knows these waters so well he can find his way blindfolded. I think you should see a car heading your way with armed gendarmes in fifteen or twenty minutes."

"What about the naval patrol boat?" he asked. "It should be near here."

"It seems to be having trouble navigating its way through the oyster beds. They don't show up on their radar. That's another factor Pleven didn't think about." She paused and then said, "Keep safe, I'll stay in touch."

Bruno pondered whether to stay on the beach and watch for a boat or head back to the track where he'd been dropped off, which seemed the most likely route for a truck. It was close to the restaurant, and there was a stretch of tarmac that was probably used as a parking lot in season. He walked up, saw a small dune and clambered up. The mist seemed to be getting thicker. There was nothing to be seen, no lights from Andernos nor from Cap Ferret, no lights of any car or truck and nothing out in the bay. He checked his watch. Isabelle's fifteen minutes were almost up. But heaven help the gendarmes trying to find their way in this mist.

His phone rang again. In his thick gloves, he had trouble pressing the right button to receive the call. He pulled off a glove with his teeth, pressed the button with fingers clumsy with the cold and dropped the glove.

"It's me," Isabelle said. "The navy patrol boat is stuck, but their radar shows a boat heading your way. Are the gendarmes there yet?"

"No sign of them." He crouched down and groped for the glove. No luck.

"*Merde,* Bruno."

"*Merde* to you, too." He was about to end

263

the call but then paused. "Hang on, I see lights on the road. It could be them."

"Keep the line open. Put your phone in your pocket and let me know if it's the gendarmes."

"I don't think it's them. It's a truck, lights far apart, so it could be a big one, moving slowly. Still no sign of anything out to sea. Phone going into my pocket now."

"I'll stay on the line," he heard her say as he fumbled the phone into the pocket without the gun.

The truck lights seemed to be wavering, but then he realized there was a man in front of them with a flashlight, guiding the vehicle to the parking lot. He heard the wheeze of compressed air brakes, and the two main lights stopped moving. That meant a very big truck. Bruno tucked his scarf down over his brow to prevent it from being picked up by the headlamps and then ducked down behind the dune.

It was a good thing he did. Somebody in the truck lit a strobe, which gave several flashes of brilliant blue light, and then Bruno was startled by the deep blare of a Klaxon, three loud bursts. Ah, thought Bruno. Sailors know about foghorns, and sound travels better than light in thick mist. The sound and the glow from the strobe must mean the boat was nearby. They'd probably be staying in touch by phone.

The truck was twenty or thirty meters from him. He turned to look out to the bay and heard the boat's motor before he saw it. His gloveless hand was terribly cold. He tucked it inside his coat and into his armpit. He might need that hand to be warm enough to hold his gun. He had a sudden, utterly irrelevant and distracting thought about Napoléons Grande Armée on the frozen retreat from Moscow. Those poor bastards, he thought. What a misery it must have been trying to reload a musket with freezing fingers.

The boat kept coming and seemed to be on the beach, or even crossing it. He blinked, disbelieving what he was seeing, and suddenly realized it had wheels and a flat bottom. As it rolled slowly past him, Bruno remembered seeing something like it in the army, a DUKW, an amphibious vehicle.

He crept out from behind his dune and followed the boat closely as it crawled up the beach, keeping out of sight of the men in the truck. He heard voices, excited and happy, congratulating one another. Now what the hell should he do? Two or three men on the truck and probably two on the boat. He pulled his gun from the shoulder holster. It felt warmer than his hand. He saw the boat begin to turn, probably to make it easier to unload the oyster cages into the truck. In the glow of the headlights he saw and recognized the boat's registration number: AC 322699.

He pulled off his other glove with his teeth and took out his phone.

"They're here," he said quietly, and heard Isabelle gasp in reply. "Boat and truck. The boat numbers match. AC three-two-two-six-nine-nine. I'll make the arrest."

"Don't," he heard her reply. "We have what we need. The roadblocks are in place."

Too late; his voice had been heard. There was silence from the truck and boat alike. He moved out into the light, realizing he'd made a mistake as he lost vision and started blinking his eyes in the glare of the headlights and released the safety catch on his weapon.

"Armed police!" he shouted. "You are under arrest and surrounded. Down on the ground, all of you. Hands on your heads."

At least his warning would be recorded, he thought. He fired a round into the air.

"Down on the ground!" he repeated, stepping out to the side where he could see them all, staring at him in shock and disbelief. Then the man with the flashlight threw it at him, darted back to the side of the truck and clambered into the cab, shouting, "Let's go."

A man on the boat hurled an oyster cage at Bruno, which missed, and the boat began reversing back down the beach. The truck began to reverse as Bruno strode forward, gun at the ready, when he was jolted forward and down by a blow to the small of his back. Another oyster cage had found its mark. But his gun was still in his hand. He aimed carefully and put two bullets into each of the front tires, watching the truck slump down onto the wheel rims.

He turned and saw the boat trundle gracefully into the waters of the bay just as a police siren sounded and a flashing blue light pulled into the parking lot, three armed men leaping out. He put his gun down on the ground and lifted the phone to his ear.

"You still there?" he asked.

"Jesus, Bruno, I heard the shots." Isabelle's voice was anguished. "What's happening?"

"The gendarmes are here. Make sure they know I'm on the ground, unarmed. The truck has been immobilized. I shot the tires out. The boat has gone back out to sea, but we have the number. I think I may have a broken rib. They hit me with an oyster cage. And tell Pleven that if he ever runs for any electoral office, I'll mount my own campaign against the stupid bastard."

LA MÈRE NOËL

The directors of the town vineyard of St. Denis were usually a contented group of men and women. But on this November day they were looking grave, even downcast. The frosts of 2017 had halved the vineyard's output and forced them to delay their plans for a visitors' center with a tasting room. The hot summer of 2018 had offered different challenges, trying to manage the wine's surging sugar and alcohol content. The year 2019, however, had seen a splendid vintage, encouraging them to buy a local vineyard that would increase their total output by 15 percent. It had seemed like a good idea at the time, even though some of the wine in the stock that had come with the sale was not up to the town's usual standards. They were selling five-liter boxes of it cheaply at local markets for twelve euros.

"The problem is that we were left short of

capital and with too little storage space this year when we were hit by Covid," said Hubert, chairman of the board and owner of a chain of wine stores. "We were hurt by the closure of bars and restaurants not just in France but also in Britain, which was turning into a good export market. They took nearly a third of our production. Then a good harvest and the new vineyard raised our output from seventy thousand liters to ninety thousand, and we can't sell them."

"What if we cut the price?" asked one of the directors, a local bank manager. She had been particularly enthusiastic about the expansion plans.

"Our prices are low enough already, and it would annoy our best clients, the people of St. Denis and the immediate region. Many of them are shareholders, and they have already bought their wine for the Christmas season at the usual prices," said the retired accountant who managed the vineyard's finances.

"We're not an *appellation contrôlée,* so none of the big firms wants to buy stock from us," Hubert went on. "We tried to sell it in bulk to the state to make industrial alcohol, but we aren't the only ones trying to do that. The state has already committed to buying two hundred and fifty million liters and can't buy any more. As it is, we got rid of five thousand liters that way. So, my friends, any ideas?" he added, looking around the table.

"Why don't we put out a pamphlet on cooking with wine?" suggested Marguerite, who ran a popular local pizzeria. "I certainly can't buy any more. My sales are down a third this year as it is."

"What if we were to try some new products, making wine vinegar, for example, or brandy, or producing our own brand of *vin de noix*?" Bruno suggested. "That new vineyard we bought has a walnut plantation that makes a good profit."

"Brandy needs two years in the barrel at a minimum," said Hubert, shaking his head. "Maybe we could think about that for the future. We might even call it Périgornac."

"*Vin de noix* might be a useful idea for next summer, Bruno," said the town's mayor. "But you know as well as I do that we need young green walnuts for that, and we won't have those until next June, so we couldn't even think about selling the stuff until late August. We'll need something faster than that, otherwise we'll have to start laying people off before Christmas or ask the shareholders for more money."

As the meeting broke up, Bruno paused

to buy a bottle of the vineyard's standard red for three euros fifty and another of Sieur de St. Denis, the vineyard's premium red, which usually sold at just under six euros a bottle. He handed over a ten-euro note, and Julien said, "Give me another five euros, and you can have one of those five-liter boxes. They aren't selling very well."

The venture of the town's vineyard was relatively new, formed when Julien, owner of the region's oldest and best-established vineyard, known as La Domaine, had launched a costly and ill-judged expansion just before his wife was diagnosed with terminal cancer. Faced with bankruptcy, he had agreed at the urging of his dying wife to a rescue package proposed by the mayor, under which Julien kept the small château and its *gîtes* and restaurant and stayed on as vineyard manager and winemaker.

"It's a shame Mère Dailloux passed away in the spring," Julien added. "She'd always take fifty liters a week for that mulled wine stall she ran in the Christmas markets."

Bruno paused, remembering with affection not only the remarkably fine taste of her product but also the way he'd always avert his eyes as he passed her stall, since everyone knew she had no license to sell the stuff. And she sold out every week.

"What about her family?" he asked. "They might have the recipe."

"Sadly not. I asked, but it seemed she took her secret to the grave," Julien replied. "I still have a couple of bottles."

"Could a decent chemist analyze it for us?"

"No idea, but it's worth a try."

Bruno thought he might have a bottle in his *cave* at home, so he drove back to find it and then set off once more, this time with his basset hound, Balzac, perched beside him. He drove into the yard of the local *collège* and climbed up to the apartment of Florence, the science teacher, where her young twins leaped upon Balzac, and Florence emerged from her kitchen to say she was just making supper if Bruno would like to join them.

"I'd love to, but I have to be at the council meeting tonight. I'm here on business, in a way," he said, and handed her the almost black bottle with its label, depicting a spry old lady raising her glass with a roguish grin. "Do you think you could analyze the contents of this? It's a very special mulled wine, but the recipe is lost."

"Mulled wine is just wine to which you add melted sugar and spices, cinnamon and cloves, mainly, and orange peel," she said.

"This was no ordinary mulled wine," Bruno replied, and explained the town vineyard's troubles, and how the renaissance of Mère Dailloux's elixir might help.

"I suppose I could make it a chemistry class project," Florence said doubtfully.

"I knew I could count on you," he said, unscrewing the cap. "This is my last bottle, but I don't suppose you'll need all that for the analysis. In my recollection it was almost as good when I drank it cold."

He poured out two small glasses, held his own up to the light. It was almost as dark as the bottle. He swirled it, sniffed it and took a sip. Florence followed suit.

"A lot of orange in there and a touch of lemon, and some herb beyond the usual cinnamon and cloves," she said, smacking her lips and looking at the bottle with new respect. "There's some apple in there, too."

"Yes, she had quite an orchard," Bruno said. "She used to sell her homemade apple juice in the market."

"Here on the label, it says DO NOT BOIL OR SIMMER, which seems odd for mulled wine," she said. "I thought it was meant to be kept simmering. I wonder why she put that on the label."

"I imagine she didn't want the alcohol boiled off," said Bruno. "I'd better go.

Thank you for doing this. Could you call me tomorrow?"

The council meeting dragged on as usual, the mayor wily enough to let the councillors talk themselves out before he stepped in to wrap matters up. As the members trooped out, Bruno mentioned his attempt to revive the mulled wine of the Widow Dailloux.

"A remarkable woman," said the mayor. "Had her first child at the age of fifteen, unmarried, of course. The father was a young *résistant*, killed in the last weeks of the war, but at least he'd come home to marry her and give the child his name. Then she had three more children with her next husband. He was the last of our *bouilleurs ambulants*, our traveling distillers, and the license to brew the stuff died with him. As a boy, I remember going with my father to the place by the cemetery where Dailloux parked his still, each of us laden down with shopping bags full of our plums, watching as he turned them into an excellent *gnôle*. I wonder what happened to his still?"

"Joe will know," replied Bruno, referring to his predecessor as town policeman. After saying good night to the mayor, he drove to Joe's old farmhouse, found him sitting by the open fire in the kitchen with his dog asleep at his feet and asked him about the still.

"It's in the museum at Périgueux," said Joe. "A lovely thing, big copper boiler and tubes, brass fittings, and they put the old metal wheels back on. He'd kept them even after he'd put rubber wheels on to make it easier for his old horse to tow."

"So he gave it to the museum?" Bruno asked as he accepted a glass of Joe's home-made *vin de noix*.

"No, Mère Dailloux kept it in her barn, polished it every week," Joe replied. "When she died, her kids put the place up for sale and were going to sell the still to a scrap merchant, but I called the museum, and the curator gave them a better price. She used to make a lovely applejack, illegal, of course, but as I've always told you, Bruno, a good cop knows when to turn a blind eye. And at just fifty francs a bottle, who could resist?"

Joe rose, went to a corner cupboard, bent down, rummaged around and came out with a bottle that had once held Perrier water and was now half full of a clear liquid. He rinsed out the glasses that had held the *vin de noix* and poured a healthy slug of the *gnôle* into each one. "Try that."

Bruno sipped, and his eyes widened. It was extraordinary, smooth and biting at the same time, with a distinct aftertaste of apples. He was fond of the *gnôle* that his friend Stéphane brewed up at the back of his neighbor's disused barn, but this was markedly better. And there was something distinctly familiar about the taste.

The next day Florence confirmed Bruno's suspicion that the magic ingredient was apple brandy, but her chemistry class analysis had found more than that. There was some star anise, a bay leaf or two and dark cane sugar. So that evening in his kitchen, armed with a bottle of Stéphane's *gnôle* and the five liters of the town vineyard's boxed wine, and with Joe and the mayor helping, they produced an uncannily accurate version of the fabled mulled wine of Mère Dailloux.

"Five weeks to go before Christmas," said Stéphane. "We have two markets each week here in St. Denis and the same in Sarlat, Bergerac and Périgueux. And then there's once-a-week markets in Lalinde, Ribérac and Eymet and Issigeac and two in Villefranche and Terrasson, Montpon and Monestier." He began ticking off the markets. "Then there's Beaumont, Pomport, Ste. Foy, St. Cyprien and Ste. Alvère. We've got nearly fifty markets a week. And over five weeks to go before Christmas."

"If we go to each market with a coffee urn to warm up the wine, we can sell it by the glass for a euro and then sell bottles," said the mayor. "If we sell twenty bottles at every market each week, that's a thousand bottles a week. We might not have to lay off any of the vineyard staff before Christmas."

"Where will we get the apple brandy?" asked Joe.

"We'll make it. There's a still in Julien's *chai*," said the mayor. "He keeps it clean to show the guests who come to his *gîtes*. And there's no shortage of apples this year."

"The only problem is that we can't sell it," said Bruno mournfully. "The *gnôle* makes it illegal."

"Who says it contains any *gnôle*?" asked the mayor, looking innocent and holding out his glass for a refill. "No, Bruno, you must never underestimate the powers of a mayor in his own commune, when armed with a solid majority on his council, the loyalty of his fellow citizens and a wide knowledge of old French laws and traditions.

"This is a commemorative local digestif, brewed in honor of a leading local citizen, the widow of a brave Resistance fighter," he went on. "We'll put a second label on the back telling their story. And heaven help any pettifogging bureaucrat who tries to stop us. And just to be sure, I'll take a bottle to the prefect myself and tell him this is how we save the town vineyard, and we'd like a distilling license, too. I like the sound of that Périgord cognac."

"Should we call it Mère Dailloux, after her?" asked Joe.

"Well, since it's Christmas," said Bruno thoughtfully, "why don't we just call it Mère Noël's Christmas Cheer?"

BOEUF NEANDERTHAL

The mayor of St. Denis and Bruno were driving back from Périgueux after the April meeting of SHAP, the Société Historique et Archéologique du Périgord, at which the mayor had achieved a lifelong dream by being elected as SHAP's new president.

"Can I ask you a favor?" the mayor began.

Bruno nodded, wondering what was coming, and said, "Of course."

"SHAP was founded on the twenty-seventh of May 1874," said the mayor. "I'd like to celebrate that date, which this year falls on a Saturday, with something special. Given your cooking skills, Bruno, do you think you could plan us an anniversary dinner for the society next month that would re-create the food of our Neanderthal forebears, but in a way that would appeal to the modern palate? And if it works, might you persuade Sylvain, your *traiteur* friend, to prepare it for the members? He's used to cooking for fifty or more people at weddings and similar events."

Bruno, in the passenger seat of the mayor's big Citroën, looked in surprise at the man who had hired him and had over the years become a friend and the nearest thing he'd ever had to a father. He had heard many unusual suggestions from the mayor over his eleven years as the town policeman, but this one surprised even him.

"Since the Périgord is the global center of prehistoric studies, with more than a hundred caves decorated with the art of our ancestors, such a feast would bring in publicity and tourism," the mayor added.

It would also, Bruno thought, mark the mayor's new position at SHAP in a striking and doubtless popular way that would certainly attract considerable publicity for the mayor, locally and perhaps nationally. Moreover, the municipal elections were looming, and even though Bruno was convinced that he would be reelected as long as he lived, the mayor never took the voters for granted.

"It won't be easy to get the right balance between historical authenticity and modern tastes," Bruno said. "We could give them raw fish followed by charred meats with nuts and berries for dessert, but I don't think that would go down very well. And what about wine?"

"Georgians were making wine in the Caucasus eight thousand years ago, and what about the pre-Roman wines at Château Belingard, right here in the Bergerac?" the mayor replied. "And we don't want it to be too authentic. I think most of us in St. Denis would have a hard time hunting aurochs and reindeer with stone axes and spears."

Bruno smiled to himself at the thought, but already he was sufficiently intrigued by the challenge to take this idea seriously. He recalled from a SHAP lecture that reindeer had been the mainstay of the prehistoric diet, along with occasional beef and horsemeat. And the earliest bone harpoons in the local museum were more than thirteen thousand years old, so fish could be on the menu.

"The problem will be some kind of sauce to go with the meat," said the mayor.

"Venison with black-currant sauce?" Bruno suggested.

"Yes, that would work," the mayor said. "We need another course. Let's try something with beef, the closest we can get to prehistoric aurochs, perhaps with a mushroom sauce? The ancient Romans thought mushrooms were the food of the gods."

They arrived in St. Denis agreeing that more research was needed. So that evening Bruno visited his friends Clothilde and Horst, professional archaeologists who lived nearby. Clothilde, a small, energetic woman with red hair and flashing eyes, was the senior curator at the National Museum of Prehistory in the nearby town of Les Eyzies. She and Horst had enjoyed, or perhaps survived, an on-again, off-again passion for each other at digs across Europe and the Middle East until Horst had retired from his teaching post at the University of Cologne and persuaded her to marry him. He now ran the Les Eyzies museum's excavation program.

Their looks of surprise were mixed with amusement when Bruno described the mayor's latest initiative over a kir. He knew he was consulting experts. The previous year, Clothilde had given a lecture at the museum on the very topic of prehistoric diets. And Horst had recently published an article in the popular magazine *Archéologie* on phytoliths, the fossilized particles of plant tissue that could be found in the middens, the rubbish dumps of prehistoric people.

"They had fire, so in principle they could

have smoked their food or dried it like the Native Americans with their pemmican," said Clothilde, thoughtfully. "And there's some new isotropic research on skeletons suggesting that fish formed up to a quarter of their diet."

She smiled at Bruno and announced, in the solemn tones of a pompous maître d'hôtel: "*Alors, mesdames, messieurs,* the chef proposes some smoked trout with perhaps a little reindeer pemmican on the side to begin."

"Remember the dig at Castel-Merle where we found the basalt stones in a clay-lined pit that you thought might have been used to boil water?" Horst said thoughtfully. "The associated pollen was nearly thirty thousand years old."

"How did that work?" Bruno asked, happy to see Horst and Clothilde getting into the spirit of the idea.

"Two ways," said Clothilde. "Scoop out a hole in deep enough clay, light a fire so the clay dries and then reline it to seal the cracks. Then light a new fire, put in your meat, well wrapped in damp leaves, cover it and — *voilà,* a baking oven. Or add water and then take red-hot stones from the fire and drop them in to boil the meat, or at least warm it."

"The people who erected the scaffolding at Lascaux in order to paint the ceilings used wood and rawhide," said Horst. "They would've easily been able to build a frame they could cover with skins to make a smoker. Or they could put flat-topped stones into a fire and cook meat or fish on top of the stones."

"Don't forget that they were very good at fire technology," added Clothilde. "That's why they were able to invent the only way to light those caves so they could see to paint deep underground. That's what they did at Lascaux more than eighteen thousand years ago. They found that rendered reindeer fat with juniper twigs for wicks gave them a smokeless light so the chalk walls weren't darkened."

"Fair enough," said Bruno. "They could have had roasted, boiled or even barbecued meat and fish. And obviously they had nuts and berries, maybe some fruit, but what else did they eat, Horst? Your *Archéologie* article said you'd found evidence of seaweed being a regular food in coastal communities. But we're more than a hundred kilometers from the sea here."

"Well, they used kelp for food and also for cordage, baskets and food wrappings, but kelp doesn't preserve well," Horst replied.

"What we found were fossils of tiny gastropods that lived on kelp, and now we've found similar fossils here inland of gastropods that lived on duckweed in rivers or water lilies in ponds. *Butomus umbellatus,* or flowering rush, grows in moist soil or shallow ponds, and the tubers are fifty percent starch, edible when cooked, although kind of tasteless. The seeds are edible raw. And we've found those in middens here."

"For vegetables we could use other tubers," said Clothilde. "Radishes and turnips are native to this region, even if they were thin and spindly things in those days. They could have eaten those, I suppose. Sorrel is native here, and so are wild garlic and nettles, so you could make nettle soup. And you know there's a new project to develop duckweed as food? People in Southeast Asia have eaten it for centuries, and it has as much protein as soybeans. I tried some once, and it was tasteless and stringy, not very appetizing, but it would keep you alive."

"Perhaps with a vinaigrette and mixed with wild-garlic leaves it could be a kind of salad," suggested Bruno.

He suddenly remembered that Pamela had given him for Christmas a modern edition of Vincent La Chapelle's famous five-volume work, *Le Cuisinier Moderne,* first published in 1742. La Chapelle had been chef to Holland's Prince of Orange. In France he'd been the personal chef for the royal mistress Madame de Pompadour.

Monsieur La Chapelle had visited Spain and Portugal to study their cooking, used the then exotic food of rice and pioneered the use of low-fat dishes. One dish Bruno recalled had used a sauce made of crushed walnuts to accompany beef, and since walnuts proliferated throughout the Périgord, he thought that might be suitable and suggested it.

"Walnut sauce would be a bit dry," Horst grumbled.

"You can't use milk or cream in the sauce," Clothilde said. "Our ancestors didn't develop the lactose-tolerant enzyme until a couple of thousand years ago."

"Really?" Bruno asked. "Didn't Neanderthal babies drink mother's milk?"

"Yes, but the enzymes were different," said Clothilde. Then she laughed out loud and said, "I don't think the mayor wants his special feast to feature a dozen topless young mothers producing the raw material for a sauce."

"I could use egg yolks to make a sauce,

and boil a duck carcass in hot water to make bouillon," suggested Bruno. "I know chickens were domesticated much later, but there were birds and nests, so eggs would have been possible."

"What about dessert?" asked Horst. "Just offering a bowl of berries or roasted chestnuts won't do the trick. You said the mayor wants this to be a memorable occasion."

They agreed to help Bruno attempt a test meal using prehistoric methods. On the following Sunday morning, at a stretch of heavy, clay-filled earth on the bank of the River Vézère on the outskirts of St. Denis, Bruno dug a pit about fifty centimeters deep. He lined the bottom with flat stones and built a small fire on top of them.

Watching him attentively was a group of Bruno's friends. Florence with her young twins, Pamela, the mayor and the priest Father Sentout, Horst and Clothilde. Bruno's hunting partner, Stéphane, was there with his cousin Sylvain. As the *traiteur* who might have to cook this meal for fifty people, Sylvain was keen to see how the experiment went.

Bruno had prepared four beefsteaks, seasoned with sea salt and tiny bulbs of wild garlic. Two were placed directly on top of flat stones in the fire and at once began to sizzle. The other two were wrapped in leaves of wild garlic that he'd left in water overnight and tied together with long strips of duckweed. When the fire burned down to glowing cinders, he put the wrapped steaks onto the ashes. To get into the spirit of the ancient cooks, Bruno was using a pair of tongs he'd made from two green sticks tied together at one end with rawhide. Then he covered the firepit with a large flat stone and examined the pile of duckweed that Horst, wearing a pair of fishermen's waders, had harvested from the river.

The mayor had brought a picnic basket containing plates, glasses and cutlery, along with a jar of homemade vinaigrette. Florence and Pamela had picked more wild garlic, sorrel leaves and very young *pissenlit,* which Pamela called dandelion. The mayor had also foraged in the woods to dig up some fresh morel mushrooms, which looked much more appetizing than his other harvest — roots of wild radish and turnip, each about ten centimeters long, thin and scrawny.

Clothilde had brought an unexpected treat, *Acorus calamus,* a plant known as sweet flag. It was native to Europe and grew on the shallow edges of ponds and in most damp soils. The rhizomes, or rootstalks, could be harvested in autumn or spring and were used as a substitute for ginger, cinnamon or nutmeg.

"In Roman times they were also candied and used as a sweetmeat, so I thought that might help with a dessert," Clothilde said. "It was a very useful plant. The inner part of young stems can be eaten raw, and the young leaves can be cooked like spinach. The mature leaves repel insects, lice and bedbugs. In medieval times, the rootstalks were used to scent clothes and cupboards. I squeezed out some of its oil, which you can use to moisten your sauce."

As Bruno cracked an egg and separated out the yolk, the first passersby stopped to watch. Within a few minutes, there was an interested gathering inlcuding Philippe Delaron, the local reporter for *Sud Ouest,* camera at the ready. He began taking photos as Bruno crushed a handful of walnuts, added some wild garlic and then stirred in the egg yolk and a little of the oil from the sweet flag. Bruno then used his tongs to turn the two sizzling steaks on the stones, and noses began to twitch with interest at the familiar aroma of charring meat and garlic.

"We are helping these eminent archaeologists to see whether we can re-create a good

290

hot meal using prehistoric techniques," the mayor explained as Philippe took notes. The mayor then bent to his picnic basket and with a flourish brought out a corkscrew and a bottle of red wine whose label carried indecipherable lettering, a little like Arabic but much more rounded.

"I have here a bottle of Saperavi, the oldest wine in the world, from Georgia in the Caucasus, where it was first made some eight thousand years ago," he declared, brandishing the bottle. "And since the grape is far more resistant to heat than our own Merlot, this may be the answer to climate change. Now that we've planted an experimental row of Saperavi vines in the town vineyard, our prehistoric foods can be washed down in the most authentic manner."

He opened the bottle and took several tiny plastic glasses from his picnic basket, enough for the merest taste, poured a little wine into each one and passed them around the assembled crowd. Then he plucked another bottle of Saperavi from his basket, opened it and filled larger glasses for each of the cooks and an extra one for Philippe.

"We'll save the wine for Bruno's pièce de résistance, which we are calling boeuf Neanderthal," the mayor said.

"Is that duckweed?" asked Father Sentout. "I never heard of anybody but ducks eating that."

"It's a delicacy in Laos and Cambodia," Clothilde said. "Full of protein."

"Who's going to eat this?" asked Mireille from the florist's shop.

"We are," said the mayor. "And if it tastes good, we might take this experiment a little further. Madame Professeur Clothilde here thought we might smoke some fish, and our own Bruno has sketched out a design for a smoker we're going to build. It looks like a small tepee covered in animal skins. We're going to try different woods to flavor the smoke, starting with applewood and chestnut."

Bruno removed the two charred steaks from the stones in the fire to a much larger stone he was using as a work surface. He had borrowed a flint knife from Horst's personal collection and used it to slice small portions of the meat. Then he stirred the vinaigrette into the salad of *pissenlit,* sorrel, wild-garlic leaves and duckweed and used his tongs to put some meat and salad onto a plate, which he handed to the mayor. Philippe Delaron photographed the mayor's first taste.

"Interesting," said the mayor, taking a

second forkful. "Not bad at all, much tastier than I expected."

"Stand back," said Bruno, donning a pair of heavy gloves so he could lift the big stone that had covered his firepit, releasing an appetizing gust of garlic-flavored roast meat that stirred some appreciative murmurs from the crowd. Bruno used his tongs to bring out the steaks in their now blackened leaves. He unwrapped them, laid them on a plate and then smeared across some of the egg yolk, oil, garlic and crushed-walnut sauce he had made. He cut each steak into bite-sized portions with the flint knife and handed it first to Clothilde, took a piece and then passed the plate on to each of the others to take their morsel before the final bite came back to Bruno.

"Not bad at all," said Pamela. "It's cooked and it's tasty."

"This nut sauce is interesting but may need some more refining, perhaps some of that sweetmeat you mentioned," said the mayor. "Still, it goes very well with the wine."

"I like it," said Clothilde. "Next time let's try it with venison and black currants. And I'd like to experiment with the boiling stones. There's some American research that says not to use granite, since the rocks can explode, so we need to get hold of some more basalt."

"I could develop a taste for this," said Horst. "When we do the barbecue, I'll bring along some bratwurst and good German beer."

"Surprisingly good," said Philippe as Bruno handed around a second plate, but the portions swiftly ran out.

"I like it," said Sylvain. "And I can make that, as long as I don't have to dig too many holes, and Bruno helps with the sauce."

"My friends," said the mayor, "I think we can say our experiment with prehistoric food and wine has been a success. We will do more next Sunday: smoked fish and barbecued meats, mushrooms with honey and crushed hazelnuts, and we'll try some different tubers and salads. Our experiments continue. But I think we can now claim that the great culinary tradition of our dear Périgord goes back some thirty thousand years, and we follow proudly in the steps of our ancestors."

And that, thought Bruno as he put aside the remainder of the duckweed for his chickens, means that the next election is sewn up.

THE COLLABORATOR

It was a fine morning in early summer, and Bruno was on his first patrol of the town's market. His basset hound, Balzac, strolled contentedly behind him, accepting with dignity the small tributes of cheese and sausage presented by the regular stallholders, who had known the dog since he was a pup. For seven centuries, the weekly market had been the basis for the prosperity that had turned the modest medieval village of St. Denis into the thriving market town of today, with its own handsome stone bridge, its long quayside and its railway station. Many local people still mourned the fact that the traditional midnight train to Paris, known locally as the cuckold's express, had been suspended by a rail system so entranced by its high-speed network that the true heartland of France was no longer served as well as it had been. Whether the cancellation of this night train had helped or hindered the stability of local marriages was still frequently debated in the cafés of St. Denis and its surrounding villages.

Once limited to the main square that opened onto the bridge, the Tuesday morning market now stretched past the church and along the length of the rue de Paris to the old parade ground in front of the gendarmerie. So Bruno's first patrol, which began shortly before the market opened at eight, took barely ten minutes in winter, but as the days lengthened and the tourist season arrived, the market grew, and he now required an hour or more to greet each stallholder with a handshake or a *bise* on each cheek, and a polite word or nugget of gossip.

The patrol completed, Bruno was heading for his office in the *mairie* to catch up with some paperwork when he saw Father Sentout and a well-dressed stranger emerge from Fauquet's café. They disappeared under the colonnades of the Hôtel de Ville for a brief moment, a shaded space where local women traditionally had the exclusive right to erect stalls to sell their rabbits, ducks and chickens. *Mairie* and "Hôtel de Ville" were interchangeable names for the same building, but after Louis XIV installed his absolute monarchy in 1692, the old elected magistrates and mayors were replaced by royal appointees, and their offices named the Hôtel de Ville.

The two men soon reappeared and strode purposefully to the modernized entrance to the *mairie*. The stranger was middle aged and wearing an elegant tie that even Bruno could recognize as Hermès. A prosperous stranger, in that case, or one whose family members were very generous with birthday gifts.

They took the elevator while Bruno trotted up the stairs. He beat them to the first floor and lingered to overhear the elderly priest murmur to Claire, the mayor's secretary, that he had an appointment. The two men were shown into the mayor's office, and after a moment Bruno heard the mayor over the intercom asking Claire for two coffees. Since he had not specified his own blend of the good coffee, it was clear that the visitors were being treated courteously but without unusual deference. Three minutes later, Bruno was summoned.

"Ah, Bruno. Bonjour, I know you are no legal expert, but you may be able to help us with the delicate question of a funeral for a very old man, born and raised here in St. Denis," the mayor began. "He left as a youth and never returned, and he was stripped of his civic rights after the war as a collaborator. You know Father Sentout, and this is Monsieur Launay, grandson of the late Emil Launay, who died recently in Germany. In his will, he expressed a wish to be buried here in the family vault with his forebears. I thought you might be able to help us with the legal position."

"Bonjour, messieurs," Bruno said, and shook hands with the stranger. "I'm not familiar with the case, but any loss of civic rights was usually for a fixed term, after which the convicted person would be restored to his rights as a citizen. The war ended more than seventy years ago, and I've never heard of any sentence anywhere near that long. I will look into it, but I should first remind you that there are several families here that remember with great bitterness the losses they suffered during the Occupation, so such a funeral might well spark some local controversy."

"I am assured that there is no legal obstacle to the burial," said the stranger. He was evidently a native French speaker, but in a stilted and old-fashioned manner, as though he had not lived in the country for many years. "My grandfather was a boy when he was taken up and courted by some prominent figures in Vichy. He wasn't even twenty years old when France was liberated, and by then he was helping the Resistance. It was a Communist Party vendetta that demanded he be put on trial. You all know how vicious the *épuration* could be."

Father Sentout and the mayor nodded. The *épuration sauvage,* or the violent purging of alleged collaborators with the Nazis and their puppets in the Vichy regime, had been widespread. More than ten thousand alleged collaborators had been killed across France in that confused period between the D-Day invasion on June 6, 1944, and de Gaulle's reassertion of legality and order in liberated Paris at the end of August. Resistance had been widespread in the Périgord, and retaliation against collaborators was swift and fierce. Women were stripped in public and their heads shaved for consorting with the occupiers. Vichy officials were shot out of hand on the town bridge and tossed into the River Vézère. The vengeance of the *libération* had been cruel. In a village just a few kilometers away, two men of the *milice,* the thuggish Vichy police, had been kicked to death by the women who'd had little choice but to give them sexual favors in return for ration cards to feed their children, while their husbands languished in prisoner-of-war camps in Germany.

"When did Emil Launay die?" Bruno asked. The name meant nothing to him.

"Just five days ago, a sudden collapse after his wife's funeral at their home in Freiburg, Germany. He'd hoped to see his one hundredth birthday, but his heart simply gave out."

"He settled in Germany?" inquired Bruno.

"He married a German woman, a refugee he met when working with the Red Cross in a displaced persons camp after the war. When he retired, they settled near Freiburg."

"Did he remain a French citizen?" the mayor asked, a coolness in his voice.

"I believe he held dual nationality, French and German, but in his work he used a diplomatic passport. He worked for the United Nations High Commissioner for Refugees, mainly at the Geneva headquarters but traveling frequently to the Middle East and Africa, so we lived in Geneva until he retired."

"A man doing God's work," said Father Sentout. "The church in St. Denis would be honored to arrange his final resting place."

"You said he was born here in St. Denis," said Bruno. "Do you still have any relatives in the district? Yours is not a surname I know, and I think I know most of them."

"There are no living relatives here that I'm aware of," said Launay. "My father's father died of wounds he received at Verdun when Emil was just a boy, and his mother died in the next war. They're both buried in the graveyard here, and my grandfather thought it right to join them."

"As I said, we'll look into this," said the mayor, rising to show that the meeting was over. "If you can give me your grandfather's full name and date of birth, that would probably make matters easier. Are you staying nearby?"

"Yes, at the Vieux Logis in Trémolat. My wife is Swiss and doesn't know this region, so we thought we'd combine a little tourism with this family duty."

"You have chosen well," said the mayor. "It's the best restaurant in the region and probably in the whole *département.* The chef, Vincent Arnould, is a genius."

"It is exceptional," Launay agreed. "Perhaps when all this is settled, you might be my guests one evening."

Launay and the priest left, but the mayor kept Bruno behind, saying, "As much as I like to be invited to the Vieux Logis, there is something here that doesn't quite add up. I'm the town historian, and I've never heard of anyone from St. Denis being charged with treason during or after the war. I'll check our civic records, and perhaps you could have a word with that friend of yours in the archives at the Center Jean Moulin."

A museum and research center dedicated to the Resistance, the center was named after a French Resistance leader who had been betrayed and then questioned under torture by Klaus Barbie, the Gestapo head in Lyon. Jean Moulin had died, probably of his injuries, on the train taking him to a concentration camp in Germany. Bruno had always found the staff at the center more than helpful in his inquiries and decided on his next visit to Bordeaux to invite Alain, the archivist who had become a friend, to lunch at his favorite restaurant by way of thanks.

"Émil Launay," said Alain when Bruno called him. "That's a complicated tale. His father received a medal at Verdun and worshipped Pétain as the general who saved France. Then his son became a symbol of Vichy youth. I have sometimes wondered what happened to him after the war."

"That's why I'm calling," said Bruno. "He died at home in Germany a few days ago, nearly a hundred years old, after a long career with the United Nations. His family wants him buried in St. Denis, but there seems to have been some kind of legal issue regarding his possible conviction as a collaborator."

"If they're waiting to bury him, there's not much time to waste," said the archivist. "But that gives me an idea. We've been thinking of doing an exhibition on youth in the Vichy regime, the way they tried to get young men into scouting and camping while the young women were barred from state jobs and were supposed to stay home, cook and have lots of babies. Emil Launay would be a perfect symbol. There's a photograph of him, a fine-looking youngster, staring worshipfully as he shook hands with Marshal Pétain. Let me look into the files, and I'll get back to you."

"Are you free for lunch tomorrow?" Bruno asked, after glancing at his own diary.

"I am, as it happens," Alain replied cheerfully.

"Then let St. Denis take you to lunch. La Tupina at twelve-thirty?"

"Great idea, Bruno. I will look forward to the meal as well as the company."

"I'll see you then," said Bruno. "One last question. Was there something like the Hitler Youth in Vichy?"

"Not exactly, but for a while Emil symbolized what the Vichy regime hoped they could do to reform the idle, jazz-loving riffraff of a corrupt and spineless democracy that had tarnished the grandeur of France and the great heroes who built her," said the archivist, his voice mocking. "Forgive me, but that's the pompous way these Vichy people liked to speak."

Bruno took the train to Bordeaux the following morning soon after ten, and he was in the central station a few minutes after noon. He strolled along the riverfront to the eighteenth-century Porte de la Monnaie, designed like a small Arc de Triomphe and named for the mint that had once produced gold and silver coins nearby. The restaurant was just behind the *porte,* and Alain was already sitting at a small table on the terrace enjoying a kir as he studied the menu. Bruno joined him, and as the waiter poured the white wine over a splash of crème de cassis, Alain asked if Bruno knew that this street leading in from the *porte* used to be known as the rue des Anglais.

"Was that when the English ruled Bordeaux?" Bruno asked.

"No, it was called that after the Battle of Castillon, when they were driven out. During the three centuries that the English were here, it was called rue des Arlots."

"But that doesn't mean anything. Was it someone's name?"

"No, it was named after the girls. 'Harlot' was the English word for those we prefer to call, given our national taste for euphemism, *les filles de joie*."

"So the English soldiers were paid with coins that came from the mint and spent them right here on girls," said Bruno.

"And on good Bordeaux wines," said Alain. "Speaking of which, do you want to share one of La Tupina's enormous steaks, or are you going for the *cul noir* pork?"

The restaurant was known for its devotion to the rare breed of black-bottomed pigs from the Pyrenees, but Bruno felt adventurous and decided to start with the little squids that looked like baby eels, followed by the veal kidneys with potatoes cooked in goose fat. Alain chose to begin with foie gras but would follow with the kidneys. They agreed to share a bottle of the house's Pessac-Léognan, and since Alain was a regular, they were shown to his usual table by the window.

"Now, tell me about Emil," said Bruno, at which point Alain brought out a small notebook and handed Bruno a fat envelope filled with photocopies of documents.

In the autumn of 1940, Alain explained,

the country's leading newspaper was *Le Temps,* which was being published out of Lyon, since Paris was occupied. The editors organized a competition for schoolchildren, an essay contest on what they hoped would come after the war.

"Young Emil wrote an idealistic piece about a united Europe, under French and German leadership, with a common rail, road and waterways network, a common education system in which every child would become fluent in at least one other language, a common legal system and a European capital on both banks of the Rhine at Strasbourg," Alain went on. "Emil's essay won the prize and attracted a lot of attention, not least in Ribbentrop's foreign ministry in Berlin. Indeed, several of its features figured in the plan Ribbentrop put before Hitler in 1943 for a European Confederation. Hitler rejected the scheme, of course."

"Was that why young Emil was seen as a collaborator?" Bruno asked.

"Partly, but also because several prominent figures in the Vichy government spoke in favor of the idea. One of them, Professor Bernard Faÿ of the Collège de France, who had just been appointed head of the Bibliothèque Nationale, invited Emil to Paris for the prize-giving and arranged a scholarship for him at the elite Louis-le-Grand lycée beside the Sorbonne. In those days, kids from humble homes like Emil's had little chance of going to any lycée, let alone Louis-le-Grand, which virtually guaranteed going on to one of the top schools like the Polytechnique or the École Normale Supérieure."

"The gateway to a glittering career," said Bruno. "Quite an opportunity for a youngster from the Périgord."

"It was the chance of a lifetime, but the association with Faÿ was the problem," Alain replied. "Faÿ was a strange man. He was fluent in English, had studied at Harvard, written some good books on American political history and contributed regularly in American magazines. He hated Freemasons, though, and organized Vichy's persecution of them, putting hundreds in jail and getting thousands of them sacked from the national bureaucracy as members of what he denounced as the Jewish-Masonic conspiracy. At the same time, Faÿ was a member of the beau monde, artistic, gay and well connected in literary circles."

"Gay?" Bruno queried. "I thought that Vichy was firmly against homosexuality."

"It was," Alain replied. "They made what

they called 'corruption of minors' a criminal offense, punishable by up to three years in prison, but a whole book could be written about the gay links to Vichy and the Nazis. Jean-Paul Sartre virtually did so in his novel *Iron in the Soul,* in which his character Daniel is entranced by the arrival of German troops in Paris and wishes he were a woman so he could shower them with flowers. And in *Funeral Rites,* Jean Genet wrote of the gay fascination with the virile German occupier. Resistance propaganda constantly attacked Bonnard, the Vichy education minister, as a notorious pederast, and, of course, Professor Bernard Faÿ, Emil's patron."

"So was this real or just anti-Vichy propaganda?" Bruno asked.

"A bit of both, and of course there were many brave gay people in the Resistance," Alain replied. "There was Roger Stéphane, head of a battalion that helped liberate Paris, and Pascal Copeau, one of the main Resistance leaders in the south, and Daniel Cordier, one of the founders of the National Resistance Council, who worked closely with Jean Moulin. There was a play performed some years ago that suggested Moulin himself was gay."

Bruno shook his head. "I never heard of

that. I have read suggestions that Moulin was almost unknown until Malraux made his famous speech when de Gaulle ordered Moulin's remains to be installed in the Panthéon in 1964."

"Ah, yes," said Alain, "When that gravel voice of Malraux began to chant the 'Song of the Partisans': *Écoute aujourd'hui, jeunesse de France, ce qui fut pour nous le chant du Malheur. C'est la marche funèbre des cendres que voici . . .*"

Alain stopped, swallowed hard and used his napkin to wipe his eyes. "Sorry, it always gets to me."

"To me, too," said Bruno, and murmured, *"Ami, si tu tombes, un ami sort de l'ombre, à ta place"* — my friend, if you fall, another friend will come from the shadows to take your place.

The two men, each born decades after France had been liberated, smiled at each other across the table, making no secret of how the "Chant des Partisans" still had this strange power to move them across the years.

Their first courses came, with a small dish to be shared of *sanguette,* the blood pudding that was one of La Tupina's specialties. The sommelier came with a glass of chilled Sauternes to accompany Alain's foie gras and poured Bruno a complimentary glass of the house white wine to go with his squid.

"There are all sorts of contradictions in history," Alain went on as they began to eat. "Bernard Faÿ is a classic example. Have you ever heard of the American woman Gertrude Stein, a modernist poet and great friend of Ernest Hemingway in prewar Paris?"

"Vaguely," Bruno replied.

"She was Jewish, so how did she manage to live out the war in France without ever being hauled in by the Gestapo?"

Bruno's eyes widened in surprise. "That seems odd. How did she manage it?"

"She had a powerful protector in Bernard Faÿ, a good friend who had translated her writings into French. Stein wrote to the court when he was tried in 1946 saying that Faÿ had been her shield against the Germans throughout the war. Her efforts to save him were in vain, since Faÿ was sentenced to life in prison. But Stein's lover, Alice B. Toklas, paid for the prison breakout that secured Faÿ's escape in 1950, and he went into exile in Switzerland, where he continued teaching until his death."

"And young Emil, was he drawn into this gay milieu?" Bruno asked.

"I don't know, but in a way it was worse,"

replied Alain. "Young Emil was also taken up by the Fascist intellectual Drieu La Rochelle, editor of the very influential *Nouvelle Revue Française,* who espoused the idea of a European confederation. Perhaps the attention went to the boy's head. Emil met Pétain, his father's hero, was sent to a Franco-German literary conference in Weimar in 1941 as the voice of French youth. He looked the part, with his fair hair and blue eyes, a poster boy for Vichy's new image of France."

Alain paused to sip his glass of Sauternes as Bruno used a hunk of bread to wipe up the last of the sauce from his plate, washing it down with some of the white wine.

"Young Emil was no fool," Alain went on. "By the end of 1941, with Hitler bogged down in Russia and the Americans coming into the war, the future was no longer looking quite so assured. Emil began going regularly to Uriage."

Bruno had never heard of Uriage and said so. Alain informed him that it was originally founded in August 1940, with Vichy support, as a training school for the future leaders of the new France that Pétain wanted to build. Hundreds of young men, civil servants, army officers, educators and promising businessmen took part in the various courses. Some courses lasted for three weeks, others for six months, in an atmosphere that was part Boy Scout camp, part religious-chivalric order. There were ninety minutes of compulsory exercise each day, and long reading lists, lectures and discussion groups were interspersed with hikes in the alpine foothills.

Uriage remained loyal to Marshal Pétain himself, but became increasingly critical of the Vichy administration, particularly regarding the persecution of Jews. Some of the lecturers, including Hubert Beuve-Méry, who was to become the first editor of *Le Monde*, said openly they wanted Britain to win the war and Germany to be defeated. The place was formally closed by a decree from Vichy's prime minister Pierre Laval at the end of 1942.

"By then the myth of an independent France under Vichy had certainly been exploded," said Bruno. "The German army had occupied the whole of France, besides which British and American troops controlled almost all of North Africa and were poised to invade Italy. And the German Sixth Army was cut off in Stalingrad."

"You're right. And many of the staff of Uriage went almost directly into the Resistance when the place was closed," Alain said. "But Emil was too notorious to be trusted by any clandestine organization, and his face had become too well known. Meanwhile, the Vichy regime was crumbling, with tightened food rationing, a freezing winter without coal because Germany wanted French coal for its war effort, and more than a million Frenchmen were conscripted into forced labor in Germany in 1943. That was in addition to the one and a half million prisoners of war Germany had held as hostages since 1940."

"Is that what happened to Emil?" Bruno asked.

"Not exactly. Emil was desperate to avoid it and seems to have used his Vichy contacts to get a job in the hated STO, the Service du Travail Obligatoire, the office that organized the forced labor system that deported Frenchmen to work in German factories."

"That sounds like collaboration to me," said Bruno.

"That's not quite right, Bruno. Emil helped to run a new system under which some of the million and a half French POWs could volunteer to become a 'free worker,' living on a French farm. For the Germans, this meant tens of thousands of camp guards could be sent to reinforce the Eastern Front. For the French POWs, more than ninety percent of whom were already in work details on German farms, this became popular as a long-lost taste of civilian life, and of course the food was better. More than two hundred thousand volunteered, and many came back after the war with German wives. It was Emil's job to go to the POW camps and help men to join."

The main course arrived, kidneys cooked on the big open fire, with heaps of potatoes straight from the great pan of goose fat bubbling in the kitchen. Their red wine was poured and pronounced excellent. Bruno sat back for a moment, enjoying the copious meal, the company and the atmosphere of a traditional French restaurant with its open fire. The walls were covered in old sepia-toned family photos in wooden frames, antlers were lined up on high shelves, stuffed pheasants were on the mantelpiece, and every so often a sonorous chime sounded from a fine old clock.

"Emil spent the rest of the war based in the German town of Trier," Alain went on as they applied themselves to the kidneys. "He felt he was despised by his fellow Frenchmen and treated with contempt by the Germans. But he used his relative freedom to exchange messages between the POWs and their families at home and, as

Germany's defeat seemed more certain, to become an informal postbox between POWs in different camps and the Resistance back in France."

"So he did join the Resistance," said Bruno. "This would have been when — in late 1943?"

"Yes, the time when it became clear to most French people that Vichy was finished and that Germany was likely to lose the war," Alain replied. "The man who arranged this for Emil was a fellow graduate of Uriage, François Mitterrand. Himself a former POW, Mitterand had worked for the Vichy regime in its department for the POWs, but by mid-1943 he had joined the Resistance. By the end of the year, he had been flown secretly into Britain and then to meet de Gaulle in Algiers. They did not get on. De Gaulle wanted his own men to run the Resistance, but a compromise was reached, and Mitterrand was smuggled back into France on a fishing boat. He built an organization to link the POWs and the forced laborers in Germany with the Resistance. He also built an intelligence network among the POWs and French workers still in Germany, in which Emil played an important role. They produced a lot of intelligence on the Nazi secret weapons, the V-bombs and jet aircraft. In April 1945, as the Reich collapsed, Emil was at the POW camp at Kaufering to greet Mitterrand at the moment of the camp's liberation."

Bruno was increasingly gripped by this strange story. "Then what happened?" he asked.

"There was nothing left in France for Emil," Alain went on. His mother had died, and a makeshift Resistance court set up by a Communist group in the Limousin had tried and convicted him in his absence for treason to France. He had found work with the Red Cross in the displaced-persons camps in Germany and fallen in love with the young woman he was to marry. But in November 1946, Emil faced a new threat. Based on the result of the earlier Resistance court, he now faced a formal trial for collaboration, one of some three hundred thousand people so accused.

"Enter Mitterrand," Alain continued. As a newly elected member of the Assemblée Nationale with impeccable Resistance credentials, Mitterrand sent a letter to the court in which Emil was being tried. He wrote that Emil had 'at great personal risk provided valuable and prolonged service to the Resistance in his work with POWs in Germany.' I have put a copy of the letter in that envelope I gave you. Emil was acquitted. And in 1985, when Emil retired from the UN, Mitterrand was president of France and arranged an advisory position for him in the European Commission's external affairs service as a consultant on refugee problems."

"What an extraordinary story," said Bruno. "Would you agree there is no legal impediment to his being buried in our cemetery in St. Denis."

"No, I don't think there is. Whatever follies or indiscretions he may have committed as a youth, the rest of his life was spent honorably. I've written a formal letter saying that. It's in your envelope."

"I'm really grateful," said Bruno, sitting back to enjoy the rest of the wine, feeling too full to do justice to any dessert. Alain said he felt the same way, so they had coffee and a small glass of *marc* to help it down. Bruno paid the check, and Alain joined him on the stroll back to St. Jean station, saying he could do with a walk.

Bruno arrived at the *mairie* in St. Denis shortly before five and found the mayor at the big table in the council chamber with several files of yellowing paper spread out in front of him that looked as if they had not been consulted in years.

"Ah, Bruno, welcome back," he said. "I have found Emil was indeed born here in St. Denis in January 1925 to Jean-Louis Launay, a war veteran on full disability pension, who was a clerk in the St. Denis post office. His mother, Elodie, born in Les Eyzies in 1899, married Jean-Louis when he was on leave here in 1916. Jean-Louis was discharged from a military hospital and from the army the following year, after losing a leg and an eye in the trenches at Verdun. He died in 1934, and to eke out her war widow's pension, Elodie found work as an assistant in a local florist's shop which was owned by the then mayor's wife. When that closed after war broke out in 1939, Elodie became a housekeeper in the presbytery, looking after the priest and two curates until her death from cancer in October 1942."

Bruno wondered to himself whether Father Sentout had known that. He'd have to ask.

"Emil was present at her funeral," the mayor went on. "We have his school reports, uniformly excellent, and the town council voted to send him a letter of commendation after he was awarded some special scholarship to the very prestigious Lycée Louis-le-Grand in Paris. In August 1944, at the urging of the local Comité de Libération, which was dominated by the FTP, the Communist wing of the Resistance, the letter of commendation was withdrawn and a request sent to the prefect for Emil to be tried and convicted in his absence for *dégradation nationale*."

"Is there anything about his being put on trial for treason?" Bruno asked.

"Not that I've found."

Bruno explained what he'd learned from Alain and showed the mayor first the copy of Mitterrand's letter and the court acquittal and then Alain's letter saying that he knew of no valid reason for Emil to be denied his wish to be buried alongside his parents.

"Emil was born almost a hundred years ago, the war has been over for the length of an average lifetime, and yet this issue is still with us," said the mayor.

"We seem to have long memories in France," said Bruno.

"Not only that," said the mayor. "It's the myths rather than the memories that govern the way we think of our history. But I think we can bury the myth of Emil being a traitor when we bury the man."

"I will be there, Monsieur le Maire. And I imagine that when we hand his grandson this treasure trove of documents about his grandfather, Monsieur Launay will be inclined to make good on his dinner invitation."

"I'll invite him and his wife to the *mairie* for a small *vin d'honneur* after the funeral and offer to tell them the full story of our combined research, along with a gift of copies of various documents from the *mairie* that I unearthed."

"A story to be told over dinner at Le Vieux Logis, I hope."

"I thought you might be thinking that, Bruno."

Bruno and le Père Noël

A Christmas Story

The last market day before Christmas in St. Denis was unusually cold. In the main square and all along the rue de Paris, stall-holders stamped their feet and blew on their chilled hands as they served the throngs of customers. Young men made jokes about global warming, and the older ones sniffed and said this was nothing; they recalled years when families had slept with the cows and livestock for their body heat. From a steel-blue sky the pale sun of December tried valiantly to give some memory of warmth. Ducks waddled over the thickening ice along the banks of the River Vézère, and a man dressed as Santa Claus emerged from the *mairie* to post on the town's official noticeboard an announcement of free firewood for the elderly.

In his usual spot by the stone steps to the upper square, Grand-père Pagnol in a Russian-style fur cap was doing a roaring trade in roasted chestnuts. Shoppers clustered around his brazier for a little heat while Pagnol cheerfully warned them all that weather such as this meant that snow was coming and they could look forward to a white Christmas.

Bruno usually felt slightly embarrassed when he dressed as Father Christmas. Today, however, he was grateful for the false beard that protected much of his face against the chill. He saluted the crowd around Pagnol's brazier before climbing the steps to greet the small band of choristers who were about to launch another of Bruno's experiments.

Pamela, a former lover of Bruno's whose striking red-bronze hair was hidden under a beret of white angora wool, greeted him with a kiss. She had once told him that there were three things she missed about Christmas in her homeland in Scotland. The first was snow, which she now seemed likely to see. The second was a proper Christmas pudding with brandy butter and a sixpenny piece hidden inside, whose annual discovery was always one of the treats of her childhood. The third was singing Christmas carols in the open air, and this Bruno had been able to arrange.

Calling on the church choir for volunteers

and fleshing out the numbers with some of the English families who lived in the district, he had persuaded Fabrice to provide the music. The young man, who played accordion at the rugby club dances, had gloves that left his fingers free. But he complained that his hands were still too cold to play. Bruno nodded with understanding and shepherded the entire choral group down to stand on the steps. He positioned Fabrice beside Pagnol's glowing brazier and signaled Father Sentout, looking even more rotund than usual with the extra layers he was wearing under his soutane, to begin.

"Vive le Vent" was the first, suitably jaunty number. To Bruno's ears it was all the more interesting since the English contingent had insisted on singing the "Jingle Bells" lyrics they knew. During rehearsals, Bruno had been happy to learn that most of the French carols had their English equivalents, and each nationality seemed happier singing their own version. So "Silent Night" also became "Douce Nuit" and "Viens, Peuple Fidèle" was twinned with "O Come, All Ye Faithful." With the unexpected inclusion in the choir of Horst, a German professor of archaeology who kept a house in St. Denis, "Mon Beau Sapin" became both "O Christmas Tree" and "O Tannenbaum." This, thought Bruno, was how Europe ought to be, with everyone happily singing the same tune in their own tongue.

As the choir launched energetically into "Rudolph the Red-Nosed Reindeer," to which the French sang "Le P'tit Renne au Nez Rouge," Bruno waved the Red Cross collection tin at all the passersby and cheered loudly at the end of each carol. Pretty soon he was using the coins in the tin as maracas to beat time. People had to stop him to put money in. More and more of them crowded around to do so, which meant that Bruno's experiment was a success. And Grand-père Pagnol had never done such trade.

Nothing in his work gave Bruno greater pleasure than to organize and cajole the townsfolk into doing things together, particularly events that brought the various nationalities into a common venture. Standing in the front row between Pamela and Florence, the science teacher at the local *collège,* was a new face. The woolen cap and scarf could not conceal the dark Mediterranean looks of Miriam. A Lebanese Christian and a devout churchgoer, Miriam had recently arrived in St. Denis to take a job as a dental hygienist. She had a young son who had enrolled in Bruno's rugby class and already showed promise. Delighted at her regular attendance at mass, Father Sentout had swiftly recruited her for the choir and given her the starring role in his choice for the finale, the ancient Latin hymn "Gaudete."

Fabrice stopped playing his accordion with relief and pushed his almost frozen hands close to the brazier. The choir launched into the chorus of the a cappella song, and then Miriam's pure soprano soared alone into the wintry air:

Mundus renovatus est, a Christo regnante.

Miriam was a woman with a burden. Bruno did not know its origin, but few could miss her air of sadness. Father Sentout had warmed to her, and Florence and Pamela in the choir had taken her under their respective wings. Fabiola, the doctor who rented one of Pamela's *gîtes,* had struck up a friendship with her. But if any of them knew what was troubling the young woman, they had chosen not to share it with Bruno.

Now it seemed that her melancholy had lifted in the pleasure and fellowship of singing. The rest of the carol singers surrounded her in congratulation. Pagnol handed her the last of his chestnuts with a courtly bow. Richard, her son, glowed with pride as he darted from the sheltering skirts of Father Sentout's housekeeper to hug his mother. The collection can in Bruno's hand grew heavy as the crowd showed their appreciation in euro coins and notes. The choir went off together to Fauquet's café for hot chocolates and coffees rich with the scent of the dark Antilles rum that Fauquet favored. Bruno stayed on in the market until his collection tin was too full to rattle.

He was heading to join them in the café when his phone vibrated. The incoming message was terse and official, from the Préfecture de Police in Paris, asking him to confirm receipt of a fax. Once in his office, he hung up his Father Christmas suit and replaced it with his uniform jacket and trousers. The black robe hanging on the rail reminded him that he had to confirm that his friend the baron would join him as Père Fouettard at the church service on Christmas Day.

Like many other towns in the Périgord, St. Denis had played host to large numbers of refugees during the war. Most had come from Alsace after 1940, when the conquering German armies had deported all inhabitants of French stock. Some had married locally and stayed; others had taken new wives and husbands home to Alsace after the war. These family connections ensured that the two regions remained close. Towns were twinned, schools exchanged visits and some traditions remained. Along with a fondness for the wines and *choucroute* of Alsace, St. Denis had adopted Père Fouettard. He was the black-clad companion to Father Christmas, who carried a cane to punish children who had been naughty. These days, Father Christmas handed out the sweets, and Père Fouettard did the same with the sours: salted biscuits, lemon drops and the Alsace delicacy called *salmiak,* a slightly bitter black licorice.

The fax informed Bruno that a prisoner on parole named Jean-Pierre Bonneval, aged thirty, had absconded from his job and the special hostel where he was supposed to live until his sentence was complete. Bruno noted that the man had only four months left of a three-year term. The second paragraph made it clear why he was being informed: Bonneval's divorced wife, Miriam, had moved with their son, Richard, to St. Denis. Bruno should keep an eye out and report at once if the prisoner were to turn up.

Christmas, Bruno thought to himself, was a time when a father might take risks to see his son, even if it meant a return to prison and time added to the sentence. The final paragraph explained that Bonneval had been convicted of aggravated drug trafficking, smuggling and receiving stolen goods.

A second sheet was a poor but recognizable photograph of a fit-looking young man, full face and profile. He had neatly cut hair, clear eyes and likable features that seemed almost ready to break into a grin. That was odd, thought Bruno. Usually anybody in a police photo looks like a villain. Studying the image, Bruno reckoned Bonneval had the solid look of a rugby player. He could understand Miriam falling for him, and he could even imagine enjoying a beer with the guy. This was foolishness, Bruno told himself; a professional con man would probably have a similarly reassuring look.

Bruno confirmed receipt of the fax and called the CIP, the *conseiller pénitentiaine d'insertion et de probation,* whose name, office and number in Paris were listed in the notes. The woman who answered the phone introduced herself as Hélène. Bruno explained that as yet there had been no sign of Bonneval, but he would visit Miriam's home and report back. Was there anything the probation officer could tell him that might be helpful?

"He was at work when he found some way

to break his electronic bracelet, and then he dropped off the radar," she explained. "He had some sort of fight with his employer and disappeared."

It was routine to request checks on all family and connections when a prisoner absconded, but the CIP added that this was an unusual case. Bonneval had been a model prisoner who had qualified for a special program of conditional release into civilian life. He was allowed to live in supervised accommodations and to work for an approved employer.

"I see he had less than four months to go," Bruno said. "Why would he go on the run at this point?"

Hélène said she was mystified, adding that Bonneval had left her a phone message on the evening of his disappearance. He'd said he was sorry to let her down, but he was being cheated of his pay by his boss. He'd complained about this before, and he had not been the first to do so.

"It's tough to get any employers to take prisoners on probation. They aren't always ideal, and this one less than most," she said. "But I thought I'd persuaded Jean-Pierre to stick it out."

By the end of the conversation, Bruno had established that Hélène came from Brive-la-

Gaillarde, a town less than an hour's drive from St. Denis. She knew the Périgord well. They exchanged mobile numbers and she also gave him the number of her mother's home in Brive, where she would be for Christmas.

"You don't sound like a gendarme," she said, a hint of flirtation in her voice.

"That's because I'm not." He explained that he was a municipal policeman, employed by the mayor of the town.

By the time he reached Fauquet's café, Miriam and her son and most of the choristers had left for lunch. Pamela sat at one of the small round tables, nursing her drink as Florence donned her coat, hat and gloves and prepared to leave.

"That was a wonderful event," he said, putting the collection can on the table and unscrewing the lid. "Now we have to count the money before handing it over."

"I have to get back to the twins," said Florence, who was the treasurer of the local Red Cross, the secretary of the local branch of the Green Party and chorister as well as science teacher. She was the kind of woman who'd probably be the first female mayor of St. Denis once her children were grown up, Bruno thought.

"If you're home this afternoon, I can drop

the money off or deposit it directly into the bank, whichever you prefer," Pamela said as Florence turned to leave.

"Whichever is easier," said Florence, departing.

With Bruno counting the coins and Pamela the notes, they added up a total of two hundred seventeen euros and sixty-three cents. He piled the money back into the can and sealed the lid.

"That's very good," said Bruno. He knew from experience that a collection for charity usually took a lot more effort to collect considerably less money. "Do you want me to take it to the bank for you?"

"No, thanks," Pamela replied. "You have that 'on duty' look as if you ought to be somewhere else, and it won't take me a minute. Has something come up?"

He nodded, without explaining. Pamela was discreet, but these things had a way of becoming known. It wouldn't be fair to Miriam or her son if one of the first details the town learned of the new arrivals was that the boy's father had been in prison. He kissed Pamela goodbye and made for his van.

He'd already looked up Miriam's address. It was a short drive to the hamlet a couple of kilometers out of town where she rented two rooms on the upper floor of a small house belonging to La Veuve Madourin. Widowed for many years and with no children in the region, Madame Madourin probably welcomed the company as much as the rent. Bruno noted the cheap new bicycle with its child seat fixed behind the saddle. Two helmets hung from the handlebars, so he knew that Miriam was at home. His knock on the door sent half a dozen chickens clucking and scuttling from the yard into a small outbuilding.

As the door opened and Madame Madourin greeted him, Bruno's phone rang. It was Pamela, sounding rushed and strained.

"Bruno, I've been robbed, just outside the bank. The thief ran away up the backstreets toward the church."

"Are you hurt?"

"No, just shocked."

"Stay where you are and I'll be right with you," he said.

He quickly apologized to Madame Madourin, put two quick questions to her and raced back to his van, scattering chickens all over again. With a final shout over his shoulder that he'd be back, he leaped inside, biting his lip in impatience for the ten seconds it took for the diesel engine to start. He turned on his flashing blue light and hurried toward St. Denis, cursing himself for not insisting on escorting Pamela to the bank. At least he'd learned from the widow that there had been no visitors for Miriam and no strangers had been seen in the hamlet.

This sort of street robbery just didn't happen in St. Denis. Nearly everyone in the commune under the age of twenty-five had been in Bruno's rugby or tennis classes. Not only did Bruno know them and their parents and uncles and aunts and siblings, but all the youngsters knew him. He'd driven them to sports events, shared their triumphs and failures and given them barbecues at his home at the end of each season. They'd grown up with him, and Bruno strongly believed that this was the best crime-prevention system he could devise. Many of them engaged in the usual youthful mischief, but theft, vandalism and criminal violence were unheard of in St. Denis. He was convinced, therefore, the thief was a stranger, which meant there was one obvious candidate.

As his van turned into the square, Pamela came out of the bank where she'd been sheltering from the cold. She looked calm.

"I was passing between those two parked cars, and somebody lunged at me. He was tall and slim and moved like a young man. He must have been waiting for me," she began. "He grabbed the collection can, pushed me back so I fell against the side of a car and darted off. By the time I looked, he'd disappeared. All I remember is that he was wearing jeans and one of those black, hooded sweater things with a scarf over his face. I didn't even see his eyes. It took me completely by surprise, and there was nobody else around."

Two hours later, after taking her statement, briefing Sergeant Jules of the gendarmes and seeing Pamela home, Bruno was going from shop to shop along the rue de Paris. He showed the faxed photo of Jean-Pierre Bonneval, asking if anyone had seen this young man that morning, dressed in a black hooded jacket.

Madame Lespinasse in the *tabac* said a young man very like that had bought a pack of Lucky Strikes. He'd then stood huddled and smoking in the shelter of her doorway while the choir had been singing around the steps. And Mirabelle, the young waitress in Fauquet's, said she had sold him a baguette when the crowd of choristers had come in from their warming drinks. Was that before Bruno had joined them? Could Bonneval have seen him counting the money with

Pamela?

"I don't know," she said. "He spent a while looking at the cakes and chocolates before he bought the bread. He looked like he was very cold."

Fauquet's was L shaped, with the counter for bread and cakes around the corner from the much larger café and bar. Bruno went to the precise spot where Bonneval had stood and found that he was hidden by a tall revolving cake stand. Through the array of chocolates, cream cakes and fruit tarts, Bruno could see into the café where the choir had been sitting and where he'd opened the collection can.

Back in his office, he called Hélène, the probation officer in Paris, and said, "He's here. And I think he just committed a street robbery."

A sigh came down the phone. "That means we can't persuade him to come back and smooth things over. We'll have to send him back to prison, and it's such a waste."

"Why do you say that?"

"He was doing so well. I thought he was going to be the first criminal that I'd really been able to help to get a job, a place to live, to straighten his life out. And now he screws it all up, just before Christmas."

"What do you know about his family?"

"His wife got a divorce while he was inside. She never visited him. I spoke to her once and she said she'd never take her boy to visit his dad in prison. It was awful because she broke with her own family too. That's why she decided to move out of Paris."

"Tell me," said Bruno. "All I know is drug trafficking and smuggling."

"Her family's from Lebanon, and her brother was the kingpin, dealing Lebanese hash, a lot of it. The police and the customs people set up a joint operation and sent in someone undercover to make a big buy. Jean-Pierre was the fall guy. Then he refused to testify against his brother-in-law, which could have gotten him a lighter sentence. He probably wouldn't even have gone inside."

In the background of Hélène's phone he could hear laughter and jaunty music. It sounded like "Vive le Vent."

"Are you having a Christmas party there?" he asked.

"Yes, it's the last day before we close for the holidays. Well, there'll be a skeleton staff. We're just having cake and a few drinks. Then I've got to get home and pack to catch the early train down to Brive."

"If I can clear up this robbery business

and get him back to you, could you smooth things over?"

"Back to me where? In Brive?" She sounded surprised.

"I was thinking in Paris, but if you're someone he trusts maybe it could work if I got him to Brive."

"I might be the only one he trusts, except for his boy," Hélène said. "Richard's the most important thing in Bonneval's life now. That's why he wants to get straight again. Every time I see him, he talks about his son."

"What does he say?"

"Oh, fantasy stuff, like teaching him to swim and taking him to football games. He had a bit of an obsession about taking him fishing like his own father did with him. He said he'd taken him fishing once on the Seine, and the boy had loved it."

Promising to call her mobile if there was any news, Bruno hung up and took his van to Madame Madourin's house. Knowing any juicy item of gossip would be all over town within a day, he simply told the widow that he had news from Miriam's family in Paris.

Miriam and her son were in a small sitting room with a sink and hot plate in one corner. They sat together on the sofa, working on a book of sudoku puzzles. Richard held the pencil, and the boy jumped up to shake hands as Bruno had entered the room, with a polite, "Bonjour, Monsieur Bruno."

Through the open door to the bedroom he could see two single beds. There was a crucifix on the wall and beneath it a TV, switched off. A small Christmas tree of silver tinsel was hung with chocolate coins wrapped in gold foil. A star of plastic crystal leaned precariously from the top.

"Sorry to bother you, but I need to know if you've seen or heard anything from Jean-Pierre," he said. "He's left the hostel and the place where he worked. I'm pretty sure he's come here."

Miriam pulled Richard to her side. Bruno could see the boy had her large, dark eyes and full mouth and had that look of the south about him.

"We just had some tea," she said. "Would you like some?"

He declined but took one of the two hard-backed chairs at the small table and said, "Perhaps you'd prefer to speak in private."

She shook her head and held the boy more closely to her. "No, I haven't seen Jean-Pierre. But I had a strange call at the dentist's office yesterday, someone asking for me. When I picked the phone up and said hello, all I could hear was breathing. I'm sure it was him. Then I called the place where I used to work, and he'd been there. They were supposed to say they didn't know where I'd gone, but the woman who replaced me was new and didn't know not to tell him." She paused and then said, a little wistfully, "He was always good with women."

"He's here, and he's in more trouble," Bruno said. "I've talked to his probation officer and we're hoping to clear this up quietly. That means getting him to go back to Paris of his own accord. Can I count on your help?"

"It's all over between him and me."

Bruno said nothing but raised his eyebrows and looked at the boy. Richard returned his gaze calmly and said, "This is about Papa. Has he come to see us?"

"Your mother will tell you about it," he said. "And don't forget I'm seeing you tomorrow morning. It's the last practice before Christmas, nine o'clock at the stadium."

He gave Miriam his card, took her mobile number and asked her to call if Jean-Pierre made contact. As he drove to Pamela's house for the evening ride with the horses, he wondered where Bonneval would sleep that night. He now had enough money for a hotel, but Sergeant Jules would already have alerted them all. There were barns enough in the area, and most of them had straw. Some had animals whose warmth he could share, if he was prepared to risk discovery by the farmer. But he was a city boy, unfamiliar with barns or animals. He wouldn't know of the hunters' hides with their old iron stoves and ready-cut firewood. Bruno decided that after dinner he'd check the bars and cafés.

When he arrived at Pamela's house, she was wrestling with what looked like a cannonball wrapped in muslin. He helped her take it out of the steamer and hang it from the thick beam above the kitchen sink, knowing it was her famous Christmas pudding. A month earlier, along with Fabiola and Florence and her twins and Bruno's friend the baron, he'd been part of the ceremony. Each of them in turn had been required to stir the thick dark mixture. It had to be stirred from east to west, Pamela insisted, since that represented the direction the three wise men had taken to reach the stable at Bethlehem. And it contained thirteen ingredients, one for each of the apostles and one for Jesus. Bruno had asked which ingredient represented Judas, and Pamela had waved her wooden spoon at him and retorted, "Salt, of course."

Bruno was to bring the goose to the *réveillon,* the Christmas Eve supper. The baron was providing the wine, Fabiola was bringing the oysters, and Florence and her children were in charge of making the paper crowns that everyone would wear at the dining table.

"Do you think we might make room for two more?" he asked. "I was thinking that Miriam and her boy might enjoy the company."

"Good idea," said Pamela. "I rather like her, and since it's Christmas . . ."

Bruno called as they walked out to the stables, where Fabiola was already saddling Bess. His face broke into a grin as Miriam said they'd be delighted to come, and what could she bring? Just some fruit juice or lemonade, he told her, whatever Richard would like to drink.

As they rode out, Bruno smiled to himself, thinking that the three of them looked like refugees, or maybe like Napoléon's troops retreating from Moscow in 1812. Pamela had a big brown woolen balaclava over her riding hat, and Fabiola had a thick scarf wrapped over her head and around her ears.

Their slim figures, made bulky with sweaters and jackets, seemed almost ghostly in the clouds of steam that rose from the horses' breath. The field ahead of them was white with frost that crackled underfoot.

"When it's like this in Scotland, we say it's too cold to snow," Pamela said, nudging Victoria's sides to start a canter. The horses responded, eager to run. She led them up the familiar route to the ridge that overlooked the valley and the great bend in the river where St. Denis nestled beneath the hillside. They paused briefly to take in the familiar view that had been transformed by the frost and the swirls of mist that rose from the water.

"It looks like a different St. Denis altogether," said Pamela. "Like a fairy tale, but one of those sinister stories from the Brothers Grimm, menacing forests and wicked witches."

She'd just been robbed, thought Bruno. She was entitled to feel that way. To him it simply looked like the same old St. Denis in a hard winter. Hector, Bruno's mount, tossed his head in impatience until Fabiola shivered and set off again. The three of them launched into a run along the ridge that became a joyous, warming gallop as they reached the firebreak through the forest.

"Wonderful," said Pamela as they rubbed down their horses in the stables and forked down fresh straw into the stalls. "Can you stay for dinner? Fabiola's making her spaghetti, and there's a chicken in the oven."

"I'll have to go and feed Balzac and my own hens first, but I can bring back some wine," Bruno said.

"Good, that will give me time for a hot bath. And bring your dog back with you."

Bruno went out briefly after the meal to check on the town's two bars that were open, looked into the church and the likely doorways where someone might take shelter. But there was no sign of Bonneval, which worried Bruno. It was the sort of night that could freeze a person to death. The sky was clear and the stars shining and brilliant. He paused to look up and picked out the familiar shapes of the Great Bear and Orion's Belt, thinking that one day he'd treat himself to a telescope and study them more closely. But he'd do so in a kinder season of the year.

The next morning, the sky was overcast and pregnant with snow. A score of youngsters had braved the weather and were jumping up and down in their tracksuits on the frosted pitch to stay warm. Richard, Bruno noted, was among them. Half a dozen unusually devoted parents huddled together in the stand to watch. Miriam, he noted, was not among them. Bruno greeted them all and brought from the back of his van some paper cups and two large thermos flasks. One contained hot chocolate for the boys and girls, and the other was filled with his own mulled wine for the adults. He'd added half a bottle of homemade *vin de noix* to a bottle of red wine, a glass of orange juice and a large glass of brandy, then heated it all with two cinnamon sticks and a dozen cloves. The parents clustered around; Bruno's mulled wine was famous in St. Denis.

Leaving them to it and hoping there would be a cupful left for him after the practice, Bruno trotted onto the pitch. He carried a rugby ball under each arm. The cold meant he'd better keep the kids running. He lined them up beneath the goalposts and started them passing the ball to one another while running up and down the length of the field. Anyone who dropped the ball had to run around the grounds before they could rejoin the line. At one point, Bruno noticed that Richard, his cold hands tucked into his armpits, had joined the long, trotting line of the droppers.

Within minutes the youngsters were glowing with warmth and a couple had shed their tracksuit tops. He moved them into three lines, one behind the other, so that the gaps between each player were longer and the passes harder to keep accurate. Then he started them in line, each turning to slip the ball back to the player behind. For a change, he formed them into two scrums, their bodies bent and locked together as each team strained to push the other back. He finished with wind sprints, twenty meters flat out and twenty meters jogging, up and down the pitch. Finally, he sent them off to the two communal baths. The girls used the visitors' changing room, and Bruno the separate shower that was usually reserved for the referee and linesmen.

Clean and changed, and feeling better for the exercise, Bruno took a cup of his mulled wine and joined the parents. The youngsters helped themselves to the hot chocolate before lining up to wish him a happy Christmas. Katrine, captain of the girls' team, stepped forward with a small parcel, neatly wrapped in Christmas paper.

"Where's Richard?" she asked, and suddenly Bruno felt the hairs rise on the back of his neck. He had last seen the boy trotting around the field. "He's supposed to hand you the card we all signed."

Despite a rush of concern for the missing boy, Bruno thought he'd better open the gift first. His jaw dropped in surprise. It was an expensive bottle of Hermès aftershave that they wouldn't have been able to find in the shops of St. Denis. He thanked them all warmly before asking Laurent, the boys' team captain, to go and see if Richard was still in the showers. He looked at his watch. Miriam would be here at any moment to pick up her son. Laurent came back to report there was no sign of Richard, and none of the others could recall him joining them in the showers.

Bruno swiftly organized three search parties: one for the showers and changing rooms, another for the stands and the storerooms beneath them and a third to look through the trees and shrubs around the rugby field. He checked the road outside and sent those parents with cars to patrol the nearby streets while he called Sergeant Jules. No cars had been reported stolen. There were only three roads out of town, and Jules could post a man at each one. Bruno then called Marie at the Hôtel de la Gare and asked her to let him know if a man and boy appeared at the station.

There was still no sign of the boy when

Miriam arrived on her bicycle. Feeling sick with guilt that he had not watched the boy more closely, Bruno led her to one side to explain that he was sure Richard was with his father. She should go home and stay there, in case the boy turned up.

Miriam took the news stoically but shook her head at his suggestion. "I'll call Madame Madourin. She can call me if he shows up. I'm going to search the town." She looked at Bruno solemnly, as if about to say something more. He braced himself for a tirade, but she bit her lip and rode off. Whatever blame she'd been about to fix on him, Bruno thought, he deserved it.

He packed up the thermos flasks, locked the stadium and showers and drove down to Antoine's campground, closed for the winter. The canoes he rented to tourists were stacked neatly on the racks and covered with tarpaulins. Antoine was in his hut, a glass of Ricard at his elbow and the smoke from a Gitane curling up from his lip. The windows were steamed up from the warmth of the ancient iron woodburning stove. He was puzzling over his accounts when Bruno entered, probably working out how far he could cheat the taxman this year. Bruno explained what he wanted and why.

"It'll be bloody cold," said Antoine. But

he wrapped himself up in an old army greatcoat and hitched his trailer to Bruno's van. They loaded a canoe onto it, took some paddles and a plank of wood and set off for the railway bridge. Bruno could not see Bonneval and his son getting farther than that.

Attached by a rope to Antoine's hand, the canoe skittered over the ice by the bank when they launched it. Bruno took the plank and laid it over the ice, which began to break as Antoine climbed across and into the bobbing canoe. Bruno followed, just managing to keep his feet dry, but already feeling the cold bite through his sneakers as they reached the stretch of clear water in the middle of the river.

The paddling warmed them, although Bruno's legs and buttocks were freezing with only a thin layer of plastic between him and the icy water. Where the current was slow, their paddles broke through the thin sheet of ice that was already forming, and the first snowflakes began to drift down. Antoine shrugged off his overcoat, laid it beneath him and then knelt on it to paddle.

"Did you never see those cowboy films?" he shouted over his shoulder. "The Indians always paddled like this. Otherwise your legs freeze."

Bruno shrugged off his life jacket and used that. Within moments his thighs were aching and his knees sore, but he felt less cold. He was struck by the way the ducks seemed to take pleasure in running from the bank to glide over the ice. They cackled in what sounded like laughter as they slid across to the channel of clear water and used it as a runway to take off, to soar over the canoe and circle and then land back in the flowing stream.

Bruno dragged his eyes from the ducks to scour the empty banks. He saw no fishermen and no sign of life, except for the discreet splash of an otter slipping into the shallows where the current had prevented ice from forming. The fields and hills to each side gleamed white as fresh laundry and on the prow of the canoe snow was beginning to settle. Surrounded by pale gray skies, white fields and ice, their red canoe offered the only splash of color in the wintry riverscape.

"Is that them?" asked Antoine as they rounded the wide bend that led to St. Denis.

Bruno squinted against the pale light and saw a bulky shape beneath the town bridge. It took him a moment to focus and identify Bonneval sitting on a wooden box, his son on his lap, holding the fishing rod. Bonneval's arms were around the boy. Richard was wearing his father's black hooded jacket. As Antoine steered in toward the quayside, Bruno pulled out his phone and called Sergeant Jules to say he could call off the other gendarmes. The boy was found. Bruno gave his location.

"I'm in the van," Jules replied. "I'll be there in a moment. I'll park at the top of the steps."

"Paddle hard," said Antoine. "We've got to break through the ice."

He scrambled forward, hitting at the ice with his paddle until he could jump onto the stone ramp, haul in the canoe and help Bruno scramble ashore.

"You're scaring the fish away," called the boy.

"I know, I'm sorry," Bruno said. "Caught anything?"

"Just a little one. Papa said to put it back." He rose from his father's knee, gave him the fishing rod and came across to shake hands with Bruno and Antoine. "Papa, this is Monsieur Bruno the policeman. He teaches me to play rugby."

Bonneval looked up, his face blue and pinched with cold, a couple of days of bristle on his chin.

"Okay, I'm ready," he said. "You're going to take me back?"

"First, we're going to get you warm," said Bruno. "Then we can talk about it."

The three men carried the canoe up the steps to the waiting gendarme van, and Richard followed with his new rod. They left the canoe at the side of the bridge, and Sergeant Jules drove them in silence up the road by the river to Bruno's parked van. Bruno called Miriam and told her the boy was fine, and she should meet them in the parking lot by the *mairie.* By the time the two police vans reached the square, she was already waiting and let her bike fall to the ground as she ran to embrace Richard.

"Look what Papa gave me," he cried, holding up his rod as she reached him.

"Give your dad his jacket," Bruno said. "It's all right, you'll see him later."

They put the bike in Sergeant Jules's van, and he drove Miriam and the boy home. Bonneval helped Bruno and Antoine load the canoe onto the trailer, and Bruno drove back to the campsite. Bruno unhitched the trailer, and the three men restored the canoe to its rack. Bruno thanked Antoine and, with Bonneval huddled beside him trying to warm up, set off for his home.

"What now?" Bonneval asked.

351

"You need a long, hot shower and a change of clothes. Then we're going to call Hélène, your probation officer. And if that works out, we'll be able to make some plans. But tell me, where did you spend the night?"

"At the back of the supermarket. They have big refrigeration units, so I thought there'd be some warmth on top of them."

"Was there?" Bruno was impressed. He'd never have thought of that.

"A little. Enough." He paused. "That's what I was, a heating engineer. I'd installed some of those units in Paris, so I knew." From the pocket of his jacket he pulled the Red Cross tin.

"I owe you thirty-five euros for the rod and bait." He put the can on the ledge above the glove box and tucked the receipt beneath it. "I had to get him something for Christmas. Somehow or other, I'll pay you back."

Back at home, Bruno watched as Balzac greeted Bonneval. The man went down on one knee, smiled for the first time and offered a hand to be sniffed and then played with Balzac's floppy ears as the dog clambered up his knee to nuzzle at Bonneval's chin. That was enough for Bruno, who reckoned that dogs were more reliable judges of character than most humans.

He picked out a spare towel and a change of clothes, showed Bonneval to the bathroom and gave him a disposable razor. He put on the kettle for some coffee and made a fire. Maybe coffee would not be enough. He took the thermos flasks from the van and began to reheat the mulled wine as he set a place at the low table by the fire and prepared eggs and cheese and *lardons* to make an omelette. Then he called Hélène's mobile.

"He's here at my place. He's taking a shower, and I'll give him something to eat."

"Is he prepared to come back to Paris with me?" she asked. "I talked to my boss, and he says we can fix this if I'm prepared to try."

"Are you?"

"Yes, but only if you agree. I don't know what sort of shape he's in."

"I think it will be okay. He just wanted to see the boy. I'll call you back when he's eaten and is ready to talk."

Clean and showered, with the omelette and baguette and two glasses of mulled wine inside him, Bonneval sat close to the fire with Bruno's dog. As if by instinct, he found the spot just under the ribs where Balzac liked to be tickled. Bruno called Hélène again and handed him the phone.

"She wants to speak to you," Bonneval said, when Bruno returned from clearing the dishes.

"He's coming back with me the day after Christmas," she said. "Can you keep him there until then? I'll pick him up at St. Denis in my mother's car, and we can take the lunchtime train together from Brive."

They agreed to meet at ten at Fauquet's café. He went into the kitchen, closed the door, called Miriam's number and told her his plan. When she hesitated, he said, "It's Christmas, Miriam."

He opened the door when the call ended and told Bonneval, "Time to work." A big goose of six kilos stood waiting on the kitchen counter. A saucepan containing vermouth was warming on the stove. Bruno turned on his oven, setting it to two hundred twenty degrees.

"You're making the stuffing," said Bruno. He pointed to a bowl of hot water filled with fat black *pruneaux d'Agen.* "Simmer those in the vermouth for about ten minutes until they're softened. Then we're going to stuff each of them with a teaspoon of foie gras, so slit them open very carefully when you take out the pits."

He handed Bonneval a small knife and said, "When the goose is done, you're com-

354

ing to Christmas dinner with some friends of mine."

"What then? Do I spend the night in jail?"

"Can you drive?"

Bonneval nodded. "Of course."

"Then you're the designated driver, which means I can drink, but you can't. You'll spend the night here in my spare room. Tomorrow morning we go to church where I'm Father Christmas and you'll dress up as my wicked companion, Père Fouettard. It's all right, the kids are used to it and know it's just a game. You have to pretend to frighten them a bit. They love it much more than when it's only Father Christmas. Something about the good cop–bad cop routine appeals to them."

He explained the tradition and the duties while Bonneval stirred the prunes. Bruno began to chop shallots and garlic and to mince a whole goose liver. When he was done, he cooked the liver and shallots together in a frying pan, placed the result in a bowl, poured a large glass of his *vin de noix* into the pan and reduced it. He added thyme, bread crumbs, salt and pepper to the liver, then poured in the thickened wine and began to blend it, adding chunks of *pâté de foie gras* until he thought there would be enough.

Bruno showed Bonneval how to stuff the first two prunes and then left him to do the rest. He salted the cavity of the goose, loosened the skin and slid slivers of foie gras beneath it and went out to feed his chickens while Bonneval worked on the prunes.

"What happens after church?" Bonneval asked when Bruno returned. The prunes were all stuffed, and he was pleased to see that Bonneval had washed the bowls and cleaned the sink. Bruno packed the prunes inside the goose, sewed it closed and then began tying the legs, wings and neck close to the body with string.

"After church, there'll be a light lunch at the priest's house, and then we take my dog for a walk in the snow. You sleep here again and on the day after Christmas we meet Hélène in the café where you saw me count the money. She takes you to Brive where you board the train for Paris. You go back to your hostel and your job for three more months. You grit your teeth and stick it out until you're a free man again."

"My boss won't take me back. He'd have to pay the wages he owes me."

"Hélène says she can arrange it, and I believe her." Bruno put the goose into the oven. "Now we brown it for fifteen minutes, then I'll turn down the heat and put it back in to roast. After we walk the dog, we take the goose over to my friend's house and enjoy our dinner. She's called Pamela. You met her when you stole the collection can from her outside the bank."

"Christ," said Bonneval, putting his hands over his face.

"You did a good job stuffing the prunes. Richard will enjoy them," Bruno said. "Do you know if he likes oysters?"

"Oysters? Richard? I doubt he's ever had them."

"We'll soon find out. Miriam and your son are coming to dinner at Pamela's this evening, and he'll be in church tomorrow to see you play Père Fouettard. Just so you know what's at stake in these next three months, Miriam knows you'll be there and she's agreed."

Bruno finished putting the bowls and dishes away and turned to look at Bonneval. He was standing at the sink but seeing nothing as he gazed through the window at the afternoon sky and the falling snow. Tears were trickling down his cheeks, and his hands gripped the edge of the sink.

"I think three hours should be enough for the goose," Bruno said, almost as if talking to himself. "Do you know how we can tell it's ready? You waggle the legs a bit to see if they're loose in the sockets. Then you put a skewer into the fleshy part, and if the juice runs out a clear pale yellow, it's done."

"Why are you doing this?" Bonneval asked, not turning around.

"I've got some bars of very nice soap that I usually take as a gift for a hostess, and some Christmas paper," said Bruno. "Maybe you could wrap one of them for Pamela, and another for Miriam. Richard already has his fishing rod."

"Why?" Bonneval repeated. This time he turned to face Bruno.

"A boy should have a father," said Bruno. "I never had one. And besides, it's Christmas."

ACKNOWLEDGMENTS

My German-language publisher, Diogenes, has for many years published regular collections of short stories by various authors, dead as well as living, on special themes. There have been collections around Christmas stories, around various holiday destinations and individual cities, about wine and about food. Anna von Planta, my German editor and now a dear friend, was the first to suggest that Bruno need not be restricted to novels and that it might be fun for him to sally out in different directions with short stories.

That was ten years ago, and the first Bruno short story was in a Christmas collection, *Bruno and le Père Noël*. Then Anna and the head of Diogenes, Philipp Keel, reported that they were getting numerous letters from German readers asking for a Bruno cookbook. To make it distinctive, the Diogenes team suggested, the cookbook should feature not only the classic food of the Périgord, but also the extra flavor of a couple of specially written short stories about Bruno.

Never having written short stories before, I did some research. It very nearly dissuaded me from the whole idea. So many writers whose work I admire have sounded ominous warnings about the challenge of the genre. Truman Capote famously called it "the most difficult and disciplining form of prose writing extant." Henry David Thoreau suggested I might be biting off much more than I could chew when he noted, "Not that the story need be long, but it will take a long while to make it short." When she noted that "the short story writer is to the novelist as a cabinetmaker is to a house carpenter," Annie Proulx made it clear that considerable finesse was required. Ray Bradbury tried to be comforting, advising us to "Write a short story every week. It's not possible to write fifty-two bad short stories in a row." Even if he's right, the prospect of fifty-one stinkers in succession was grim.

Three of these short stories have appeared in the two German-language cookbooks, and four others have appeared in various Diogenes collections. Several have been published in English as Kindle shorts. Readers in Australia and South Africa and some other countries wrote to complain that for reasons of copyright, they have been unable to download or read them, which made me want to find a solution. Six of these tales are new stories, especially written for this book. I enjoy writing them because it enables me to explore new themes and places and try out new characters and situations without having to fit them into the novel I'm working on at the time.

These stories and the Bruno novels would never have existed without the food and wine, the history and climate, the landscape and atmosphere and above all the people of the Périgord. Their kindness and forbearance, their wisdom and courtesy, have been and remain an inspiration, a comfort and an unending gift.

As always, I owe to my wife, Julia, a debt I never could repay for all the love and help and support and advice (not just on Bruno and his cooking) that she has provided me over the years. Our daughters, Kate and Fanny, have been involved in the tales of Bruno from the beginning as first readers, critics, publicists, website curators and supporters. I am fortunate to have good friends as editors, Jane Wood in London and Jonathan Segal in New York, who have as always whipped things into shape with courtesy, subtlety and dispatch.

Martin Walker, the Périgord

ABOUT THE AUTHOR

Martin Walker proudly carries a British passport, supports Scotland in rugby, England in cricket, the United States in national parks and the Périgord in food, wine and the sweetness of life. He had a prizewinning career in international journalism with Britain's *The Guardian* and with United Press International, reporting from every continent except Antarctica. His writings have also appeared in *The New York Times, The Washington Post, The New Republic,* Spain's *El Mundo,* Germany's *Die Zeit,* and Russia's *Novaye Vremya.* He published nonfiction books on Mikhail Gorbachev's Soviet Union, on British and American politics, on the international press and on the history of the Cold War. He enjoyed a second career in think tanks on geopolitics and economics and has now published fifteen novels in the international best-selling series of Bruno, chief of police. The

Bruno novels have also led to two cookbooks, written with his wife of forty-three years, the food writer Julia Watson. Each one won the Gourmand International Award as Best French Cookbook of the Year. He writes regularly on wine and is a *grand consul de la Vinée de Bergerac,* a body founded in 1254. With the help of wine-making friends, he produces a very agreeable Bergerac red wine called Cuvée Bruno. He has been elected to the Académie des Lettres et des Arts du Périgord and was awarded a gold medal by the French republic for his services to tourism. In 2021 he was awarded the Prix Charbonnier by the Federation of Alliances Françaises for his services to French culture. Covid permitting, he and Julia divide their time between the Périgord, London and Washington, D.C.

The employees of Thorndike Press hope you have enjoyed this Large Print book. All our Thorndike, Wheeler, and Kennebec Large Print titles are designed for easy reading, and all our books are made to last. Other Thorndike Press Large Print books are available at your library, through selected bookstores, or directly from us.

For information about titles, please call:
(800) 223-1244

or visit our website at:
gale.com/thorndike

To share your comments, please write:

Publisher
Thorndike Press
10 Water St., Suite 310
Waterville, ME 04901